ROBIN SCHADEL

Liam's Doom

First published by Cursing Raven Books 2021

Copyright © 2021 by Robin Schadel

First edition

ISBN: 978-1-63684-297-4

This book was professionally typeset on Reedsy.
Find out more at reedsy.com

To my dearest Nixie for her love and support.
I love you all the lots

Chapter 1

"So, it's true. He really did those things to our daughter," Sarah Ellison said as tears fell from her eyes, giving them the appearance of vintage green glass bottles. She was a plump, mousy woman who kept her brown hair in a messy bun as we sat in the sitting area of her small one-bedroom apartment, decorated with a mix of thrift store and hand-me-down furniture, on the northern edge of Butcher's Bend, South Carolina. She was in her mid-twenties and going through a nasty divorce to an abusive asshole who's skirted through life by being the mayor's son and the grandson of our state senator. Southern aristocracy at its finest. When she fled with their four-year-old daughter, daddy sent the local cops to take their daughter, Lisa, back to her father on the promise that they would not charge her with kidnapping.

I nodded, "Yeah. I'm so sorry, and I wish I had something to say that didn't ring hollow, but," I shrugged, "all I got is that you were right and that he won't be doing this much longer."

I took a sip of the sweet tea she offered me when I arrived. I drank it out of politeness; I never could stomach it. Tea should be hot with just a hint of honey, or, better yet, replaced with hot, strong, black coffee. I watched as she placed the photos I showed her back in the manila envelope along with a flash

1

drive containing them and the video. As she cried, I moved onto the arm of her chair and placed an arm around her. I sat in silence for a few moments. She needed this.

She looked up at me and said, "And the video? That's him – and them – doing those things to her? How did you get this? My lawyer said when they searched his computer, it was totally clean."

I nodded and smiled as gently as I could. "I didn't search his computer. Whether it was always clean or he had someone wipe it, I can't say. I can say that the arrogant S.O.B. didn't believe in closing the shades on her bedroom window on the third story of his home. Made getting this disgusting evidence easy."

Those words tasted like bile in my mouth. What Henry Planter did to his daughter and then took money from other men who did the same things to her was beyond disgusting. In some of the smaller towns around here, he would've been shot for doing that, but being the heir to a powerful and wealthy family, meant that crimes often got swept under someone else's rug. But there was no way in Heaven, Limbo, Hell, and the Otherworld that I was going to let this bastard get away with this monstrous perversity. It didn't matter whose son or grandson he was.

She wiped her eyes and looked at me, the mascara streaming down her face. "And you'll be in court for us next month?"

I smiled and shook my head. "Not for you but with you and in a three-piece suit, ready to testify."

"It's okay if you're not, Miss Hain," she said. "My hours at the diner got cut this week. I don't know if I can keep paying you."

I stroked her back gently. "You've paid enough," I replied.

"You focus on giving your daughter a good home with a loving mother, and your lawyer and I will worry about keeping him away from both of you. From this point forward, I'm pro bono."

"Bless you, Miss Hain," she said as she grasped my hand. "You're an angel."

I shook my head, smiling as I countered, "There are a lot of people who say the opposite. Well, you know where to find me if you need me, Sarah. I've got to get back to the office. Try to get some rest, okay?"

The clock on my Civic's dash read half past seven, and since I actually adjusted it for the time change this fall, I knew it was accurate. I stayed later than I intended, but she needed me. Mom was always right: no one's ever "just a client" with me. I massaged the steering wheel as I turned the key in the ignition, hoping the love I've shown would keep this fifteen-year-old car going for at least another three or four months. The engine sputtered for a bit, but the old girl started purring unevenly. As I left the Section 8 complex where she lived, I called my assistant, Destiny.

"Hain Private Investigations, this is Destiny speaking. How may I help you?" she chirped happily on the phone.

"Des, it's me. I'm grabbing a pizza at Sal's before heading back. You want the 'Quattro'?"

"Uh, yeah! Sausage, onion, bell peppers, and jalapeños so spicy and balanced you'd think he got the recipe from an old Sicilian strega, sign me up for that any day." We both laughed. As thunder rumbled in the distance, she added, "Hey, be careful in the rain. You still need to get the brakes checked, Sam."

"She'll hold together. See you soon." After ending the call, I stroked the car's dashboard gently and whispered, "Hear me,

3

baby? Hold together."

By the time I returned to our office, it was one of those Bulwer-Lytton nights. I briefed Destiny on my client meeting while we ate pizza and drank root beer. Given the hour, we sat in my office and chatted, losing track of time as we both waited for the storm to pass before driving home. Sometimes it's good to work with your friends.

"Dark and stormy tonight, Sam – just like your birthday! Which–" Destiny said as she peered out of the window beside my desk in our small, two-room office on the third floor of the Oberon Center at the corner of Willow and Yew.

"Is five days from now, Des," I replied, rolling my eyes. "Yeah, I know the irony. After all, my father named me after the Celtic festival commemorating the end of the harvest season. And, given that it's the day when the Veil is at its thinnest, the fact that I was born on a dark and stormy night bursts with more gothic flair than an over-tightened Victorian corset."

"Not that you'd complain about that," she winked.

I sighed, rolling my eyes at the quirky woman with attractive, if stereotypical "German," features; although her hair was too unruly and short to keep in plaited braids these days, I have seen pictures from her childhood in Hanau where her mother disciplined that mess of blonde curls into perfect plaits. Now, she kept her hair chin-length, which, along with her charcoal suit adorned with a Gardevoir pin on the right lapel and sea foam blouse, made her ice-blue eyes sparkle in both the warm sunlight and the flickering florescent lighting of our office space. Destiny Grimm – yes, one of those Grimms – has been an invaluable friend and ally in this strange venture of mine.

"So, any plans for your Big Three-Oh?" She asked in a sing-song voice.

"After everything that went down with Rachel last week, I'll probably do what I did last year: sit in my office, eat cake, and see if a potential client shows up. Then, I'll probably go have a round or two at The Four Winds and talk to Mom before I snuggle in bed with Sandy. I lead such an exciting life." I laughed.

"You do," she replied flatly. Her voice took on the melodramatic flair of a soap opera narrator as she continued, "The Great Private Investigator: Sam Hain, born on a dark and stormy full moon on the last night of October, entering the mortal world as the Veil between our world and the Otherwold wanes to its thinnest, the legendary 'Fixer' for those who need help outside the normal channels, daring fashion icon who combines the sensibilities of modern life with vintage flair and style, whose razor-sharp wit and hair-trigger temper prove too much for the average damsel to bear, who – like a werewolf under a full moon – turns as basic as a PSL at the first sign of fall. Also, you make a mean whiskey sour."

We both laughed. And honestly, yeah, I do have a pretty interesting, if not unconventional, life. I mean, my father, Donal Hain, was the Arch Magus for the Astrum Argentum before he retired, and he, with sound mind and body, and I'm told no malice, pronounced the ultimate dad joke by naming me Samantha but only ever calling me "Sam" unless I was in trouble, because I was born on Halloween. He regularly sent letters to my teachers stating that I had requested to be called "Sam." Of course my teachers, the local goths kids, and a few nerds got the joke growing up, and all of them, and I mean all of them, felt the need to point out how funny they thought it was. While working on becoming a college dropout during my grunge phase, I went by my middle name, Blake, which my mom gave me in honor of her older brother who passed away an hour before I was born. I could've finished that Comparative Literature degree, but after mom's accident, I ran off to Ireland in '12 to track down a morally deficient, drunken leprechaun who was bankrupting an underground gambling circuit run by county and parish officials and never went back. But that's a story for another time. That was my first "Fix," and I've gained a reputation with Veil Crossers as the go-to solution for problems that might draw negative attention from the Veil Watchers.

Now, to be clear, Veil Crossing hasn't been a crime since pretty much every country signed the International Supernatural Entity Recognition and Rights Treaty while at some big retreat that the media said was about climate change, which we still haven't tackled yet. Six years ago. Liechtenstein refused for reasons unknown, but I suspected it was so they could see their name plastered on international news for once. The treaty acknowledged that we share our world with undead, shapeshifters, lycanthropes, angels, djinn, demons, and fae; it also legitimated the civic defense powers of the Veil Watchers and provided a means for these non-mortal entities to enter, live, and thrive in our world while keeping their identities secret. The treaty even legally formulated the rules of consent for vampiric and lycanthropic feeding and reproduction, and it mandated severe penalties for those who violated these laws. We're still working on explaining other forms of consent to assholes. Thanks to my father, I've always known that these beings existed, but I've taken on a professional interest in more recent years. They're powerful, sure, but they're people too. They have problems just like everyone else, but when they get into trouble, the Watchers usually kill without question. And that's not fair.

I smiled as I mused over my life, only snapping out of my memories when Destiny said, "Oh, but tonight's the full moon. That's why you're still in the office instead of at home with your evening coffee pot and Netflix subscription."

"Yeah," I answered, nodding. "I'm waiting to see what trouble walks through that door." I pointed to the wooden door that had "Hain Private Investigations" written in a Helvetica arch above my logo: a silver waning sliver of a moon at the edge of a black disk. "Always happens on the full moon, so let's see what shit I get asked to fix tonight."

"If anything," she said, "I mean, we've been quiet on that front for three months."

"But it's October's full moon, Des," I replied. "All the little ghosts and goblins will be roaming free."

"At least it's not Devil's Night, right?" She closed her eyes. I nodded, remembering the carnage of October 2019.

"That would be more predictable. More dangerous, sure, but more predictable." I walked to the front room to refill my coffee mug, a simple black mug with "Failure to plan on your part does NOT indicate an emergency on mine" in bright yellow letters, when the door opened and a short, squat ginger with a patchy beard and dazzling peridot eyes entered. His navy pinstripe suit was a tad oversized, wrinkled, and perfectly dry while his crimson fedora seemed soaking wet. He looked me over and, in a heavy brogue that cracked like a teenager's voice, said, "Good evening, Miss. Might you direct me to Mister Sam Hain? I've a matter that needs fixing."

* * *

"I'm Sam Hain," the woman replied and then emphatically added with a dagger-hurling smile, "Samantha Blake Hain, Private Investigator. How may I help you?"

Taken aback, the short, red-haired man removed his crimson hat and bowed respectfully. "Forgive me, Miss Hain, but I assumed from your clothes that you were the sec—"

"The secretary. I've heard it before. Don't let the stilettos and stockings fool you. I can smuggle a selkie out of a public aquarium just as easily as I can tango at twilight."

Sam slid onto Destiny's desk and crossed her legs. On this autumnal night, she wore a burgundy wiggle dress with a keyhole opening and lace sleeves. The tops of her seamed stockings, held in place by garters, peeked from beneath the hemline. Running the pale fingers of her left hand through her victory-curled brown hair, she sipped her coffee, drawing it into the smirking mouth beneath her broad nose before winking at him. She set the mug on the mahogany-tinted IKEA Malm desk and grabbed a legal pad and pen.

"So," she stared beyond this potential client's eyes as she asked, "what do you need fixed?"

The man nodded. "Well - I - you know why I'm here, so I guess you know who I am, right?"

Sam looked him over again before replying, "I doubt you'll tell me your name, but you're a ginger, have dazzling eyes, and are wearing a red fedora that's soaking wet while your wrinkly suit is dry. You're one of the Fair Folk. I'd wager you're a redcap?"

He nodded in assent. Destiny Grimm emerged from Sam's office. She stood a few inches shorter than Sam, and, although they were the same age, her more conservative dress often made her appear older. She sat behind her desk and shook the mouse, waking her computer and causing the overhead lighting to flicker. The redcap's eyes widened, and he backed toward the door.

"What in all of Faerie, the Otherworld, and the Nine Hells is she doing here? I'm not talking anymore with one of them in the room!"

"Really?" Destiny rolled her eyes. "I work here. I'm not in the family business" she turned her gaze toward the desk and hastily added, "Not anymore."

"Des is my friend and assistant," Sam added. "She's a Grimm, but she's no Veil Watcher. Besides, she'll draw up the contract that we'll sign, should I decide to help you. You can protest all you want, but none from Faerie seek me out during the full moon unless they're waist-deep in wet shit." She folded her arms across her chest and cocked an eyebrow. "I'd wager you're out of other options, so tell me what you need fixed."

A defeated sigh escaped the redcap's lips. He nodded. "Very well. It's not me - it's a friend, Niamh O'Cuinn. She was spotted by a serving girl from Castle Gealladh while out singing in the Emberheath Bog a fortnight ago. Seems the girl, a Mabd something-or-other, got a clear video of her on her cell phone. A bunch of amateur ghost hunters descended on the area, which is annoying on most nights, but we can normally fool them and get them to leave. Seems, however, that quite a few of them have gone and died out in the bog which got the Gardaí involved, and then, well, it drew their interest."

"The Duilearga." Sam responded.

"Aye," the redcap replied.

Sam nodded. Named for Séamus Duilearga, one of the earliest collectors of Irish folklore, the Duilearga served

9

as Ireland's branch of the Veil Watchers, an organization that ensures that instances of "Veil piercing", when mortals accidentally learn that they share a world with the creatures of folklore, are contained. Destiny's eyes darted up in concern as Sam ran her fingers over a spot on her left shoulder where her dress covered a scar from a Duilearga agent's blessed silver bullet during an altercation while confronting that leprechaun. Of all the Veil Watchers, the Duilearga had a reputation for quick, decisive investigations, leaving little time for Sam to resolve the situation before, like all other branches of Veil Watchers, the Duilearga closed their investigation through a body count.

"Shit! How long have the Duilearga been on the case?" Sam asked.

The redcap shuffled nervously and replied, "A few days, I'd wager."

Both women narrowed their eyes at their visitor. Sam shook her head. "I don't deal with lawyers after normal business hours, Mister Redcap–not since last week."

The redcap looked confused. "I'm no barrister, Miss Hain. I'm a gardener."

"Then either you stop speaking in faerie circles and tell me what the actual fuck is going on or get the fucking hell out of my office! With a 'few days" lead, the Duilearga might already have a bead on your friend there, and that means that she, the girl who discovered her song, and all the amateur ghost hunters and police officers might be dead. So, let's go over your story–starting with you giving me a name by which I can contact you, since I know you won't tell me your true name–and, this time, why don't you give me all the important details that you've conveniently omitted so I can do what I need to do?"

Sam and the redcap stared at each other, unblinking, for several minutes as Destiny's fingers clicked the keys on her keyboard. Sam shot the redcap a razor-sharp smile as she drummed her fingers slowly on the desk. "Well, Mister Redcap, the choice is yours. It's late, and time is, well, blood money." She winced as she said that, but continued. "I'm out of coffee, and Netflix has a new season of The Great British Baking Show with my name on it. What's it going to be?"

The redcap sighed and stared at the floorboards while shifting from one foot to the other. "Very well, Miss Hain. You may call me Dagh Mobh, and here's all that I know. Niamh was out on the Emberheath Bog at night singing. This was before the moon's first quarter. She usually picks stormy nights with heavy fog, so humans think she's the wind or a bird or something. You mortals will believe anything to avoid the truth. Don't look at me like that! You know I'm not talking about you lot. Anyway, she was really into her song and didn't notice this Mabd approach and get a clear video. Girl posted it to her Inster or Facegram or TokTik or whatever magical media is popular. I can't ever get them straight. That's what brought in all the ghost hunters who chased out into the Emberheath Bog after her. Several ended up dead – she never attacked them–not one, I swear."

"Then what killed them?" Sam asked as she took notes.

"I didn't see all of them die, so I don't know. I assume most died of shock. I mean, you can hunt for stuff like this but seeing it, well, that's got to be a right shock to the system. There was some gunfire and growling, so maybe hunting accidents or a bear or a big cat. Well, the lot of them that survived talked up what happened at The Tipsy Tenpenny. The village got in an uproar, and you know gossip spreads like the flu, which –"

"Drew the Duilearga's attention," Sam interjected.

Dagh nodded. "Aye, Miss Hain. And that's all I–Titania, Queen of the Summer Court! What's that noise?" The redcap dropped his fedora as Destiny's printer growled to life before spitting out a handful of pages.

"Here you go, Sam. One contract for the safe removal of one banshee and the protection of the young girl named Mabd as well as unnumbered and unnamed other mortals to be completed before the 31st of October to minimize the dangers posed by Duilearga involvement."

Dagh's eyes shot wide as he sputtered, "I never said she was a banshee!"

"Remember, I'm one of those people? It's my job to know these things." Destiny's tongue shot forward. She sneered at the redcap as Sam took the contract from her.

"If there are no corrections, Mister Mobh, my fee for this is seven thousand U.S. dollars. I expect half up front and half on completion. I take cash, check, or electronic transfer. Faerie gold is not accepted here."

"Seven thousand! That's robbery. I was told your rate was five thousand. I won't pay."

"Under normal conditions, you would be correct, Mister Mobh. However, given that I must travel to Ireland and that I have – how should I put it? – only a 'few days' before the Duilearga 'take care of the matter' – if they haven't already done so, travel expenses and rush job fees have been factored in. But," she paused as she gently placed the contract on the desk beside Destiny's Indigo League pen cup, "the choice to engage my services remains with you."

The redcap ran his fingers over his fedora's brim and through

12

his mass of red hair as he contemplated his decision. He walked over to the desk and slowly perused the contract. His brow furrowed and his shoulders slumped forward as he opened his wallet and produced thirty-five one hundred-dollar bills. Signing the contract, he said, "I have little choice if I'm to help her, I suppose. Alright, Miss Hain, you've got yourself a deal."

Sam signed the contract and accepted the payment. As she slid the paperwork back to Destiny, she smiled. "A pleasure doing business with you. I'll make my arrangements and leave for Ireland."

"You hurry," Dagh nodded as he walked toward the door. "We'll be watching you."

As the door closed behind him, Destiny glowered. "You didn't have to go so hard on him, Sam. We're barely scraping by as it is. Your car needs repairs. We need electrical work and new equipment. You almost lost this case."

Sam shrugged and sighed. "Then I could have a drink and go home in peace. Des, it's not like it's some chosen destiny bullshit. They seek me out because I'm good at what I do. It's purely financial – especially given most of my mortal clients can't pay that much."

"And yet you never turn them down," Destiny replied flatly.

Sam furrowed her brow. "They're women in need of help, Des. The police won't do anything without a body of evidence, and in many of these cases, that could prove fatal. They come to me, and I help them, taking only what they can afford. So, 'Fixing' makes up for it."

Destiny snorted. "I may be your assistant, but your destiny seems to be having a heart that bleeds for the suffering of others. That's not a bad thing, Sam." She chuckled as she placed a hand on her friend's shoulder. "Besides, Ireland for your birthday. There are worse places to be, I suppose. Plus, we all know you have a thing for redheads."

Sam growled in mock annoyance. "You google any information you can find on this castle and the nearest town while I head to home to fix Sandy's dinner, pack, and get a nap in."

"Gotcha, boss. I'll book you a flight. Nothing before ten, as always?"

Sam shook her head. "Can't fly this time," she said. I'll lose almost a full day if I travel by plane. And since our little redcap friend likely left out other details, I've got to do a little predeparture digging. Besides, I need a drink. Mind looking after Sandy while I'm gone?"

"I'm on it. Text you in a few hours," Destiny replied.

* * *

An insistent but plaintive meow from a calico cat pacing at her apartment door greeted Sam as she returned home. The two-bedroom apartment was cozy. Or at least that is what Sam told herself to justify refusing her father's repeated offerings of help with affording a larger place. Without a second thought, Sam scooped the cat into her arms, held her close, and kissed the top of her head. She flipped the cat over and cradled her, stroking her orange paws–the only part of her fur with that coloration. She gave the cat a final kiss before gently setting her on the wood floor and going to get her dinner. "I missed you too, Sandy Paws, best Christmas present I ever received."

Sandy followed Sam through the cramped den with the tattered tan couch that Sam had had since college and that Sandy preferred to her scratching post and the dining area

14

where Sam stored her pile of unread books on the small dining table. An impressionistic but attractive watercolor of the Stubai Alps around Wilder Freiger. Sam paused to stare wistfully at the painting for a moment, remembering one of the happier and more relaxing moments since her mother passed. They headed into her bedroom where Sam grabbed her blue and brown leather dress bag as Sam packed for her upcoming trip. After an hour of playing with Sandy, moving Sandy out of her travel bag, and lint-rolling the clothes Sandy sat on, Sam packed her clothes, passport and permits for the return trip, the leather map case in which she carried her silver rapier, a pistol, two clips with normal and blessed cold iron rounds, and–just in case–a hunter's kit. She hung a blue and orange paisley A-line dress, coordinating orange knit cardigan, and pale tights from the hook atop her closet door. She placed a pair of brown riding boots beside them. She sighed, mentally listing all she had to pack after her nap. She scratched Sandy's chin, smiling as her cat purred, and then took a relaxing bath before setting her alarm, curling up in bed with Sandy, and taking a nap.

After hitting the snooze button twice, Sam took a quick shower, made a cup of coffee, dressed, packed her makeup, and carried her traveling goods into the room she used for an office, locking the door behind her. As she entered the room, a vibration from her backpack announced a text message; Destiny determined that the nearest town to the castle was Bannagh in Sligo County near Benbulben Mountain, a small town of about four hundred people. She said it had one bed-and-breakfast called The Slouching Giant, a single pub, and a train station about a mile to its southwest. Destiny identified the young girl as Mabd Donovan and said she posted the banshee video on her TikTok under the handle of "Smyling_xEirex_Eyes," stating that the video has been viewed almost one million times. Sam cursed this last bit. Destiny warned that tracking the girl down may prove difficult, if her recent inactivity on social media proves to be an indication. She ended with, "I booked you the last room at the B&B, seems to be crowded with a few ghost hunters and some history professor from Trinity. Be safe."

"Hmm," Sam thought. "I wonder if it's Professor Kennedy." She thanked and reassured Destiny that she would be safe. Sam then turned her attention back to the task at hand in her office. Aside from the mahogany writing desk and matching shelf overflowing with leather-bound books, nothing else in this room furnished with four large white pillar candles set atop black marble pillars in each of the cardinal points; a wooden table dressed with a black cloth, a pair of black and white taper candles, a leather-bound book – a gift from her father – whose pages were mostly empty, a dagger, a censor, a wand, and a silver pentacle; and a large circle comprising multiple lines of runes, sigils, and sacred words in whose center the wooden table held vigil.

Sam moved her traveling gear into the circle, lit the candles on the table, and cleansed the area by walking the edge of the circle, holding the white candle in her hands. She knocked thrice on table and forcefully pronounced a string of divine names. She then opened the book to the fourth page with writing on it and chanted, *"Per obscurum noctis, per clara die, ego tibi aperire viam praecipio,"* six times. A wind blew through the chamber, snuffing the candles. After the wind stopped, a small point of silver light appeared on the eastern wall. The point drifted, leaving a light trail that outlined the shape of a door.

Sam heard the click of the locking mechanism's release as the line completed tracing the shape. She closed the book on her table, picked up her gear, and stepped through the door.

* * *

A husky voice singing "Diamonds are a Girl's Best Friend" greeted Sam as she entered the bar. The voice's owner, a statuesque, curly-haired, caramel-skinned woman whose elegantly curved horns signaled her unearthly origin draped herself across a grand piano adorned with a landscape of wax from the three-pronged candelabra that stood near the music stand where a classically handsome man with Semitic features and thick black hair accompanied her as she entertained the mixed crowd of Veil Crossers, humans and non-humans who can move across the Veil in secret, whose candle-shadowed faces watched the performance with rapt attention. The bartender, a handsome man in a white shirt with a charcoal vest, slicked black hair, three-day stubble, and piercing green eyes, called out in a voice that sounded like an aristocratic Londoner, "Welcome to The Four Winds where all who enter are welcome to sit, drink, and share their stories. We only have one rule, and that's–Oh, hello, Samantha, come have a drink."

She felt the eyes of several of the barflies follow her as she found an empty section of the bar and sat down. As the bartender approached, she leaned forward. "Good morning, Nick. I'll have my usual."

He nodded and produced a whisky sour. Leaning against the bar, he smirked. "And what have you brought me this time?"

Sam swirled the cocktail a few times before taking a long, slow sip. As her shoulders relaxed, she smiled quickly before furrowing her brow. She turned back toward the stage and said, "It's good to see Lilith and Gabriel are back to working together."

He chuckled and allowed an elongated canine to show briefly. "Yes, but you're dodging the question. What have you brought me?"

Sam slapped her hand on her chest and opened her mouth in mock surprise. "Now, Mister Scratch, can't a lady such as myself and a gentleman such as yourself just engage in a bit of friendly conversation without it immediately turning into a business transaction?"

He smirked and leaned toward her. "A lady most certainly may. However, if I truly believed that you, dear lady, had developed the Southern belle's patience for small talk, I might have to close this bar. So, what did you bring me?"

"I'm glad you're not one of the lawyers I regularly stare down, Nick." The rim of the glass muffled Sam's voice slightly. She set the glass on the napkin Nick had placed atop his polished mahogany bar and then said, "Banshee on social media has left a trail of bodies, and the Duilearga are about to descend on a small Irish village."

"That explains the recent influx of mortal souls here." Nick crossed his arms over his chest.

"So, you already knew?" Sam's eyes flashed with excitement.

"Not exactly," he chuckled. "I knew of the banshee, and they understood how they died. However, for those who 'hunt' for proof of the afterlife, the fact that my establishment exists—the fact that I exist—seemed to be quite the shock to their systems."

"They're here? Can I speak to them?"

He shook his head. "They were, Samantha, but Michael came to collect them about an hour ago. Well, all but one. Hermes

18

came for him."

"Damn! I could've used the lead."

"True, but at least now I know that your mortal technology can capture the Fae. That could prove useful in coming negotiations." Sam raised her left eyebrow from behind her drink, but before she could query, Nick touched his left hand to the center of his chest three times and winked. "You know where I keep my cards, Samantha."

"And you know that you can call me 'Sam,' Nick, but I'm sure you've gathered I'm not just here for a drink."

He leaned back against the shelf of scotches and crossed his arms over his chest. "Well, Private Investigator Samantha B. Hain, given what possessions you have with you, what you've told me regarding this banshee situation, and what I've gathered from the ghosts of her hunters, I would surmise that mortal methods of transportation are not fast enough for your lack of patience and desire to conclude this matter before your special day. Am I correct?"

"You could have simply said 'before my birthday,'" She sighed, pinching the bridge of her nose.

"I could have, but it's not just a birthday, is it? It's the one day each year that you get to spend time with your mother, and, per our agreement, we've got a private booth reserved."

Samantha gave him a genuine smile. "You're not so bad, Nick."

He frowned mockingly and said, "Don't tell anyone, my dear. It'll ruin my reputation." A woman called him from across the bar. He turned and nodded before turning back to Sam. "Excuse me, dear. The wife is calling. Finish your drink, and I'll return in a few to help with travel arrangements." He sauntered away.

Sam stared into her slowly emptying cocktail glass as her mind sipped on snippets of memory. Traipsing through a forest of thick oak, birch, and rowan trees in County Cork during an Irish spring when she had her first encounter with a Duilearga agent. His warning that the "wee lass" should return home and play with her "dollies" spurred her on to find and help that leprechaun more than the five hundred dollars she was offered if she succeeded. She expected him to try to out-think her, but she did not expect him to shoot her while attempting to complete his duties. She lied to Amanda about the wound, saying she accidentally startled a hunter while walking through a faerie ring. They became nothing more than roommates after Amanda discovered the lie, and when their lease expired shortly thereafter, they parted ways. Sam wondered what this trip to Ireland would cost her.

"Drink rarely has the prophetic answers you mortals so often pray it to have," came a heavily accented Austrian woman's voice from behind her. Sam jerked her head around to see a beautiful but solemn woman with black hair, pale skin, and burgundy lips wearing a perfectly tailored pencil dress and blazer. She appeared to be no older than twenty. The woman sat on the stool beside Sam and leaned forward, smiling. "Tell me, Sam, what do you seek?"

Sam blinked and jerked her eyes up to meet the woman's. "You don't really care for details on this case, 'Milla. So why ask?"

The woman, Countess Carmilla Karnstein, shrugged and smiled. Her index finger circled the rim of Sam's glass as she said, "Such mortal concerns are beneath me, true, but I care for your safety. Though a good age, is thirty not when age begins to 'creak up on you' as they say?"

Sam rolled her eyes. "Your cheeks are flushed, 'Milla," she said. "You're not hungry, so what's your angle?"

Carmilla chuckled and licked her lips. With a smirking wink, she brushed the tip of her perfectly manicured index finger with its burgundy-polished nail against the back of Sam's hand and replied, "There is always room for dessert."

Sam bit her lip and swallowed hard as she pulled away slowly. "Countess Karnstein, we've discussed this. It–it wouldn't work."

The woman furrowed her brow and pursed her lips in a mocking pout. "Forgive me, Sam. I forgot that you were involved with that Rachel woman. Unless –"

"We're no longer together," Sam interrupted, running her fingers through her hair. "And it's not that, 'Milla. And it's–it's not even that you drink blood to survive. It's that you literally are a corpse during the day, and I just can't handle waking up to that. It felt cold and lonely."

She whispered into Sam's ear, "There are ways, Samantha, to ensure our schedules align." She squeezed Sam's hand briefly and then pulled back, sitting upright on her stool. "But I will not press the matter, because I find great value in your friendship. However, my offer remains on the proverbial table–from one night unto eternity."

Sam gulped her whiskey sour and asked, "How are things in Austria? Are you still painting? You really should think about selling your work."

The vampire chuckled and said, "I am, but I don't think the Grimms would take kindly to one in my position dancing across the Veil with such abandon."

Sam thought for a moment before responding, "But you wouldn't have to do anything you don't normally do. You could be this reclusive artist who only makes appearances at night, hosts exhibitions in abandoned churches and castles, and who seems to live on a diet of red wine and passion. Besides," she leaned in and sipped her cocktail, saying, "It's not like when you were my age. You can just set up an online shop and some social media for advertising, and let things go from there. You're talented, 'Milla. You don't have to follow tradition and rely on investments drawn from centuries' old family money."

Countess Karnstein looked into the distance for a moment. She nodded and said, "I will consider this, Sam. It is new territory for me, and one my age adapts slowly to such new ideas."

They talked for another hour before Countess Karnstein left for her home. As the crowd at The Four Winds thinned, Nick returned to Sam, a broad, cocky smile on his face. "I hope I didn't interrupt anything, Samantha."

"Long conversation, Nick. Seems you had one too. Or were you ignoring me for your other patrons?"

"I admit," he replied, "that I did serve a handful of my guests, but I spent most of my absence tending to my wife's every need."

"Horny fucking devil," Sam replied under her breath.

Nick laughed and replied, "Damned as charged. But you needed some assistance in traveling to Ireland, correct?"

"I do," Sam nodded. "I need to get to a train station just south of Bannagh in County Sligo."

"Bannagh? That's near Castle Gaelladgh, isn't it?" Nick mused.

"Yes," Sam bolted upright. "Know something?"

Nick grinned hungrily. "Many things, Samantha Blake Hain. However, few are freely given. I've not been to Ireland in some time, and I don't recall there being a banshee attached to that castle; however, most of my time there was spent playing cards with the Tottenhams and the Friars of Saint Francis of Wycombe. Those were the days. You have your grimoire with you, yes?"

She shook her head. "Why bother? I'm not my father's successor, Nick. I've only got like three or four spells in it."

Nick pinched the bridge of his nose and took a deep breath. "No, Samantha, but the spells he convinced you to learn would benefit you by keeping you safe. You're dealing with the Fae. Tell me, how do you plan to remain safe should the banshee wail your name?"

Sam pulled a small tube from her pocket. "Ear plugs, Nick. Modern invention–no magic required."

He shook his head. "Those ghost hunters can be forgiven for their ignorance of the truth, but you, Sam Hain, your legacy implies that you know better than to trust mortal inventions in the face of non-mortal threats. Be careful – unless you're planning to spend more time with your mother than the current agreement allows." He cocked an eyebrow.

Sam's cheeks flushed as she sputtered the last watered-down drop of her drink. Thrusting the empty glass toward him, she growled. "How can–I am thinking no such thing!" She straightened herself. "For someone who values knowledge so highly, you really should buy a clue. Which door will get me to my destination?"

He snatched the glass from the bar and pointed to the western wall. She smiled professionally, nodded her head, and said, "Always a pleasure. I'll see you on my birthday."

As she slammed the door behind her, Lilith sauntered over and sat on the bar. She leaned over and kissed him deeply, her hand flicking open a few of the buttons on his shirt. As she pulled away, she said, "Samael, why did you say that too her?"

He poured them both a glass of deep burgundy wine. "Her thoughts betray her, darling. And Countess Karnstein brought her own concerns to my attention after the last time they spoke. The Countess fears that someone may use it against her. And I do not trust the Fae. I do not lie to mortals. Don't give me that side eye, darling. I simply bury the truth in mountains of legalese that few have the time, the intellect, or the desire to surmount. Thus, they damn themselves by their own hubris or laziness. It's nothing personal for me–simply business. The Fae, on the other hand, will deceive and trick for the sheer joy of doing so. Those sociopathic little monsters need to be brought to heel, and until Titania and Oberon gain the courage and power to do so, the unruly denizens of their courts will endanger mortals." He sipped the wine and continued, "She doesn't need to be Donal's successor, but she needs to accept that she is his heir. That could save her life.

Chapter 2

"Alright, Miss Hain, you're all set. You'll be staying in Room 12 at the far end of that hall." The balding, silver-goateed owner of The Slouching Giant whose pale skin had reddish undertones said as he smiled warmly and handed me the room key, pointing at the hall on his right with his hand that seemed large and calloused, like a farmer's or a carpenter's hand.

"Thank you very much for your help, Mister O'Gill. I'm sorry it was such an early morning booking for you." I replied.

"Oh, not a problem at all. The missus and I get up with the sun to have coffee on the back porch every morning. You're a bit earlier than expected." He said.

I furrowed my brow and clenched my jaw before asking, "Oh? What do you mean?"

He shook his head, "Oh nothing, Miss. When your assistant called and said you'd be coming in today, I assumed you'd be flying out from America at a more reasonable hour. Seems you were already on your way." He must have seen me relax before adding, "Did you think I was going to take a cheap jab at your name?"

I snorted. "Everyone else has. All. My. Life."

He nodded and pointed to his nameplate that said, "Darby." With a smile, he replied, "My name's Darby O'Gill. Thanks to that motion picture by Mister Walt Disney, every Yank asks me how often I see 'little people.' For years, I couldn't go anywhere across the pond without it happening every time I'd pull out my card to pay for something. Before the Missus and I met, I disappointed so many women by looking more like Albert Sharpe than a young Sean Connery. With all the talk of a banshee, things are going to get a lot worse."

"Banshee?" I feigned ignorance and tried to sound like a tourist. "So there really is a haunted castle around here?"

He sighed heavily. "The Good Folk of the Woods are likely real enough, so I wouldn't seek them out. But don't believe the stories they print in the brochures about ghosts and demons in and around Castle Gaelladgh. And I know I should be playing up the stories for business, but I don't want you getting the idea to go running off into the bog in the middle of the night and getting killed like those idiots have been doing. If you want to go hiking in the mountains or walking the woods, do so during the day with one of the guides."

"So what riled everyone up? Just an old tale or something? I studied comparative literature in college, so I love hearing good stories." I batted my eyelashes furiously while smiling.

"Nah, there's been no talk of banshees around here – a faerie ring in the bog or in the woods, sure–but never a banshee. This girl, Mabd Donovan, sweet girl, really, who serves the O'Cuinn family that lives in Castle Gaelladgh, well, she posted some video on whatever this TikTok thing is claiming to be a banshee's song. Got to be faked. I mean, we could fake things like that with a little petroleum jelly and our eight mils back when I was about your age. I figure, with the computer programs the kids learn in school these days, it can't be real."

"So, the people who died in the bog, they didn't die from

fright or 'mysterious circumstances,'" I asked.

He shook his head. "One died in a hunting accident. A few of the older ones probably had a heart attack, but most of them had major cuts on their bodies that looked like giant claw marks. Most reasonable people believe it was a large cat or a bear or something. It's not common, but it does happen."

I feigned a disappointed sigh. "What a shame. As cheesy as it may sound, given my name and all that, a good ghost story this time of year is a true treat."

"Aye," he smiled, "They are. If you want to hear a good yarn or two, head on down to the Tenpenny later and listen to some of us old timers and some of the songwriters there. You'll hear a good tale or two–just don't go traipsing about at night and become one." We both laughed.

He told me that they served breakfast from six to ten in the mornings, and that they kept coffee and tea supplies in the sitting room for when guests needed them. I smiled and thanked him again as I headed down the hallway toward my room. As I left the lobby, I heard him muse that I remind him of his granddaughter. I smiled. He seems like a nice old grandfather, and I never got to know mine that well on either side–especially after mom's accident. Maybe I'll work on that in the coming year.

The Slouching Giant had gorgeous cream-colored walls with bright oak flooring and wrought iron light fixtures in its wider-than-expected hallways. I had assumed a bed-and-breakfast in a town this small would just be a converted old house; maybe it is, because its owner, at least Mister O'Gill–haven't met Mrs. O'Gill yet, though he did mention that he had a wife–really made me feel welcome here. While walking, I texted Destiny to let her know I had arrived safely. Fortunately, I haven't had teleportation sickness in a few years, but I still get a bit nauseous when stepping through some of those portals. I suppose I owe Nick a thank you for having me emerge in a public restroom stall this time. Before I looked up from my phone, I bumped into someone walking the other way. "Sorry," I blurted quickly as I turned to look at him, but he kept walking, allowing me only a glimpse at a thick mess of curly brown hair and his left hand as he waved what seemed to be a "Don't worry about it" reply while mumbling about "bloody American kids these days." And then my eyes fixed on the ring on his index finger: a signet ring. There's only one thing that could mean, and that's what I was afraid of. I bet he's already got a body count.

Irish country charm greeted me as I opened the door to my room. It wasn't my preferred decorating style, but for a bed-and-breakfast with "quaint and cozy country charm," there was more space than expected. The O'Gills placed an apple cider air freshener in the room that smelled like real cider. I hung my dress bag in the closet and set my suitcase beside my bed. I ran my fingers along the varnished wood of the four-poster bed and smirked; I could have some fun here if I were on a pleasure trip. Maybe in the future. Now, I needed about four more hours of sleep to investigate properly.

* * *

"I know what I saw, Des. The fucking Duilearga have at least one agent here already. Big guy too, brown hair and chubby fingers. Didn't get a look at his face," Sam spoke into her cell phone after she woke from her post-teleportation nap.

"Are you really surprised, Sam?" Destiny responded. "That

redcap guy told you they said they would handle the matter on the thirty-first, so…"

"I know it makes sense," Sam spat out. "It just complicates matters, because I don't fucking know if he recognized me or if…"

"Or if he's the guy who gave you that shoulder scar that you routinely hide with clothing that's too warm for our North Carolina summers."

"Can't be him," Sam said as she glare and snorted into the phone. Through gritted teeth, she replied, "He was too portly, but I am not thinking about Michael fucking Cormack with his cocky, patronizing attitude and 'shoot first' policy."

Sam angrily recounted her first encounter with a Duilearga agent, which, although it happened almost nine years ago, she remembered the details as if it occurred recently. While Destiny's verbal responses suggested patience, her constant eye rolling and the fact that she focused more attention on navigating Butcher's Bend's streets during rush hour suggested her attention was focused elsewhere. As Sam recounted the potato overload she had during her recovery in Mallow General, she paused and asked, "Des, are you still listening?"

"Perfect attendance as always, boss." Destiny replied with a practiced smile.

"Des, why did you let me rant like that again?" Sam asked.

"Same reason as always, Sam: you needed it." Destiny replied. "I know you're stressed with the time crunch and then seeing a Duilearga agent your first hour in Ireland. And when you're stressed, you have a tendency to ignore the information around you, and that's not good for an investigation. So, because I'm your friend, I wanted you to get this out of your system before you headed out to investigate. Speaking of, what's the game plan?"

Sam sighed, collapsing on the bed. "I don't have a fucking clue. I don't know where to start, and I'm not sure what I can do to fix the situation without anyone dying. Right now, all I've got planned is to chill in the sitting room with a book, listening to some of the ghost hunters talking and maybe strike up a conversation to get some information before heading out to the pub to see if the locals can help me find that Mabd girl who seems quiet on social, right?" Sam cocked her head to the side, trying to recognize the low-volume music coming through the phone.

"Mabd Donovan. Yeah, she hasn't posted anything in about a week. Last thing I could find was a Tweet about how viral her banshee vid went. I'll keep stalking and text if I find something. So, which ghost hunting cutie is going to get that infamous Samantha Hain charm?"

Sam gagged audibly. "From what I've seen, Des, ghost hunting seems to be a sausage fest. Isn't that more your thing?"

"What? I'm German! Of course, I love sausages. I just wish most of the ones I've had lately didn't require so much preparation." She sighed. "Hold on," she paused to unlock the office door, "I wish I were back home right now. I love you, Sam, but Germany in the fall is heaven for me."

"Why didn't you take off for Oktoberfest this year like you always do?"

"I had a feeling that something weird would happen while I was gone. And then your dad showed up with that lady with the yellow ribbon choker and a story right off Creepypasta. And it's been nine years since your mom's passing–three times three–that's a big deal in our old stories. And then, well, this."

Sam winced. "Dad always has impeccable timing, ugh.

Anyway, next year, you're going. Hell, I might take off and come too. I had fun last time."

Destiny chuckled. "You weren't as bad as some Americans can be, and my family loves you. Just don't spend half the time talking about work with my father."

Sam smiled, "But that made the entire trip tax deductible. Fine, Des, fine. I'll actually have a vacation next year. Anyway, let me get going and start this investigation. And you probably want to get back to that tropical island you brought to work with you."

Destiny took a quick glance at her desk and saw that she forgot to mute her Switch Lite, allowing Sam to pick up on the background music from *Animal Crossing: New Horizons*. With a sheepish grin, she replied, "Gotta have some company while I sit and wait for the phone to ring, boss. Anyway. Time is blood money. Bye!"

"She'll never let me live that drunken quip down," Sam said to herself as she placed her phone in her purse. "But in my business, time is often blood money. Hopefully, saving someone's blood instead of spilling it." She headed into the sitting room, locking her door behind her.

A handful of patrons rested in the rustic wooden chairs in The Slouching Giant's sitting room. While giving her the welcoming tour, Mister O'Gill said that his great-grandfather made the furniture himself, and that the family has taken it upon themselves to continue with the furniture's upkeep. Sam settled in an open chair near the hearth where flames from the spiced cider and mulled wine candles sitting atop the mantle swayed gently. Keeping her boots off the soft, heather-filled cushion, she curled up, removing her book, *Werewolves of Wuthering Heights*, from her purse, and began rereading, her ears actively listening for any interesting conversations.

Thirty pages into her halfhearted rereading, Sam overheard two male ghost hunters whose accents placed them from somewhere in Cornwall arguing. They appeared to be several years older than Sam and dressed in matching gray sweater vests with embroidered logos and driving caps. The older one, a portly man with umber skin, thinning salt-and-pepper hair, and three-day stubble, leaned toward the younger, clean-shaven brown-skinned man and said, "Look, Frank, we both saw the bloody video of that thing, but we've been out here almost a week and haven't found nothing. I say it's time to pack up and head home. We've both used enough holiday time out here, and, well, I'm concerned one of us'll die if we keep this up."

Frank shook his head. "I don't know, Nigel. I think we're on the edge of something big–something that'll put Cornwall Spiritualist Society on the map. Let's head back to the castle and talk to the O'Cuinn lady. I think she knows something she ain't telling."

Nigel ran his fingers through what remained of his hair, "I don't know. I'll think about it. Anyway, I need to call Meg and see how she and the kids are doing. That'll make my decision for me. Back in ten or so." He walked down the hallway toward his room.

Sam watched from over the top of her book as Frank exhaled deeply, furrowed his brow, and stared at the spiral-bound notebook he had with him. Sam waited for a few moments before walking toward his chair and sitting next to him. "Excuse me, I'm on vacation, and I heard you and your friend talking about ghosts. Are there any good ghost stories from this town?"

32

Frank chuckled as he looked her over. "You're really not from around here – not even this millennium." He paused before adding, "I don't mean it in a bad way. The look suits you, but it's clear you're not a local."

Sam bit her lip quickly and leaned toward him. "Do I stick out that badly? Guess it can't be helped. Still, you haven't answered my question. Know any good ghost stories from here?"

"That seems a rather pointed question, Miss, er, oh! I never got your name. I'm Frank Caldwell of Cornwall Spiritualist Society, and you are?"

She held out her hand and said, "Samantha Burnside. So, a Spiritualist Society. Do you just chase ghosts, or do you hold meditation retreats or something?"

Frank shook his head and laughed. "We try to document the existence of paranormal phenomena and, when necessary, help people who are being attacked by spirits of all kinds."

"So, I guess I happened to luck out," Sam smiled at him. "You seem to be the person with the stories. I know Mister O'Gill said something about a fake banshee video from around here, but the websites I saw as I planned my trip said something about a haunted castle which no one seems willing to talk about. It sucks, because with Halloween coming up, a good ghost story would be amazing!"

Frank laughed. "I can't disagree with that last part. Well then, let me tell you the strange tale of the Banshee of Emberheath Bog."

Sam listened intently, feigning surprise as Frank recounted the basic story of Mabd Donovan seeing and recording the banshee with her cell phone before uploading it to her TikTok. Apparently, when it turned toward her, she hid inside the

O'Cuinn-Gaell Pathway, a portal-shaped megalithic structure amidst the dwarf cornel, juniper, and bog rosemary, which the local legends claim is a pathway to the Otherworld. From her vocal commentary, Mabd believed this allowed her to avoid the banshee's gaze, which she credited with saving her life. Sam wondered if that were some local legend, given that tradition warns of the danger of hearing the banshee wail one's name. Frank continued by telling her that, as the video's virality increased, scores of amateur ghost hunters from Ireland, England, France, Germany, and even a few from the United States swarmed the small town and began searching for this banshee. None have found definitive evidence of its existence, and a handful have died out in the bog. As a result, the local police have posted patrols throughout the forest, the hills, and the bog to keep more people from dying.

"Fascinating," Sam replied. "Is the young girl okay? I know that, if all this happened because of something I posted on social media, I'd be a jagged ball of emotion."

Frank shook his head. "I can't say. We didn't speak to her, and only the first teams who got here had the chance before she went missing. And the survivors have all gone home."

"Missing?" Sam's eyes shot open. "That's terrible!"

Frank closed his eyes and nodded. "Yeah, seems she was on her way home from the Tenpenny after work and decided to walk by Old Tom's Hill – a shortcut or something – and just never made it home."

Sam tilted her head and cocked her eyebrow. "Old Tom's Hill? Strange name for a hill. What is it, someone's grave?"

"Nah, place of local legends. Some say it's a place where the Good People of the Woods would hold court. Others say it's where Liam O'Cuinn made a pact with the devil back in the thirteen hundreds. Most people discount that last one bit now, given that it likely started from anger over Liam's loyalty to the English throne, but they still believe in the Good Folk of the Woods."

They continued talking for a few more minutes when Frank's partner Nigel returned. Frank looked up and said, "Oh, Hey, Nige, how're Meg and the kids?"

"They're fine. I see you've attracted some attention, Frank." He extended his hand to Sam and said, "Nigel Dalencourt, pleasure."

Sam returned the greeting and said, "Samantha Burnside. And, I admit that I heard part of your conversation, and Frank was gracious enough to tell me some of the local ghost stories. 'Tis the season, after all."

Frank rolled his eyes and chuckled. "Aye." He turned his attention to Frank. "That said, Frank, I'm packing up and heading home. Meg's starting to get frazzled dealing with the contractor for the sitting room addition. I won't force you to come too, but I'm taking most of the gear. Your call."

Frank nodded. "I'm going to stick it out one more night, I think." He grinned wickedly and shot Sam a raised eyebrow. "What about it? You like the stories, so care to investigate if they're true?"

Nigel grunted. "You can't just bring a random girl you fancy on an investigation. What if she gets scared and runs off into a wet patch in the bog? Our goal is to document instances of the paranormal and not to create them."

This led to a heated discussion between the two men. After ten minutes, Sam rolled her eyes, sighed, and interrupted, "Gentlemen, while I appreciate the concern for my safety, the only question asked was one seeking my interest in the matter.

I was neither given the chance to answer that question, nor was I asked if I even thought I possessed the ability to handle the mythical banshee that, well, no one in this conversation seems to have found." She smiled sweetly.

Nigel grimaced and glared at her. "My apologies, Miss. Yes, I'm doubting your ability. I mean, to be honest; however, you look like a teacher, and we do this for fun – we don't have insurance in case something goes –"

"Wrong and I decide to sue." Sam smiled sweetly. "I understand, and I understand risk. After all, I'm a young woman traveling abroad alone to a village where several strange deaths have been happening lately. I'm not stupid, and I've learned to live with more risks than at least half the population believes exists. And, if we're going to judge by appearances, Mister Dalencourt, you have the body and hairline of an old high school quarterback who spends too much time at the bar lamenting his glory days. Of course," she smiled and stroked his shoulder to soften the ego blow. Frank laughed, and Sam continued, "talking to you for only a few minutes has revealed you to be far more than that. Books and covers, you know?"

Frank shot Nigel a challenging eyebrow and a smirk. Nigel nodded. "Quite the mouth on you, Miss Burnside. I'm not your father, so I can't make you stay home. If you think you can handle it, then I'll leave the decision up to you. It's your arse that'll suffer if you're not. But I'm heading home. Nice meeting you. Frank, let me know when you head home." Nigel walked over to Mister O'Gill and checked out.

Frank turned to Sam and asked, "So, fancy hunting for ghosts tonight?"

Sam winked. "I'll think about it. Ask me this afternoon."

"How about dinner at the Tenpenny around sunset? My treat." Frank blurted out quickly.

Sam smiled, "You don't have to be so gallant, but I would like a companion for supper. I'll see you then."

"Great! I've got some afternoon investigating to do, so I'll see you then." He shook her hand and then walked away.

Sam's eyes widened, and she sent Destiny a quick text, "I think I got asked out. By a guy. What should I do?"

* * *

Like most European villages, Bannagh was built for pedestrians. The streets had been paved to account first for bicycles and then for automobiles, and about half of the buildings had distinctly modern architecture. However, many older stone buildings remained, and some even had thatched roofs to give them that quaint village feel that so many tourists sought to have an authentic experience. As the thought crossed her mind, Sam rolled her eyes. A few of the older residents eyed her as she walked the streets, smiling idly. She found her way to The Prints and the Paper, Bannagh's only bookstore. A bell tinkled as she opened the door.

"Welcome to The Prints and the Paper, how are you–oh! You're new in town. How are you, dear?" The middle-aged woman with curly blonde hair and graying brown roots said from behind the register.

"I'm doing alright, ma'am. How are you?" Sam replied with a smile.

"I'm well, dear. So, what can I interest you in?" The woman asked.

Sam paused thoughtfully before replying, "Well, it's a bit

cliché, but you can't beat a good ghost story this time of year. So, what do you have in supernatural folklore, local legend, or something similar to the old Scary Stories to Tell in the Dark type thing?"

The woman frowned and shot a searching look at Sam. "You're one of those ghost chasers, aren't you? Here about the banshee?"

"Banshee? You mean that story that Mister O'Gill told me couldn't be real? I didn't hear about it until I checked in at The Slouching Giant. I decided I needed a vacation and googled 'small Irish towns with ghost legends', and Bannagh popped up a few pages in. I looked up some photos of the town and thought it looked like the perfect remote little place to relax in. Then I arrived, and, well, I learned what's been going on."

She raised an eyebrow. "Are you sure? There's something about you that says you'll go rushing into the bog looking for romance or terror, not caring which you find. Let me give you this advice: You don't have to believe in the Good Folk who live in the bog and the woods to know it's best to not go stirring them up against you. Don't step inside a faerie ring, don't walk through the O'Cuinn-Gaell Pathway, and don't, for the love of God in heaven and all his saints, don't go climbing Old Tom's Hill after dark."

"That's what that girl from the castle, um, Mary Donovan did, right?"

The woman sighed. "Mabd, but yes. Sweet girl, but she doomed herself when she walked up Old Tom's Hill alone."

Sam tensed her lips. "So, what's the story with Old Tom's Hill? I did talk to one of the ghost hunters staying here, and he said something about a deal with the devil happening there that no one believes."

She shook her head in response. "That devil stuff may or may not be true, but that place has been dangerous even before St. Patrick ran the snakes into the sea."

As she walked down the row of shelves marked "Gently Loved Books," Sam noticed what appeared to be a prosthetic leg emerge from beneath her green and blue plaid maxi skirt. She grabbed an older, leather-bound book, handed it to Sam, and said, "Here. Maryanne Logue donated this as part of her late father's library when he passed on. God rest his soul. Seems he collected local legends from here and our neighbor counties. There's some good stuff, but he also wrote in the margins like a madman, so you may have trouble reading some parts. It's a one-of-a-kind, though used, so forty euro."

Sam looked at the ceiling, trying to convert the currency in her head. "Sure." She handed the woman her card.

The woman ran the card, and as she handed Sam the receipt to sign, she said, "Hain, that's an Irish name. My husband has a cousin–second or third, I can't remember which–named Donal Hain."

Sam paused. "Well, my dad always said I have family all over Ireland. Anyway, thank you so much, I'm going to go enjoy this with a cup of coffee."

After exiting the shop, she exhaled slowly. "Great," she thought, "I hope she's not close enough to call dad and ask about his daughter. I do not have the time to deal with him right now."

Her phone vibrated, and she saw Destiny had replied to her text with, "What? Since when?"

She shot off a series of rapid texts explaining how he was one of the ghost hunters she spoke with at the bed-and-breakfast that he invited her to have dinner with him at his expense to discuss the possibility of her joining his last night of searching for the banshee. She rolled her eyes as she responded to texts reminding her to be charming, to shave her legs, to smile, and to wear something to accentuate her bust and her eyes. And then Destiny asked, "Well, is he at least cute?"

Sam thought for a moment before replying, "I guess, if you're into symmetrical features save for a hairy wart on the right side of his chin, nice eyes, and men."

"Well, have fun, be safe, use protection," Destiny replied with a winking emoji. Sam glared into the phone as Destiny added, "and I don't mean a gun."

Sam walked to the local coffee shop, Café O'Day, placed her order, and found an empty seat in a quiet corner. Sitting alone, she opened her new book and noticed the handwritten words "Cosaint, Onóir, Dualgas" on dedication page. Recognizing the Duilearga's motto of "Protection, Honor, Duty," she mused that the notes, though written in Irish, might be more useful than the legends. Grabbing her small teal notebook and a black pen from her purse, she muttered to herself, "Now I wish I'd have bothered to learn more Irish from Professor Kennedy."

After an afternoon spent reading her new book, drinking four large mugs of black coffee, and eating chocolate mince-meat bars, Sam started her return to The Slouching Giant to prepare for her paranormal investigation date tonight. On her way back, she passed by Old Tom's Hill, where several bright yellow signs instructed residents and guests to stay away from the area. The grassy hill itself stood taller than any of the buildings in town, like a border gate between the human world of Bannagh and the natural world of the forest just beyond the town. Sam recalled the bookstore owner's admonition against climbing the hill at night, and since it was only afternoon, she took a quick look around and climbed the hill.

The dried grass crunched beneath Sam's feet as she ascended the lonely hill. A single rowan tree provided shade at the hill's summit, and beneath its branches, sat a large stone, flat and irregularly shaped, and a ring of large gray mushrooms. Sam estimated that she could easily lie down in the circle without touching a single mushroom. A goat bleated from a nearby farm as a cool wind gently brushed against Sam's right side. Walking the summit's perimeter, she saw another ring of mushrooms at the north base. It was smaller than the first one and had a patch of dead grass on its eastern edge that left a mushroom-free opening. She knelt on the grass and found nothing that resembled the markings of either shoes or boots; the only tracks visible were large hooves, which she reasoned were caused by farmers grazing their animals.

Finding nothing, she descended the hill and headed back to The Slouching Giant to change for the evening. While her blue swing dress and orange cardigan were stylish, since she planned to accept Frank's offer of banshee hunting tonight, she needed something more practical. Drawing inspiration from Marlene Dietrich, she chose a charcoal vest and trouser with a subtle white pinstripe, a white blouse with a silver lavaliere hanging just below her collarbone, camel leather riding boots, and a camel knee-length trench. Standing before the bathroom mirror, she darkened her lip and winged her liner, muttering to herself, "No amount of contour will fix this nose, Sam. Anyway: be charming, don't lead him on, and be careful." She placed her Walther P-38 in her purse as she locked the door and headed to The Tipsy Tenpenny.

* * *

Locals crowded into Bannagh's pub on this Thursday evening. Though the wrought iron fixtures and other essentials were modern, The Tipsy Tenpenny maintained the look at feel it had when it opened in 1781. She walked to the bar and ordered a White Hag Black Pig stout and surveyed the room. Sam mentally noted the groups of men, and the occasional woman, wearing matching shirts, marking them as likely ghost hunters, and the older men in sweaters–some speaking in Irish, which she barely understood–talking among themselves and laughing louder than the others. A fire warmed a cauldron filled with apples, cinnamon, clove, and coriander, perfuming the pub as a trio of older men sat around the hearth playing fiddle, flute, and guitar. She saw Frank sitting alone at a two-seater near the far wall, made her way through the crowd, and stiffened only slightly when he stood and pulled her chair back for her.

"I thought you'd forgotten," he said as he returned to his seat.

"Sorry, I'm late," Sam replied. "I got a little too engrossed in this old book of local legends I found at the bookstore that some local scholar, I guess, made notes in, but since I really can't read Irish that well, I can't get a lot from them. Then I figured I needed to change into something a bit more practical if I'm to accompany you tonight."

"We could always return to the Giant for you to change," he said, sipping his deep amber beer. "Wait–did you say, 'accompany me'? Does that mean that you've decided to come with me?"

Sam smiled and shrugged. "I thought it might be fun. I've never gone on a ghost hunt before–not with someone who's part of a ghost hunting team. So, what's our first step?"

"Our first step," Frank replied, "is to have dinner. Don't laugh! I'm serious. We're going to be out there until dawn, and so having a full belly–and a lot of coffee–are essential. We can also discuss research now and get to know each other better–for team-building purposes."

Sam looked around the bar. "Have all these guys been here since the video went viral?"

Frank shook his head, sipping his ale. "Nah, most got here within the last week. We only got here four days ago. So far, lots of nothing."

Sam cocked an eyebrow as she sipped her stout. "Well, I'm always up for a good meal, but I doubt I found any info you didn't already know. Like I said, I buried my nose in a book on local legends, since everyone I ran into today kept warning me to stay away from Old Tom's Hill."

Their server, a middle-aged woman with silvering red hair and whose facial features suggested she and the bartender were related, arrived with their orders. Frank ordered a massive plate of shepherd's pie, and Sam ordered a crusty bread bowl of beef stew and a side of garlic mashed potatoes, which she claimed was to protect her from any Irish vampires they might encounter after dark. She downplayed Frank's jab that she was mocking him as the server refilled their water glasses and left them alone.

"So, what did you find out about Old Tom's Hill," Frank asked.

"Just a bunch of old stories about disappearances and missing time," Sam replied. "I mean, there was this old legend about how some ancestor of the family who lives in the castle sold his soul for money or love–no one I talked to seems to believe that, though." And then she thought, "Shit, I hope he's not onto me."

"Yeah, that's old English hate," Frank spoke through a full mouth. "I can't say I blame them. England's done a lot to them over the years. Why'd you look into that?"

Sam shrugged. "Well, every older person I met pointedly warned me to stay away from it. So naturally–"

"You got curious," Frank interjected.

Sam smiled sweetly and batted her eyes. "It's who I am. Plus, I'm honestly more concerned about that girl Mabd going missing. I mean, finding a banshee would be cool, but making sure she's alive and safe, now that seems like a great thing."

"It would," Frank agreed, "but we'd be bloody lucky to find her. Bobbies couldn't find nothing over there. She was seen there, but now no one can find hide nor hair of her. Even the GPS on her phone isn't helpful. Nah, we're going back into the bog, sneaking past the official 'caution' lines, and finding that banshee." He winked. "It'll be an adventure. Excuse me, I've got to use the loo."

He stood and headed to the restroom, giving Sam a chance to check her buzzing phone. As she predicted, she missed a call from her father, who left a voice message, and Destiny texted to ask how her "date" was going and sent her a meme of Jabba the Hutt trying to kiss a disgusted-looking Leia, accompanied by the words "When you've had a bad date, but he tries to kiss you anyway." Sam chuckled but replied that had Frank been a woman, this would be a nice first date. Sam's conversation distracted her from seeing that Mister O'Gill approached Frank for a brief conversation. As Frank returned, Sam shot a quick, "Heading to the bog. Research Old Tom Hill. Ask Nick Scratch. Thanks."

"Your boyfriend back in the States?" Frank asked with a smirk.

"No," Sam replied with a smile, "my best friend and cat-sitter. Just checking up on me."

"You've got a cat," Frank said.

Sam smiled, "Yes, and why did your voice drop? I've had Sandy Paws for twelve years, and she's been with me through a lot. I guess you don't want to see a picture?"

Frank shook his head. "Sorry, never been a cat person. Dogs: now that's a man's best friend!"

"Well," Sam sipped her beer, "I'm no man."

"No, you're not, and it seems that Mister O'Gill has taken a protective shine to you. He warned me not to let you go 'traipsing out on the bog at midnight' like some gothic heroine."

Sam smiled. "He did mention that I reminded him of his granddaughter. He's just being sweet."

"So," Frank leaned forward, his eyes searching her as he asked, "You've got a best friend, a surrogate Irish grandfather, and a cat. What do you for work?"

"Shit," Sam thought as her heart rate increased, "What do I say?" She pursed her lips briefly and replied, "I'm a social worker. I specialize in domestic violence and child abuse cases – especially those people whom no one else seems able or willing to help. What about you? Does ghost hunting pay the bills?"

"Oh, wow, that's pretty heavy. Nah, I don't get paid to hunt ghosts. I work in insurance. Boring job mostly, but the pay's good."

Sam consciously mirrored his lean and asked, "So what got you started? Movies? Knockings in the attic? Demon possess your little sister?" She giggled, hoping that last one did not

45

happen.

He laughed. "Gran thought she was for a while: rebellious, tattooed at sixteen, dropped out of uni to start a punk band, that sort of thing. But, to tell the truth, I got interested in this when my gran passed. She raised me and my sister after our mum died in a plane crash on her way back from Madrid, and then she took ill and never got better when I was at uni. About a year later, I started seeing things when I came home–seeing her, actually–and sometimes hearing her voice. There was this club on campus that talked about talking to ghosts through EVPs–you know, Electronic Voice Phenomena, where we use recording equipment to try to pick up faint ghost voices. I really just wanted to talk to her again, and the process gave me the bug, as they say."

"My kind of girl," Sam mused. Frank cocked an eyebrow. She reached out and put her hand on his and nodded. "I lost my mom when I was at college. An accident. Dad was never really in my life much before that–off and on–due to work and the divorce. He tried to be more active around that time, but it didn't stick. So, I get it; the chance to talk with a loved one just one more time. Yeah." Her voice trailed off. After a moment of silence between them, she asked, "I'm sorry, but I haven't asked about your day. How'd your day at the castle go?"

Frank pulled back and folded his arms across his chest. "Not as good as I'd hoped, honestly. Lady O'Cuinn, to her credit, cares more for finding her employee than she does for finding out about the banshee. Odd, given that a banshee wailing often portends death–and her granddaughter who lives at the castle too is with child, so it could be a bit of a problem for the family. And, to be fair, she's always listening to opera, and that puts me to sleep."

"Oh, a great-grandbaby on the way and opera. Well, they say classical music is good for children's development." Sam shrugged.

"I've heard," Frank replied. "But Lady O'Cuinn used to be something of a singer and actress in Dublin. But, let me settle the tab so we can get started, eh?"

Chapter 3

It was a clear and starry night. A gentle breeze escorted our heroes to the edge of the sleepy Irish village set against the Emberheath Bog. As their shadows joined the great darkness beyond Bannagh's final streetlight, they spied a humanoid shape walking past a window on the second floor of Castle Gaelladgh and then disappear. Ahead of them, a series of bright yellow signs placed at regular intervals warned them to stay out; the Gardaí obviously couldn't wrap caution tape around the entire forest and bog. Our heroine, a plucky young American woman with penchants for sass and fashion, dressed like she stepped out of a feminist reimagining of a Lovecraftian tale. Our hero, a taller, dark-skinned man from the English region of Cornwall, wore a black leather trench coat, a charcoal Cornwall Spiritualist Society sweater, faded black trousers, and black hiking boots. As he rummaged through his backpack of supplies, a silver pendant with an eight-pointed star fell into my view.

Taking hold of the pendant, I raised an eyebrow, "This is pretty. Special meaning to you?"

"It's just a good luck charm I've had for a while." He rushed his words as he hid the pendant beneath his sweater.

"Oh, okay. Nothing wrong with having luck on your

side," I nodded. Liar! That specific eight-pointed star is the symbol of the Astrum Argentum. Being the daughter of Donal Hain, I grew up around that symbol being hidden in plain sight. He tried repeatedly to get me to join the Order, but my stubbornness–inherited from him–and my growing resentment over his regular absences in my life only strengthened my resolve to avoid that group of pretentious mages and magic entirely. I wasn't entirely successful in the latter; I'll concede my father had a point on teaching me a few basic rites and protective spells. That said, my new friend Frank didn't strike me as a ranking magus. If he were, he probably would have recognized me by now. Though, at least he won't be totally unprepared if we do run into trouble from Veil Crossers. Let's hope we can avoid all that, the police, and the Duilearga.

I may have partially lied when I told Frank I'd never gone ghost hunting before. I mean, I never went ghost hunting as part of an organized team, but I've hunted ghosts and, given that we're looking for a banshee, fae before. It's just that I've gone into the field alone, and since I already knew they existed, I didn't need all these gadgets to try to prove their existence. I'd love for Destiny to join me, but she's pretty adamant about not getting so directly involved again, given who her family happens to be. I almost declined to join Frank, because I was sure that I knew more of what we might come into contact with than he did. Given that he's Astrum Argentum, maybe I've got more of a partner than a bumbling sidekick.

As expected from a member of the Over-educated Occult Order, Frank thoroughly explained every piece of equipment we would be using and the standard protocol for the night's investigation. While Nigel returned home with most of their equipment, he left Frank with a digital recorder, an EMF detector, a full-spectrum digital camera and, fortunately, two flashlights. Frank gave me a thorough description of each tool and a crash course to train me in how they were to be used. My favorite part was his diatribe against using a spirit board, because, "Those things are fake at best, working on psychosomatic principles, but, on rare occasions, they may actually contact demons–never the spirits of the dead." My father would be so proud. I rolled my eyes at that thought.

Seeing my breath as I walked through the cold has always been a favorite thing of mine. We'd have another two or three weeks before weather like this came to Butcher's Bend, so I really couldn't complain about being led into the Emberheath Bog on this clear, starry October night. We couldn't see much beyond what our flashlights allowed, and so my eyes kept scanning the edges of my field of vision. A gentle wind guided us as we left the well-worn paths to slip past the police search parties trying to keep people away from the bog until they determined the area was safe for night walkers again. A barn owl hooted from a lone rowan tree to our right. Under normal circumstances, this would be a nice place for a night's walk. I may have to come back.

I knew that peat bogs had a distinctive rancor about them, but I honestly thought being around my father's collection of repulsive-smelling protective and banishing incenses–and the fact that I've had to slog through a charnel house of the rotting victims of a vampire suffering from synthoflavin psychosis–would have better prepared me for the reek ruining the beauty of the cool night air. My nose wrinkled as I coughed from the smell. A police search light flashed in the corner of my eyes. I blinked and lost sight of the drier ground as we

50

traversed soggy peat-and-heather-covered soil that undulated like a heaving chest, grasping for air. Instinctively, I called out for help as my calves sank into the stinking wetlands, and Frank grabbed me and pulled me to drier ground behind one of the few trees in the area.

He pushed me to my knees, pointed toward the searchlight, and whispered, "Lights down. Stay still."

I followed his lead and lowered my flashlight to minimize its brightness. I wasn't tired, but I made use of this rest to catch my breath and let my heart rate return to normal after that slip. Slowing my breath, I forced my eyes to stop blinking as I followed the patrol's flashlights as they moved closer toward us. I crouched lower behind the tree like I hid behind our blue sofa with a gold paisley pattern when I was kid sneaking out after bedtime secretly to watch Saturday Night Live or whatever cheesy Lifetime movie my mom was watching that night. Only this time, if I got caught, being sent to my room could mean death for a lot of people—Frank included. Old Tom's Hill didn't seem to have this many cops and caution signs when we walked past it, but he wouldn't listen to me.

As the patrol came within a football field of us, my phone vibrated. Shit! Tonight was not the night to leave it on vibrate only instead of full silence. The officers quickened their pace as they moved toward us. Frank glared at me. I reached down, grabbed a stone, and hurled it as far as I could toward my left. It skipped a few times on the hard ground and then splashed as it landed in a pool of murky water. The officers stopped and turned toward the sound. I sucked in my gut and clenched every muscle in my body as we waited to see if my instinctive reaction worked.

One officer turned back toward us, his flashlight searching

the area five feet in front of us. After a few minutes of searching, the patrol turned and walked toward the sound. We watched them for a few minutes before breathing a sigh of relief. Frank looked over and nodded before hissing a whispered response, "Good save. Important message?"

I pulled my phone out of my purse as I responded, "It's probably;" I paused when I saw the name Donal Hain illuminated beneath the word "Voicemail". "Nothing important," I said as I quickly returned the phone to my bag.

We continued across the bog in silence for about half an hour before Frank suggested I switch on the full spectrum camera and record video. As the camera powered on, I pulled my earplugs from my purse and pressed them into my ears. I saw, but couldn't hear, Frank chuckle and shake his head before leaning in and saying, "I doubt that'll help much against a banshee's wail."

"Do you have any other suggestions?" I shot back with a smile. "Because you haven't offered any so far."

He shook his head as we continued our search. After what felt like half an hour, the O'Cuinn-Gaell Portal loomed like a giant eye from atop the hill ahead of us. Frank pulled out his digital recorder and began asking the banshee vague questions in English as I slowly swept the digital camera across the area. I honestly don't know how much longer I can continue this charade; I know this banshee of Niamh O'Cuinn is real, and I'll be damned to join the Astrum Argentum as my father's heir if he can honestly say that he does not know her to be real as well.

We approached the Portal, and I'll just say that this megalith left me unimpressed compared to others I've seen. The O'Cuinn-Gaell Portal was a dolmen, and, as its name implied, it was a giant doorway made of five massive stones: four support stones and one large capstone. However, as the hair on my arms and the back of my neck raised, I realized there was something to this place. Frank held his left index finger to his lips, which was a relief, as his constant droning of those vague questions annoyed me. I moved closer and started examining the stones themselves for anything that could prove helpful. As I knelt by the support stone closest to me, Frank stage-whispered, "Pst! What are you doing? You let the camera drop."

I raised the camera up and, glowering toward the stone, turned it toward the bog. "I'm seeing if there's anything on the stone that might give us a clue what we should expect. A name. Ogham script. Something."

"You read Ogham script?" Frank snorted in disbelief.

"No," I replied, "but I know someone who does. And with you chanting questions to contact the banshee, having a name seems like something that would make that easier."

He smiled. "A pretty face and good instincts. If you can cook, you'd be a total package."

I growled and glared, causing him to backpedal about that being a joke. I shook my head and continued searching the stones. Neither that book of local legends nor anyone I spoke with mentioned a purpose for this portal, but Mabd hid within this portal when the banshee appeared, leading me to believe that there's something about this stone doorway.

* * *

Destiny Grimm spent a quiet day in the Hain Private Investigations office filing paperwork, making phone calls, and, mostly playing games on her Nintendo Switch. Sam's request for her to research Old Tom's Hill arrived an hour after she returned from lunch. As she prepared to clock out for the day, the phone rang. "Hain Private Investigations, this is Destiny speaking. How may I help you?"

A deep, stern voice responded, "Destiny, why is my daughter in Ireland?"

"Oh, hello, Mister Hain," she replied. "I didn't expect you to call today. She's working on a case. How did you know?"

"A distant cousin who lives in Bannagh emailed to say that a young woman named Samantha Hain purchased Thomas Logue's collection of County Sligo legends. What's going on?"

"Details of all cases are confidential, sir." Destiny continued in her practiced, customer service voice. "And as you are also aware, she tends to take a particular kind of case around the full moon each month. You rarely call to inquire about them, sir, so why do you want details about this one?"

Destiny heard Donal Hain growl through the phone. He breathed deeply and then said, "Damnit, Destiny, this isn't about investigator privilege. There are ancient dealings in that county that have caused numerous historical and present troubles, and the High Council of the Astrum Argent–yes, I've returned to the Order at the Council's request. Look, that's not important. Getting her home before her birthday: that is what's important. I've got to go–Council meeting–but bring her home soon. Bye."

Destiny grabbed her cell phone and opened her messages. She calculated the time in Ireland and then placed her phone in her purse. "No," she thought, "I'll message her if I get something concrete. Time for a drink."

After feeding Sandy Paws, Destiny unlocked the door to

Sam's office and stepped inside. Though less trained in or knowledgeable on ritual magic than Sam was, Destiny knew that if she traced the sigil of Samael on the wall of a room used for ritual magic, then either summoning him or opening a door to The Four Winds was possible. As she finished tracing the last point, she intoned, "Samael, Left Hand of God, First of the Fallen, Lord of Hell, open to me a door to The Four Winds Bar."

As she finished speaking, a blue flame ignited on the bottom left corner of the paper containing the sigil she traced. The flame descended to the floor and then traced the outline of a door which then clicked to signal that it had been unlocked. Destiny quickly tidied up the room, grabbed her purse, and walked through the door.

Three-pronged golden candelabra stood proudly atop each table in The Four Winds as Destiny walked through the portal. No one at the bar seemed really interested in hiding their true identities tonight as conversation replaced Lilith's sultry voice as the primary sound heard throughout the room. The demons present all had their horns and tails visible, and a handful displayed their leathery wings. Dancing lights glittered around the fae, whose red, orange, and brown clothing marked them as members of the Autumnal Court. Countess Carmilla Karnstein and the two other vampires seated with her had their gleaming fangs revealed as they sipped blood directly from the necks of willing mortals. The pack of werewolves, whose hybrid forms revealed the beautiful diversity of their fur, ate raw meat and drank beer while chatting with a pair of kitsune sipping their sake from ceramic cups. Krampus sat at the end of the bar sipping on glühwein. Destiny clutched her purse tightly as she strode toward the bar. All eyes turned toward her, and then, as if in recognition, all faces quickly looked down to avoid her gaze.

Nicholas Scratch, Samael, maintained the most human form of any of the demons, displaying only two slender, elegantly curved onyx horns. Sensing the mood change and the door close behind Destiny, he wiped the bar clean, leaned forward, and said, "Welcome to The Four Winds where–oh, if it isn't Wilhelm's heir. To what do I owe the pleasure of your visit? After all, it's not often one of your blood steps into my bar–especially after the events in Berlin."

The werewolves growled. Destiny held her purse close to her chest as she hurried to the bar and stood on her toes, replying, "Yes, well, I need a drink, and Sam thinks you know things." He cocked an eyebrow, causing her eyes to widen as she inhaled sharply. Her cheeks flushed as she shook her head rapidly. "I didn't mean it that way, Mister Scratch. She thinks you might know something about Old Tom's Hill."

He laughed as he poured a crisp white wine into a crystal glass and set it before her. "Riesling: dry, crisp, with just a hint of sweetness."

Destiny took a sip from the glass and threw her head back and moaned as her shoulders melted. "That is the perfect Riesling. Damn, you're good."

His eyes gleamed like glowing embers as he smiled. "I've had practice. Now, why don't you tell me what you have to offer in exchange for the information Ms. Hain desires?"

She scratched her neck beneath her left ear and cocked her head. "But I thought the first one was always free." Her gaze shot to her glass and then her jaw slacked as she rose her eyes to meet Mister Scratch's smile. She tensed her lips and glared. "I fell for a bait and switch by someone who lost a fiddle contest to a Georgia hillbilly. Unbelievable."

Nick glowered and then cocked his head wistfully. "Did I lose? Perhaps I lost the contest, but that victory caused a young man's pride to swell to where, upon his death, I took possession of his soul. I warned him of that eventuality, but you mortals often fail to see the long game when it is played upon you." He paused dramatically before adding, "Like a fiddle."

"I didn't plan for this," Destiny thought. She gulped wine down before asking, "What would you accept?"

Nick Scratch stroked his chin for a moment before responding, "Well, if money is all you have, I suppose I could accept that. If you're unimaginative, your soul is always a viable option. However, word has reached me that our mutual friend Miss Hain has been contemplating a plan to spend more time with her mother than our current agreement allows. Why don't you enlighten me on that?"

Destiny swallowed hard. "Is there anything else you would like to know?"

He smirked and leaned forward. "There are many things I would like to know, but this particular rumor is one I would value equal to the answers she desires. So, if you have knowledge of equal value to that, then, by all means, speak."

"What should I say?" Destiny thought, staring into her wineglass as her heart rate increased. "Sam asked me to keep that secret after I found the first draft of her note in the trash can of her office. I can't just tell him."

"Your quickened breathing betrays you, Miss Grimm," Nick Scratch purred. "You entered my place of business to find answers for Samantha Hain. I have stated the price for the information. It's nothing personal, my dear; it's simply business – unless you have something else of equal value to offer."

"Would the fact that Donal Hain has returned to," she began.

"The Astrum Argentum," he finished. "I'm afraid I already know that, dear. So, what do you have to offer?"

Destiny took five sips of her wine in rapid succession. "I can't tell him," she thought. "I promised Sam, but I promised her I would get the information." She looked into his eyes and said, "Do you have a restroom I could use? What's with the Disney villain laugh?"

Nick's smile revealed his slightly elongated canines as his laughter became a dark chuckle. He pointed toward the south wall. "The restrooms are over there, my dear. Of course, mortal cell phones do not work here."

"Excuse me," Destiny said as she rose and walked to the restroom, cursing herself for not realizing that she could not get cell phone service in a pocket dimension.

Destiny flushed the golden handle on the black marble toilet before stepping from the stall into the well-lit restroom. Peering into the silver-framed mirror as she washed her hands, she noticed she was alone. Her nose wrinkled at the stronger-than-expected scent of lavender that hung in the cool air. As she turned to leave, she gasped as she saw Countess Karnstein, her cheeks flushed and vibrant, standing right behind her.

"Oh, Carmilla," Destiny stammered. "I'm so sorry. I didn't see you–oh, yeah, vampire in a mirror."

Carmilla smiled and nodded. "There is no offense, and yes, this is a silver-backed mirror, so you would not be able to see me."

"Uh, the stall's empty if you need to–can you–you know, go?" Destiny winced at her own words.

"I have no need for the, how do you say it, facilities?" She replied as her fangs bared in a smirk. "I came for you."

Destiny's eyes shot wide as she backed against the sink, her hands gripping it tightly. "I'm not–I'm flattered–but I'm not into that." Her voice lifted as she spoke, creating a frightened tone that sounded almost questioning.

Carmilla waved her hand dismissively. "Did you observe nothing as you entered the public house? No, little Grimm, I overheard your conversation with our charming devil of a host, and," she switched to German, hoping to put the young woman at ease, "given that the information he seeks is a secret that our friend Samantha requested us to keep, I thought perhaps I could provide you with something of value to trade for the answers you seek."

"And you're just going to give it to me?" Destiny searched the vampire's face.

"No. I would like something in return," she said. "However, that which I am willing to accept is far less intrusive or damning."

Destiny's shoulders relaxed. "What–what do you want?"

"Well, you know what I want, but I am willing to accept spending a few hours with Samantha in my castle. I promise to do nothing that she does not allow, but I would like to have her company there." She retreated a few steps.

Destiny thought for a moment before replying, "I'm not going to trick Sam. You understand, right? I'm going to tell her about the offer and let it be her choice. No matter how much I ship this."

"Of course," the Countess replied as she lowered her head. "I would not dream of having her against her will."

Destiny took a deep breath. "Alright. If we're clear, then

thank you. I could use the help."

Carmilla glided to Destiny, who tensed as the vampire whispered something into her ear. Destiny shot Carmilla a quizzical look; the Countess simply nodded and smiled. Destiny gulped and exhaled slowly. Carmilla waved her hand dismissively. Destiny nodded and exited the restroom. As she sat down at the bar, Nick Scratch leaned close to her, allowing her to smell his cologne–leather, pipe tobacco, and burning leaves–before asking, "Well, do you have something to offer me in exchange for the answers Samantha seeks?"

Destiny took a few deep breaths and sipped the last bit of her wine, her eyes closed in a moment of desperate prayer to whoever would listen. She looked into Nick's eyes and said, "As I searched our files, I noticed something that I'd forgotten. A Veil Crossing client mentioned that the Order of the Dragon has obtained the Tepes Signet Ring, which means that they will be able to enter the sealed crypt and awaken Vlad Dracula. Is that enough?"

He searched her face after she finished speaking, watching every eye movement and muscle twitch. He leaned against the bar's shelves and stroked his chin. Destiny's heart pounded as she could hear nothing but her heartbeat and her breathing. He smirked and chuckled. "That is interesting. It's not what I wanted to hear, but I will give you this in trade. Tell Samantha that one of the answers she seeks lies buried beneath Old Tom's Hill, but she will need to be careful in its extraction. I have never spent time in County Sligo, but many have. She will have a choice to make. Also, she would do well to remember the wards her father taught her. That," he folded his arms across his chest, "is what you have earned."

Destiny smiled as she slid her empty glass toward him.

"Thank you, Mister Scratch. I will tell her. Have a nice evening." She stood and left for home.

* * *

"Is there anyone here with us?" Frank asked as he tiptoed in slow circles around the O'Cuinn-Gaell Portal, his digital recorder held at chest level.

There was no audible response to Frank's questioning. Sam rolled her eyes and growled as she crawled to the third support stone. The first two stones, which stood taller than her and almost twice as wide, had nothing on the exterior faces beyond centuries of weathering. She traced the contours of each stone – all cold and rough to the touch – hoping for any anomalous sensation that would suggest human artifice. She sighed and moved to the fourth support stone as Frank asked the banshee that haunts this bog to give them a sign of her presence. Silence answered his questions.

A flash of light caused Sam's gaze to jerk from the stone toward where Frank raised his arm to cover his eyes as a ball of blue fire erupted at chest level in the air. The ball pulsed until it settled on the size of a softball. Frank thrust his recorder toward it and asked the banshee to use the power of the flame to speak her name. In the silence that followed, the ball of fire floated off into the air and dissipated. Frank cursed and walked over to the dolmen, shaking his head and punching the air.

Sam peered out from around the megalith and asked, "Are you okay?"

He shook his head and sighed. "Just bog gas. I got excited."

"Is that the thing people thought was a will-o'-wisp?"

Frank nodded. "Yeah. And it bloody fooled me too. Well, there's nothing here. Let's turn back."

Sam narrowed her eyes and inhaled deeply. "You're probably right. We've been out here for hours." She paused as she turned toward the dolmen, her flashlight illuminating the underside of the capstone, illuminating a series of patterned markings. "Wait. There's something written on the stone."

"Wait!" Frank shouted as Sam crawled into the Portal to examine the markings.

"Just let me snap a quick pic," she replied as her phone's camera flashed.

A distinct chill filled the air as the moisture in the air thickened into a fog. Sam emerged from the other side of the Portal as the north wind swirled through the landscape; the sparse brush crackled in the wind. The air acquired a floral-tinged earthy scent. The nocturnal animals fell silent. Then Sam and Frank turned an ear toward the wind as both heard a faint cry. As the cry grew louder, they heard its musical cadence and recognized it as a lament. A shadow began moving through the fog toward them. The fog seemed to part as it approached, allowing them to see the outline of a woman who appeared to be combing her long hair as she sang. As her movement continued, they saw she was an older, matronly woman dressed in a burial shroud and an old gray cloak.

Frank held out his arm to stop Sam from moving closer as he walked toward the woman, his recorder at chest level, and asked, "Are you the banshee?"

Sam rolled her eyes as the figure ignored him and continued moving past them. He followed it, continuing question it, but regardless of his topic, the spirit ignored him and continued on her way. After a few moments, Sam shook her head, glared at Frank's back, and asked, "An t-ainm atá ort Niamh O'Cuinn?"

"What?" Frank sputtered as he turned and stared at Sam.

The spirit stopped its song and turned toward her, replying in Irish, "I am."

Sam nodded and continued. "My name is Samantha. He is Frank."

Frank hissed and whispered, "Don't say our names! Raise the camera!"

She waved his concern away. "Dagh Mobh says you are in danger. Let me help. Why are you here?"

The spirit of Niamh O'Cuinn turned toward the castle and continued her journey. Before she returned to her song, Sam heard the words, "Liam's doom is come."

Frank's jaw hung low as he approached Sam. "You–you speak Irish?"

Sam shrugged. "About as well as a ten-year-old."

"Well," he flung his arms wide. "Don't keep me in suspense. What did you ask her?"

Sam breathed deeply. "I asked her if she was Niamh O'Cuinn, the ancestral matriarch, and she –"

"Wait," Frank interrupted. "I never told you that name. What made you ask about it?"

Sam winced before responding, "I told you I found a book of local legends. That name got mentioned in several of the ones about Old Tom's Hill. And one of the few margin notes I could understand said that if a banshee ever showed up for the family, it would probably be Niamh's spirit. And I chose to use what little Irish I know, because your questions were getting us nowhere and I figured that she may prefer her own language to that of her people's oppressor."

She smiled and felt his gaze search her in the darkness; she hoped he chose not to press the issue. He put his recorder in his pocket and stroked his chin. "Hm. Something seems off, Samantha, but I don't know what. Is that all?"

Sam shook her head. "The last thing she said was something about Liam's doom coming. So, are we heading to Old Tom's Hill?" She started walking toward Bannagh.

"What? No," Frank called out as he moved to catch up to her. "We're going back to The Giant and get some sleep. I've got to analyze all we've collected, because we've done it, Samantha! We've got proof of the banshee. You talked to her. This is amazing."

"But what about Mabd?" She asked as they continued walking. "What about the O'Cuinn family who must be in serious trouble if a banshee is coming to warn them? You're just going to let them suffer?"

"What are we going to do?" Frank asked. "No one can find the girl, and we can't stop this mysterious doom. We have evidence, which we need to analyze to learn more about banshees and supernatural creatures. That's why we came out here, remember?"

Sam spun toward him, her face flushed and her eyes blazing. "You're all alike," she seethed, "All of you!"

"What?" His eyes were wide and his jaw slacked. "Men?"

"Oh, you're worse than just a man," Sam spat.

As she opened her mouth to continue, her phone buzzed again. As she removed it from her purse to see who was calling, Frank caught a quick glimpse of the caller's name as it flashed across her screen. He took a step back and cocked his head. Sam doubled her pace as she shoved her phone back into her purse. Frank looked around for a few seconds before rushing to catch up to her. He grasped her wrist; she spun around and thrust her elbow into his face. He grunted in pain as he pulled away.

"Never grab a woman from behind," she said as she pointed her finger at him.

He rubbed his face and replied, "I'll remember that. Are you that pissed off at me? And why was Donal Hain calling you?"

She growled. "At you. At him. At this whole situation. And he's calling me, because he's an asshole who thinks that after years of barely being involved in my life, he can suddenly be my father. Pick your jaw up, Frank. Burnside is my mother's maiden name. I use it when I travel alone for increased safety and because my name–"

"Samantha Hain, Samantha Hain," Frank repeated absent-mindedly. "Sam Hain! You're Sam Hain, and it's," he gasped, "almost Samhain."

"Well, look at the big brain on Frank," Sam replied as she increased her pace. "It's obvious you're a member of the Astrum Argentum."

Frank sprinted to match her pace. "How did you know? Oh, the pendant. But you're Sam Hain, the legendary fixer. Even Probationers like me know of you, because the Arch Magus–"

"Former Arch Magus," Sam interrupted.

Frank shook his head. "No, he returned to the Order the equinox before I joined." Sam sputtered, and he continued, "I guess you don't talk to him that much. Anyway, he repeatedly tells stories of your exploits. So, this is no vacation for you, is it?"

Sam stopped and breathed deeply. "No. If you want the truth, a Faerie friend of Niamh's approached me and asked me to fix the situation. I almost didn't take the case. I'd been dealing with personal things and a mundane case that was just shitty on all fronts. And, since my birthday is coming up, I really wasn't looking for any more trouble. But I knew it would come. And, full disclosure, I was more of a bitch to him than usual, because I really didn't want to deal with faerie troubles. Ultimately, I had to help Mabd, because I know that if I were her, I would be terrified right now. And the faerie told me the Duilearga had promised to handle the matter on my birthday."

"The Duilearga? The Veil Watchers are looking into this?" Frank asked.

"What did you expect?" Sam asked. "A banshee goes viral on social media. A bunch of amateur ghost hunters descend on a small town. Some of them die."

"Do you think the Duilearga killed them?" Frank's face started losing its color, and his hands trembled.

Sam shrugged and sighed. "I don't know. I don't think so, but I have no evidence yet. I've heard that a few had heart attacks and that most of them had terrible claw marks. Neither method is Duilearga M.O. But since one agent is already in town, I don't know."

"One's already here? How do you know this?"

Sam shook her head and continued walking toward the village. "I literally bumped into him as I walked to my room. I think he's staying in the room opposite me. So, part of the body count may be his."

As they reached the edge of Bannagh, Frank said, "Look, the lights at the Tenpenny are still on. Care for a nightcap?"

"I'm buying my own," Sam replied, "but sure."

The Tipsy Tenpenny had almost as large a crowd at this hour as when Sam and Frank left on their little adventure. A few of the older residents had gone to sleep, but most of the younger crowd and the ghost hunters were still there. Frank chose another pale ale, but this time, Sam ordered a double whiskey and a water. They moved to a table in a far corner and sat down. Frank rubbed his jaw. After a few sips, Sam visibly relaxed and said, "I'm sorry about your jaw. It was a reflex, but I should've been more in control. It's not like there was anyone out there but you."

He winced and nodded. "Accepted. And you were right, I should've known better than to grab you from behind." He chuckled. "If I would've known who you really were, I may have been more inclined to expect that reaction."

Sam sighed and sipped her whiskey. "The last thing mom and I did together was take a self defense class. She had her accident a week later."

Frank nodded and sat for a few minutes. "I'm sorry."

Sam swallowed deeply and nodded. "That class is one of the few things that really stuck from college."

They sat in silence for a few moments, both thinking about their departed loved ones before Frank asked, "So what's our plan now?"

"We do nothing," Sam replied. "You are going back to Cornwall, and I'm going to continue my investigation."

"You don't want a partner?" Frank countered. "I could be a benefit."

Sam snorted into her glass. "You saying that bumbling ghost hunter schtick was just an act?"

Frank lowered his head. "I was following protocol. I'll admit that we didn't even think about the language barrier. That was a good call, Sam."

She smiled. "I think she probably knew English, but I don't

think she wanted to communicate in it. At least I have a little information to go on when I go talk to Lady O'Cuinn tomorrow."

Frank took a swig from his pint glass and sighed. "She won't talk to you. She's not talking to any more ghost hunters."

Sam winked as she sipped her whiskey. "Good thing I'm not a ghost hunter, isn't it? I'm a private investigator who was hired to investigate the situation. I didn't come here seeking to find 'evidence' of the banshee. I came to stop death from happening. That's my priority, and, based on what you said about her earlier, I think she'll appreciate my concerns."

Frank nodded. "Perhaps. Are you sure you don't want a partner?"

At that point, a large man with curly brown hair walked over to the table, his left hand in a pocket of his brown tweed blazer and a pint of a red ale in his right hand. "Post-investigation rendezvous, Frank? I haven't seen you in the company of such a lovely lass before."

"Uh, no," Frank replied. "Professor Creevy, this is—"

"Samantha Burnside," Sam interrupted, extending her hand with a smile. When the man shook her hand, she asked, "Professor, eh? You wouldn't happen to know Padraig Kennedy, who teaches history at Trinity College?"

Taken aback, Professor Creevy said. "He's a colleague and friend of mine. How did you?"

Sam smiled. "When I booked my room, Mister O'Gill said a professor from Dublin was staying here, and Professor Kennedy is a family friend. Just thought I'd ask."

Creevy nodded and turned back to Frank. "Seems you found something that's not a banshee. She's not even a ghost."

"No," Frank replied, "but she did accompany on my investigation tonight, and I think it was pretty productive evening."

"Was it now?" Creevy glanced at Sam.

She shrugged. "All I got was wet and dirty. We did see some swamp gas that did that will-o'-wisp behavior, so that was kind of cool. But, sadly," she sighed, "there'll be no screaming women this night."

Frank opened his mouth, but Sam kicked him under the table, causing him to wince. He glowered at her, and she responded with a pointed look. Creevy laughed and said, "Well, perhaps that'll change in a few minutes."

As he walked off, Frank whispered, "What did you do that for?"

Sam rolled her eyes and gave an exasperated sigh. "Think, Frank, think. Someone–at least one person–in this town is a Duilearga agent. The best way to stay alive is to not be on their radar. I can protect myself, but I can't protect everyone who may be on their list. Go home, check in with your buddy, tell your family you love them, and be safe."

Frank punched his palm and swallowed a third of his pint in a single gulp. "Damnit, Samantha, that goes against everything I believe as a man. I can't leave you to face them and whatever else is out there alone. It's just not right."

Sam pinched the bridge of her nose and sighed. She reached out and touched Frank's hand, smiled, and said, "I appreciate your concern, but this isn't my first investigation. And you've even admitted to being only a Probationer. What will you do if we have to stare down an angry fae like a dullahan? What happens if it's something worse? What do you plan to do if a Duilearga agent pulls a gun on you?"

Frank sank into his chair, his shoulders and chest fallen. "I didn't plan for any of that. Honestly, Nigel and I just thought we'd spend a few nights out here, catch a few sounds at best, and then head home. We had no idea–I had no idea–that this would put us in the middle of an investigation involving both Veil Watchers and the Arch Magus' daughter. I don't know. I'll think it over and let you know tomorrow at breakfast. Fair?"

Sam nodded. "I can't force you to leave, Frank. I came prepared, because I knew what I was getting into. You came prepared for what you thought you were getting into. Now that you know what you've actually gotten into, I hope you're smart enough to know that you're not prepared."

He nodded. "Well, will you at least share that pic you took of the Portal?"

She nodded and reached into her purse for her phone. She saw a series of texts from Destiny, which she would read later. She slid the phone over to him. He leaned in and squinted as he looked at a pattern of markings that looked to have been carved by a small tool, markings that appeared to read either "ZOZO" or "SOSO" in angular letters. He sat up and cocked his head back. He exhaled in exasperation and shrugged his shoulders. "Led Zeppelin fan maybe?"

Sam shrugged. "I don't know. There were no other markings on it, so I thought it might be important."

They finished their drinks and headed back to The Slouching Giant. The streetlights elongated their shadows as Frank jokingly suggested they head to Old Tom's Hill; he sputtered when Sam agreed. A quick scan suggested there were no patrols in the area, which made sense, given that local legends strongly suggested avoiding the hill at night. They reached the summit and saw a distant light in the forest; Frank claimed it was probably just a hunter or a farmer looking for a lost animal. When they heard a gunshot in the distance, Frank confirmed it to be a hunter.

All was quiet in Bannagh. Frank produced his digital recorder and said, "Let's continue this investigation." He then stepped into the ring of mushrooms at the top of the hill and sat down.

"Frank, get out of there," Sam said. "I don't think annoying the Fae is a good idea."

He laughed. "The woman who rushed out to talk to a wailing banshee is afraid of a few dancing Faeries?" He set the recorder down and said, "Alright Faeries, I'm going to get up and dance. Why don't you care to join me?"

Frank gyrated in a manner that suggested lower abdominal and back pain, his arms stretched at his sides and mirroring the motion of waves. His feet two-stepped from side to side as he cavorted around the ring's center. Sam laughed; although, her eyes focused on the light she saw in the forest as it traveled through the woods, appearing to move closer to them. Frank began jumping in circles to regain her attention as a cold October wind rustled the red, gold, and brown leaves on the trees.

Another gunshot rang through the air, and Frank cried out in pain. He grabbed his left shoulder and collapsed in the ring's center. Sam rushed over to see blood pouring out from his shoulder. She pulled a handkerchief from her purse and pressed firmly on the wound as Frank, wide-eyed and trembling, panted rapidly. She winced as she felt the scar on her own shoulder open into a fresh wound. She choked back tears as she reached for her own shoulder; there was no blood. Cursing herself she leaned her body on to Frank, hoping to increase the pressure on his wound.

As she grabbed her phone, she pleaded with Frank to remain

calm. Her hand shook as she dialed. "Shit! Fuck! Why am I dialing 9-1-1? What do I dial here? I know it. It's, uh."

"It's 1-1-2, here, lass. And I've already called them." Sam spun her head around and saw Professor Creevy panting as he trudged up the hill, cell phone in hand.

She breathed a sigh of relief and said, "Oh thank you, Professor. How did you know we would be here?"

He chuckled. "I didn't really. I was heading back to my room when I heard a gunshot followed by a scream. I called out to the Guards on patrol before calling for an ambulance. It'll be here within twenty minutes." He knelt beside Frank and helped apply pressure to the wound. "Stay calm, son. I know you're scared, but staying calm just might keep you alive."

At that moment, an older man came racing toward them. He looked to be in his mid-fifties with coal-black eyes and only a few wisps of white hair peeking from beneath his camel and gray hounds tooth deerstalker hat. His jowls hung below his chin, and he wore a dark gray knit turtleneck and a tan pair of trousers. He had a hunting rifle in his hand and a lantern in the other. He knelt and added pressure with his right hand. He offered a weak smile and said, "Seems my shooting gets worse as I get older. Gunshot wounds are nasty business. If he weren't playing in a faerie ring, luck might be on his side."

Some of the police patrolling the area arrived after a few minutes to investigate, and an ambulance arrived shortly after they did. While the paramedics loaded Frank into the ambulance and did their best to keep Sam calm, the officers took statements from Professor Creevy; the hunter who identified himself as George Crowley; and Sam. George stated that he was out lamping for foxes. The ambulance drove toward Sligo University Hospital while the officers continued their investigation. One of the younger officers offered to escort Sam back to The Slouching Giant, but Creevy said he would keep her safe as she headed back to her room. As they left, she caught a quick glimpse of a large signet ring on George Crowley's left hand, but she was unable to identify the design.

She thanked Professor Creevy as he opened the Giant's door for her. Sam smiled weakly at Mrs. O'Gill and walked to her room. As she unlocked the door, she turned to Creevy and said, "Thank you again. I didn't think I would panic, given I've been shot before."

He smiled. "That may be why you panicked, lass. But think nothing of it. You're a friend of a friend, so that makes you a friend. You sleep well tonight."

She thanked him again. As she opened the door to her room, she saw a small white envelope on the floor. She picked it up as she locked the door, finding no writing on the exterior. Tossing the envelope on the bed, she removed her clothes and makeup, took a quick shower, and then climbed into bed. Opening the envelope, she saw a familiar three-word motto at the top of the stationary and then, written in blotchy, blue ink, was a single sentence, "We'll see you soon."

Chapter 4

My phone, which I swear was on vibrate when I went to bed, rang. I flailed around the bed for a few rings until I found the damned thing on the nightstand where the room's alarm clock blazed 7:02 a.m. in red. Did I turn the ringer back on in case Frank called me? Did I give him my number? Or would it have been one of the Garda? I blinked a few times before seeing Destiny's name, and then it made sense. She's the only living person on my Favorites list, so I'll always hear calls from her. I sat up and rubbed my temples, "Hey, Des? What's up? It's gotta be like two in the morning for you."

"Hey, Sam," she said through a yawn. "I just didn't hear from you, so I wanted to make sure you were okay. Sorry, I dozed off for a bit, or I would've called before midnight over there."

I yawned, "Fuck, you're making me yawn. But yeah, I got the texts. Sorry, last night was intense."

"Intense? As in 'your secret threesome fantasy that I only know because you spilled it to me while you were drunk on New Year's Eve came true' intense or as in 'Run from your life because of the cannibals chasing us' intense?" She asked.

"Frank, my ghost hunter friend, was shot while dancing in a faerie ring." I replied through yawns.

"Wait? What?" Destiny squeaked. "Is he okay? Are you okay?

Was it the Duilearga?"

"I'd rather not talk about it," I snorted. "Look, Des, you need some sleep. I'll read the texts and call you later. Apparently, I need to call my father, who messaged and called me last night, but his ass can wait until I've had my coffee."

"Call me tomorrow," Destiny said. "I have a date tonight."

"Tinder?" I asked.

"No," she replied. "His name's Alex. It's a blind date my mom and one of her friends 'suggested.' He's an accountant."

I smirked into the phone. "Well, have fun, be charming, and use protection. And I don't mean a gun. I'll call you tomorrow." I hung up as she blew a raspberry into the phone.

I turned on the lamp, wincing as the light seemed brighter this morning than it did last night. I guess this would be Carmilla's first reaction to waking up before sunset, followed by searing pain and agony. I fumbled around the room and prepared a cup of coffee. Unlike most hotels I visited in the States, this place had in-room coffee that I could stomach when served black, which is how coffee is meant to be served. I grabbed a sweater and jeans, throwing them on the bed, as the coffee maker worked its magic on the pod, filling my room with the rich, roasted smell of my favorite beverage. As I grabbed the plain, white, ceramic mug provided, I scanned Destiny's texts. So, it seems that my father wants me to abandon the case, something "ancient" is rising or whatever, and I need to get under Old Tom's Hill somehow. My choice is simple. I have to save Mabd.

I sat on the bed and drank my coffee. Without thought, I grabbed the St. Benedict medallion my mother gave me after I ran into her bedroom crying because of a nightmare. I had watched the VHS tape of Return to Oz, and I dreamed that

Jack Pumpkinhead and Princess Mombi had teamed up to take my head. This medallion is the only thing that has seen me through more struggles than Sandy Paws. I almost placed it in mom's casket when I said goodbye. If mom hadn't had her accident while I was in college, would I be doing this today? I'd love an answer to that, but I wish mom were here now. One day each year is not enough. I squeezed the medallion as salty tears stung my eyes and streamed down my cheeks. Releasing the medallion, I wiped my eyes and said, "Sorry, Benedict. It's hard to have faith when you have knowledge."

I showered, dressed, grabbed both my purse and the map case, and headed toward the sitting room for breakfast. As I passed by the desk, Mister O'Gill stopped me and said, "Morning, Samantha. You'll have the run of the place today."

"Oh? Am I the only one here?" I asked.

"Not exactly," he replied, "but we only have four guests right now. You, the ghost hunter friend you made—who I hear is in the hospital in Sligo—and Professor Creevy. Oh, and a man who just arrived about half an hour ago. His last name's Hain as well. I doubt you know him, but it'll give you something to start a conversation that's a little safer than ghost stories. How are you holding up?"

I smiled. "I appreciate your protectiveness, Mister O'Gill. It was an interesting night, and I'm as okay as I can be, given what happened on the way back here. I'll call after lunch to see how he's doing. I don't think I'll be going on another hunt with him again. And I certainly won't be stepping into a faerie ring and dancing."

He nodded and smiled. "At least you're safe. You do remind me of my granddaughter. It was a struggle, but she turned out alright. I hope you do too."

"Thank you," I said. Damn. *This nice man is going to make that mascara earn its waterproof label.*

I walked into the sitting room and headed straight to the buffet, grabbing myself a full Irish breakfast. I would never tell Destiny, but I think bangers are better than bratwurst. I filled another mug with coffee and sat down at one of the smaller tables. After a few bites, I scanned the room and saw him sipping his tea while reading some old leather-bound book in a chair by the hearth. He was a fat, middle-aged ginger, but you wouldn't know that, given the overall lack of hair on his head, save for what emerged from his ears and his bulbous nose. It seems he didn't see me, so I tried to eat faster.

Unfortunately, I was wrong. He closed his book and walked over to me, and in his condescending baritone said, "I see you're enjoying your last breakfast here, Samantha."

I slowed my chewing pace, swallowed, and took a long, slow sip of my coffee before responding, "Well, good morning to you too, father." As he sat in the chair opposite me, I added, "Please, have a seat."

He reeked of Brut aftershave and wore a shit-brown sweater vest over his pale blue button down and khaki slacks. "You're going home, Samantha Blake."

"So we're already at first and middle names. Guess I've been a very bad girl," I snarled as I glared at him while slicing the tip of my last banger with a single stroke. As I stabbed it with my fork, I said, "Oh, I'm sorry, I know you haven't really been involved in my life since I was six-years-old, but in case you've forgotten, I will be thirty in three days. I don't have a curfew, and you don't get to boss me around like your little underlings in the Order. There's a young girl in danger, and I can't abandon her to them."

He leaned in and lowered his voice as he replied, "Samantha Blake Hain, the Duilearga are the least of your worries. I can't explain right now, but there are forces–"

"Moving that do not respect the Treaty," I interrupted. "Yeah, dad, Destiny told me you called at work. I've gotten more information from Nick Scratch than from you or anyone else."

He leaned forward and lowered his voice, "Some things are best left uninvestigated, Samantha. And when the Council heard what happened last night, I felt it best to come and collect you myself."

I growled as my eyes narrowed. "Collect me? Like I'm a pet, a child, a trophy? You think I'm happy that Frank was shot last night? He may have been one of your little wizardlings, but he was genuinely a nice person. The only member of your little pretentious boy wizard club I have any ill will toward is, well, you."

"From what I understand, Mister Caldwell is in surgery as we speak." He leaned back in his chair and folded his arms across his chest.

My fork clanged against the plate. "What? Oh, no! Is he going to make it?"

My father shook his head. "It's a critical time for him. Seems the bullet wound punctured an artery, and he lost a lot of blood. Had your wound been half an inch higher, well, you would have been in his situation. So, go home."

I took a deep breath and closed my eyes for a moment. Shaking my head, I replied, "I can't do that. This young girl needs help, and whatever ancient forces are out there, and whichever Duilearga agents are coming to join those already here, can move out of my way. She doesn't deserve to be left to that fate. No one does. Your stupid Order always talks about humanity coming into the 'divine light of knowledge.' Well, while you wait for it to happen, I'm going to go out into the darkness with a candle and an extended hand. So, why don't you start talking, father?"

His thick fingers pinched the bridge of his nose as he sighed. "You're lucky that I have a distant cousin who happens to run a bookstore where you bought a book of local legends collected by Thomas Logue. Had she not asked about you, I might have not known you were here and in danger. I called your office, because I thought Destiny would talk to me before you would."

"Can you blame me?" I asked through a mouthful of beans. "You were barely in my life after you and mom divorced. I tried to give you a pass, but when I learned that you had access to teleportation portals, I realized the distance wasn't the issue. And when I hit thirteen, you quit calling me. I didn't hear from you again until after mom's accident." I threw my fork onto the plate as my hands started shaking. "And you waltzed into my life and acted like you hadn't missed a day."

"It wasn't an accident, Samantha, and you know that," He said, his eyes coldly logical.

"Fuck. You." I shot back, draining the remaining half of my coffee mug in a single gulp.

His shoulders sank as he sighed. "I made mistakes, Sam, with you and with Amelia. I can't fix those the way you fix supernatural problems. All I can do is try to do what's best for you from day to day. Give me a chance to do that."

"I need more coffee," I said as I rose from my seat. My heart rate was faster than I needed it right now, and my mind raced with things to say to him. I did not need this now. I only had three more days until the Duilearga took care of the situation. And every fucking one offers a cryptic warning about some ancient power, but none of these know-nothing assholes seems to think that it's a good idea to fill me in on the details. As I poured more coffee, I sighed. I returned to my seat, sipped my coffee, eyed my father cautiously, and asked, "Since I'm sure you know I'm not leaving until I close this case, what do you plan to do?"

He folded his arms across his chest. "Then I have no choice but to stay and protect you."

I rolled my eyes. "Look, Donal, I've been doing this for almost ten years, and not once–even on my first fix–have I had my father holding my hand. I'm an intelligent, capable woman. So, you can go back home to Dublin, or the Grand Temple of your precious Order in London, or to Hell, or to the nearest Tesco. I really don't care. If you know something that I need to know, why don't you just tell me?"

"It's not that simple, Sam." He rubbed his temples with his right hand. "There are too many sides of this conflict to say what knowledge is needed. I know it seems like a tall order, but I am asking you to trust me."

I leaned back in my chair. Everyone seems more worried about me than usual, and I've had more strangers do things to warn me or look out for my safety than I've had in my entire life. Maybe there is something to what they're saying. As I mentally ran through every time my father had broken a promise of help, Mister O'Gill passed behind my father as he refreshed some of the dishes on the breakfast buffet. He gave me one of those grandfatherly looks that said, "You know what you need to do."

I sighed and said, "Let's do something we've never done, dad: compromise. I'm going to speak to Lady O'Cuinn alone. You can do whatever you want to do. I'll text you when I'm heading back, and we can discuss things. Then, and only then, we'll go from there."

He nodded. "I'll take it, Samantha, but do give me a chance. I know what's best for you."

* * *

Lady O'Cuinn's butler, an older gentleman with a Roman nose and whisky barrel stomach, escorted Sam into the sitting room of Gaelladgh Castle and left to tell the Lady she had a guest. The vaulted ceiling and large windows provided ample natural light, and the pale oak flooring kept the room feeling light and open. Portraits of ancestors and other family adorned the walls. Sam sank easily into the plush green velvet cushions of her chair, noting that the burnished bronze trim matched the leafy scrollwork on the green wallpaper. She smiled as she stroked the velvet armrest and sighed contentedly as the smells of rosemary and baking bread wafted into her nostrils. Sam heard the faint sound of unfamiliar music from another room; it was beautiful, but sad.

After a few moments, Sam stood and greeted Lady O'Cuinn as she entered. She stood a few inches taller than Sam. Although her face had the severity of a bitter Dickensian widow, her smile was warm and gentle. She kept her silver hair in a neat bun, allowing only a single, small ringlet to fall on the left side of her face. Her half-moon glasses clung to the bridge of her nose, even as she pushed them up repeatedly. She wore a tan cable-knit sweater and a navy maxi skirt. They shook hands and sat in chairs across from each other. The butler poured tea in chipped green cups with golden scroll-work that mirrored that of the wallpaper before taking his leave.

As Sam sipped the rose petal and black tea, Lady O'Cuinn said, "You must understand, Miss Hain, that had you not provided proof of your occupation, I would not have seen you."

"Of course," Sam said. "When I first arrived in town, I heard how almost all of these amateur ghost hunters descended upon your lovely home and that their only concern was authenticating the banshee video. As such, I was hoping I could conduct my investigation without disturbing you, but I've hit a wall."

"And with the nasty incidents that have befallen them," Lady O'Cuinn stirred her tea slowly. "I did not appreciate the ghost hunters and their incessant questioning, but I have never wished harm on any of them."

Sam inhaled deeply as she stared at the floor. She nodded, "Yeah, from what I've heard–and seen–things have gotten nasty."

Lady O'Cuinn nodded in understanding. "Well, if there is anything I can tell you that will help you find Mabd, I will. She may be an employee, but she is like a granddaughter to me. My only granddaughter, her perpetual boyfriend, and myself are the only family she has within a hundred kilometers."

Sam smiled. "I'm sure she appreciates that. Do you have a photograph of her I could see or copy? I'll be honest, I don't know what she looks like."

Lady O'Cuinn nodded. "May I use the email on your card? Good."

She searched through the photos on her cell phone for a moment before selecting one. Looking at Sam's business card, she squinted as she typed the email address and pressed the send button. After a few moments, Sam saw the email on her phone and opened the attachment. The image showed Lady O'Cuinn and three other people – a middle-aged couple and a young woman–at a party. The middle-aged woman resembled Lady O'Cuinn in bone structure, so Sam focused her attention on the younger woman–an attractive-enough, mousy girl with fair skin, brown hair and eyes, and a slightly upturned nose.

"The one seated behind the cake is Mabd," Lady O'Cuinn said. "It was her twenty-third birthday, and we wanted to show her we love her. She's one of the lucky ones."

"Oh? What do you mean?" Sam asked.

"Well," she said, "as I'm sure happens in the States, when an orphan remains unadopted, they often find themselves in a precarious situation when they reach adulthood."

Sam nodded. "Yeah, I've seen the results of that a few times. It's probably different here, but it's likely not great. And I wouldn't have recognized Mabd if I'd seen her already. And that leads to the day she disappeared. Can you recall anything unusual? Did she say anything? Do anything?"

Lady O'Cuinn narrowed her eyes and pursed her lips. After a moment, she shook her head. "No. Aside from walking up Old Tom's Hill. Yes, she can return to her room here, but one has to go out of their way to pass by the hill."

"Given the local legends and how fervently people warn others about them," Sam said as she jotted notes in her small spiral notebook, "I'm surprised she risked it."

"Well, after surviving that encounter with the banshee–oh, yes, she showed me the video, so you can stop pretending you don't know the full story–well, she became much bolder than she once was."

Sam picked up her jaw. "Okay. How did you know? I don't exactly keep 'Expert Veil Crossing Fixer' on my business cards."

She smiled into her tea. "I have a cousin married to a Councilman in Cork who mentioned your name a few years ago when they had some trouble with a little leprechaun."

Sam nodded. "That was almost a decade ago. You have a damned good memory."

She nodded and smiled. "Well, I do. Decades of theater and opera made that a necessity. But, in Christian honesty, it was the fact that your name really is Sam Hain. It's hard to forget that."

Sam smiled while rolling her eyes. "That's really my only reason for going by 'Sam' instead of either Samantha or Blake, which is my middle name." She shifted in the chair. "But this does make what I'm about to ask you a little easier. Since you watched the video, did you understand anything the banshee said?"

Lady O'Cuinn shook her head. "It was a beautiful, sad song. I think it was in an older version of Irish. I'm not fluent, but I can sing in it. Why?"

Sam leaned forward. "To be honest, Lady O'Cuinn, I walked the bog last night with one of those ghost hunters, and we met the banshee. Seems none of the ghost hunters thought to speak to her in Irish, and so my broken Irish caused her to stop for a conversation. Does the name 'Niamh O'Cuinn' mean anything to you?"

Lady O'Cuinn paused and stared into her teacup. "Niamh's a family name, so there are quite a few of us who have it. Did you understand anything else?"

Sam sighed. "The only other thing she mentioned that I could understand was something about Liam's doom coming?"

Lady O'Cuinn leaned back in her chair and sighed. After a moment of silence, she whispered, "Liam's doom. I feel like

I should know that. I feel like I do know that, but it's just in the shadows of my mind. With my granddaughter nearing her due date, I'm sure you understand."

They shared a smile. Sam nodded. "Your first great-grandchild?"

"Possibly my only direct great-grandchild. My granddaughter has PCOS."

Sam nodded and smiled. "You know, they say classical music boosts a baby's intelligence, so might I ask what you have playing while I've been here?"

Lady O'Cuinn's eyes became glassy as she smiled and nodded. "Gluck's Orfeo ed Euridice." She sighed and turned her attention to the portrait of a man with a thick brown beard and green eyes that hung on the wall behind Sam. "Today marks the twenty-first anniversary of my husband Reginald's passing. When we were much younger, I performed the role of Euridice at the Irish National Opera. After opening night, Reginald presented me with a bouquet of roses and an engagement ring. And now, every year on this day, I listen to the opera, and I feel like he is with me for a brief moment."

Sam carefully wiped a tear away and whispered, "Mom." She smiled and nodded. "That's really beautiful, and someone willing to do all that for love is a special find."

"It is," Lady O'Cuinn replied. "Love makes us do strange things." Her voice trailed off as looked into the distance. She gasped. "Liam's doom. Please excuse me for one moment, Miss Hain. I think I just remembered something." She rose and left the room.

A few moments later, Lady O'Cuinn returned with a worn leather tome with silver fittings. She returned to her chair and opened the book. With a heavy sigh, she said, "As we discussed

Orpheo, it triggered a memory from my wedding day of my own grandmother telling me the story of how our family came to be. It's an old family legend that I thought was a good yarn, but in no manner could it be real. And yet, here we are.

"As the story goes, Edward III, King of England, awarded the land to Liam for his aid in helping the king's son Lionel subdue some of the autonomous lords. As I'm sure you know, that didn't sit well with many Irishmen. This led to numerous problems and riots, which Liam handled through bribery, blackmail, and brutality."

"The 'Three B's' of government," Sam interjected.

"Aye," Lady O'Cuinn shot her a quick glare. "Well, as he grew older, he recognized that he needed an heir, and he had his heart set on a younger woman, Niamh Connacht, the younger daughter of a long-established noble line here. According to his journal," she held up the book, "there were mutual feelings of affection between them, but her father wouldn't hear of her marrying a 'traitor to the Isle,' as many called Liam. And while he could have forced the marriage, Liam knew that angering a Connacht would cause greater strife than he and his allies could handle."

"As the story goes, Liam was hunting in the forest beyond Bannagh one day. He sat at the base of Old Tom's Hill to cook the pheasants he killed. A strange wind blew through the woods, and uprooted a large yew tree, which fell on Liam's groin. As he pulled himself out from under the tree, he cursed, believing he would never have an heir. He claimed that, at that moment, the devil approached and offered him medicine that would restore his virility. He said his virility would mean nothing if he could not have the woman he loved. Well, the devil promised him both if he would grant him a favor in the future. He agreed. Liam and Niamh married the next summer, and they celebrated the birth of their first son the next spring."

"That's a lovely faerie story, Lady O'Cuinn," Sam said. "That doesn't explain this 'doom' that is coming or give me a name to research or anything."

She shook her head. "No, and I have scoured Liam's journal, hoping to find more details. All I could find is a reference to a bargain made and signed with the devil that was buried somewhere at the base of Old Tom's Hill."

Sam sighed. "That's not the first time someone's told me to look beneath that hill. It's not an answer, but it's a step closer to that answer." She stood and added, "Well, best wishes for a safe delivery and a healthy baby. Thank you for your hospitality, Lady O'Cuinn. I won't take up any more of your time. I hope to wrap this up by the 30th both for Mabd's safety and because my birthday is the 31st."

Lady O'Cuinn shook her hand and laughed. "You were born on Samhain. I'm sure you were ribbed a few times over that. Well, thank you, Miss Hain, and I wish you all the luck in our land."

As Sam left Gaelladgh Castle, she saw she had a text message from her father. "We have a private room at the Tipsy Tenpenny reserved for noon. Be there." She noted the time was a quarter past ten, so she headed to Old Tom's Hill and dig for an answer. On her way, she stopped at the local hardware store to purchase a trowel, knowing that such a tool would be less conspicuous to carry than a shovel.

* * *

Were it not for last night's events, Old Tom's Hill would have remained as quiet and innocuous an appearance as it had the first time Sam climbed it alone. The caution signs blazed their warnings into her eyes as she recalled the terror on Frank's face as he bled on the grass. She ran her fingers through her hair as she stared at the ground. Her heart began pounding in her chest, and her breathing quickened. She massaged the scar on her shoulder. When she realized what she was doing, she shook her head and blinked.

"Let me give the hospital a call," she whispered, reaching into her purse for her cell phone. She searched for the number for Sligo University Hospital and dialed. When the receptionist answered, she said, "Hi, I'm looking for a patient–admitted last night with a gunshot wound–a Frank Caldwell. No, I'm not family; we're just friends."

"We can't give out records. I'm sure you understand," the receptionist replied in a supportive yet perky voice. "But I can tell you he's in surgery right now. Don't know how long he'll be there. Gunshot wounds are nasty things."

"I understand. Thank you." Sam ended the call.

She stared at the hill for a moment, her muscles tense, and her breathing again quick. She clenched her jaw and took a single, deep breath before walking around the eastern side of the hill toward the small, broken ring of mushrooms on its northern side. The western wind felt harsh against her skin as the overcast sky loomed above her. Her nose wrinkled and tears formed in the corners of her eyes as the bitter, metallic smell of iron rose from the grass. Her mind flashed to Frank's blood-soaked shoulder and her attempts to stop the flow. Her eyes glanced at her trembling hands and saw them wringing. She whispered, "Damn," as she breathed deeply.

Surveying the broken ring, she ran her fingers over the

reddish-brown grass on its eastern edge where no mushrooms grew. The dry, brittle grass crumbled in her fingers before the breeze carried it away. She sniffed the dust that remained; it smelled like the cold ash that remains in a fireplace at the end of a long winter. The grass immediately outside the ring also felt dry, but it did not crumble in her hands. She rested her chin between her thumb and index finger for a moment before shaking her head. Scanning the area to be certain no one saw her, she took her trowel and began digging.

After half an hour of digging, Sam's trowel scraped against metal. She increased her pace, scraping and poking to find the edges of whatever had been buried. Ten minutes passed, and Sam realized that she had found a flat-topped metal container with tarnished bronze fittings, dull gray, and the size of a briefcase. The density of the metal hindered her excavation of this metal box. The box appeared sturdy with intact, though rusted, fittings; the barrel-shaped padlock appeared rusted and frail. Sam tapped it with the butt of the trowel a few times before it broke, allowing her access to the box's interior.

Tattered and soiled remains of velvet cushions lined the interior walls of the box. A long piece of parchment, bound in rough cord and sealed in wax, rested on the ruins of its bedding. The parchment, light beige, felt supple when Sam ran her fingers over it; this surprised her, as she had assumed the document would have become brittle after being buried for nearly seven centuries. The outline of a heraldic lion stood proudly against the midnight blue wax that sealed the knot of the black cord surrounding the document. She easily flicked the wax seal away and untied the cord. She scanned the text of the document and exhaled when she recognized the text to be in Latin; she was less-than-fluent in Latin, but she read Latin better than she did Irish.

Scanning the document revealed that it was the written record of a pact struck between Liam O'Cuinn and a being who signed their name in a sigil unfamiliar to Sam. The specifics suggested it was not an infernal contract, which meant that Samael spoke truthfully when he claimed noninvolvement. The circular language seemed fae, but something that Sam could not identify felt out of place. She chose not to dwell on that, because, buried in paragraphs of dense, metaphor-laced, poetic prose, were the terms of the contract. So it seems that this being promised that Liam would be allowed to wed Niamh Connacht and produce an heir; in exchange, this being would claim the first daughter of the thirteenth generation born in Castle Gaelladgh, and the O'Cuinn bloodline would end with her.

Sam leaned against the hill's gentle slope and exhaled. "So that's Liam's doom. Fuck." She grimaced and said, "I guess I'll have to ask dad who this being is, because I don't recognize that sigil. Double fuck."

She stared at the contract for a few minutes before a shrill voice with a thick brogue whispered from the woods, "There is another way to find out the truth."

Sam's mind flitted from thoughts of her mother, to Mabd, to the unborn great-granddaughter of Lady O'Cuinn, to Frank, to her father, and back to her mother. They danced a widening gyre that caused her hands to tremble and her eyes to water. The voice spoke at a normal volume, "There is another way to find the truth."

After a moment of silence, the speaker whistled, but Sam failed to hear as memories and imagined conversations played out in her mind. The speaker, a short, squat man with a thick, unkempt red beard, a clay pipe in his mouth, brown breeches, and a matching green tailcoat and bowler, rushed toward her, grabbed the parchment containing the contract, and raced into the forest while giggling. This snapped Sam from her thoughts. She spun toward the giggling and saw the tiny person rushing off with the contract. She slammed her fist into the dirt and cursed, "Fucking leprechaun!"

Sam chased him into the forest, paying little attention to the branches that scratched at her skin as she pushed through the dense, autumnal foliage. She breathed rapidly, wincing slightly from the combination of branch scratches and the slapping of her purse and map case against her body. Birds ended their songs as they scattered as she passed them, her eyes narrowed, and her brow furrowed as she gained on the leprechaun whose run turned to skipping. The western wind blew cool against the left side of her face. She stopped, pulled her gun from her purse, and fired a warning shot over the leprechaun's head.

"That's the last warning you get, you fucking thief. You bring that back now," she demanded.

The leprechaun chortled as he turned around, smiled, and walked up to her. She squinted as he approached, breathed a sigh of relief that she followed by cocking her head and raising an eyebrow. He bowed and said, "It's a right pleasure to see your smiling face again too, Miss Hain."

"Again?" She asked before her eyes widened. "Wait! You–you're Flann Mac Maghnus. Well, I see you're still alive after all these years."

He shrugged, "It's only been a few days for us, lass. And that's a fine greeting that I didn't expect from you."

She returned her gun to her purse and lowered her gaze. "Sorry. Why didn't you just say something before stealing that contract?"

He folded his arms across his chest and replied. "Why didn't you listen when I tried to get your attention? Whatever's going on your head is distracting you at a time when you don't need that. So, I'm here," he said while smiling and flinging his arms open.

Sam shook her head and asked, "I doubt you're here to be my counselor. So, can you identify that sigil for me?"

He unrolled the parchment and scanned it while mumbling to himself. He whistled and shook his head. "No, I can't do that. But you did me a good turn when my gambling habits got the better of me and kept me safe from the Watchers' guns, not that yours are much safer. So, I'm going to do you a good turn right now and help you find what you need."

Sam reached forward and snatched the contract from his hand. "How? You just said that you don't know who this being is."

The leprechaun winked and replied, "I know someone who does." He held out his pocket watch. "Come on. Time's ticking."

Sam checked her phone. "I've got to meet my father for lunch in half an hour. Can it wait until after?"

"This'll only take ten minutes, I swear." He replied.

Sam stared at the contract for a moment before turning her head toward Bannagh. She sighed, and her shoulders sank toward the earth. She gathered her possessions, stood, and said, "Alright."

She walked toward him, and Flann led Sam deeper into the woods. The winds rushed through the forest, ripping leaves from the trees. The red, brown, and gold leaves swirled around them as the leprechaun led the way through a thick patch of mushrooms whose earthy colors glowed with translucent blue, green, and, golden lights. The air smelled of fresh apples and rich cinnamon and clove spices; its smell grew more intense as they moved through the mushroom field, exited the forest, and reached a white sand beach where a simple rowboat floated in readiness. They stepped into the boat. Flann untied the boat from its mooring and rowed into the sea.

* * *

"She's late, Donal," Professor Creevy said as he glanced at his pocket watch while sitting in one of the leather and mahogany chairs surrounding a circular mahogany table in The Tipsy Tenpenny's private room. A crystal snifter of brandy sat before him, and he held a cigar in his right hand. Its thick, earthy aroma wafted through the air.

"She'll be here, Seamus. Being late is not like her, but she will be here." Donal Hain said, sipping the peaty, amber Scotch in his glass and mumbling, "Where are you, Samantha?"

"Let us hope, for her sake. Our other associate will arrive shortly, and they will not wait forever – even though they could."

The two men talked for a few moments, before the door's shadow lengthened to touch that of the table. The two men heard the click of a locking mechanism, and the shadow door creaked open. Lavender and patchouli punched through the portal as a slender being with long black ringlets, ruddy but fair skin, long and pointed ears, and one lavender and one coppery-brown eye flounced into the room, twirling into one of the empty chairs. Their high cheekbones sparkled with multicolored diamond dust as they summoned a glass of sparkling pink wine into a slender hand that emerged from the oversized handkerchief sleeve on their gauzy white shirt.

As the two men rose and gave a polite bow, Creevy said, "Welcome, Fosiri Bha'esi, Count of Autumn's Twilight and Thane of the Queen of Earth and Winter. I am Professor Seamus Creevy, Knight-General of the Order of the Dragon, and this is Donal Hain, Arch Magus of the Astrum Argentum and representative of the High Council of said Order."

The Fae noble gently waved their empty hand while sipping their wine. Their voice emerged as a flute's trill amidst a thunderstorm. "Yes, and where is our fourth? The wild card?"

"Regrettably, Honorable Count Bha'esi, she may not be joining us." Creevy said, glaring at Arch Magus Hain.

Donal Hain nodded. "Yes, Count Bha'esi, perhaps the fault is mine, for she and I have not had the most positive relationship. And since I asked her to join us, she may have chosen to ignore my request."

"Ignoring an order from a superior is an unacceptable trait, Arch Magus." Count Bha'esi said, crossing their legs and leaning over the side of the chair. "No matter, we shall continue without her."

The Fae noble clapped their hands four times, and the low, sonorous clang of a gong sounded in the room. Hundreds of tiny orbs of green light danced in the air until, in a flash of light, a tiny human-looking Fae with wasp wings and emerald hair emerged, seated at a wooden scribe's desk with quill and parchment. Bha'esi looked at the insignificant creature and nodded. The creature dipped its quill into a pot of ink and waited. The two humans nodded.

"Well," Professor Creevy said, "Let us begin. Let the record show that this meeting is attended by Count Bha'esi, representing the Court of Autumn; Arch Magus Donal Hain, representing the Hermetic Order of the Astrum Argentum; and myself, Professor Seamus Creevy, representing the Order of the Dragon. The fourth invited to this meeting, one Samantha Blake Hain, has chosen not to attend. And while it may be regrettable, this action marks her as an enemy of our cause."

The scribal faerie furiously wrote every word spoken as both Creevy and Bha'esi noticed Donal's fallen expression. Bha'esi then leaned forward to speak. "It is regrettable, but it is the nature of such revolutions, is it not? And as such, let the record show that both the Queen of Air and Summer and the Queen of Earth and Winter have violated the Ancient Laws of the Seasons by seeking alliances with those from other planes. The Queen of Air and Summer is currently in negotiations with Samael, Lord of Hell, and the Queen of Earth and Winter is currently negotiating with Fuqtus the djinn; there is no intelligence at present demonstrating Iblis knows of such negotiations. Their stated purposes are identical: to respond to the 'changing world around us.'" Bha'esi growled and rolled their eyes. "Thus, herein, we enter into a pact."

Creevy's eyes widened. "I thought we had already reached our agreement, most noble Count."

Bha'esi chuckled, his elongated eye teeth bared to the men. "We have, good professor. This is simply the formal declaration of our intents to enter into a mutually beneficial arrangement. As such, you possess with you the required documentation of promises for you and your respective orders, correct?"

They nodded. Arch Magus Hain reached into his gray leather briefcase and produced a silver disk about the size of a dinner plate upon which he had inscribed a series of sigils and runes.

He pushed the disk to Bha'esi and said, "The Hermetic Order of the Astrum Argentum promises to provide support during your conquest of Faerie. We will use our magic to seal off the portals, preventing any from entering or exiting without your approval. Additionally, we shall use our magic to locate and detain all who give aid to your enemies and to lay siege to their strongholds. In exchange, your powers will add to ours as we infiltrate and ascend to stewardship over the Western Hemisphere."

Bha'esi held the disk in their right hand for a few moments. Their left hand traced every line, circle, curve, and point etched into the silver. They smirked. "Excellent. Of course, you do realize that you may have to kill your own daughter should she oppose our designs?"

Donal Hain swallowed and replied, "I am aware of that possibility, yes."

Professor Creevy produced a golden disk of similar size and design from his black leather messenger bag. He pushed the disk toward Bha'esi and said, "The Order of the Dragon, once we have resurrected our great leader Vlad Tepes Dracula, will provide ground troops to supplement your own during your war. In exchange, your powers will aid us in subjugating the Eastern Hemisphere, bringing those unruly mongrels to heel. And thus, with East and West in true alliance, there will be order and peace."

Bha'esi smiled as they accepted the golden disk. "Then our business this day is concluded. I will send a trooper to your respective orders when the time of your service is at hand. Be ready."

The three rose and bowed to one another. Count Bha'esi and the scribal faerie exited as they entered. The two men sighed, and Donal Hain sank into his chair and downed his Scotch. Creevy patted him on the shoulder and said, "Tough business, bringing peace to the world," before returning to his seat and adding, "tough but important work."

"Yes," Donal Hain replied, his eyes turned toward the inactive screen on his phone. "And needed, given the recent wars, continuing civil unrest, and that pandemic from last year, the world needs leaders who can force them into order and enlightenment if needed."

"No gods but true masters," Creevy nodded, sipping his cognac. "But, how's the boy doing?"

Donal nodded. "He's in surgery. Touch and go with bullet wounds. Thank you for assisting in getting him to the hospital. He's got promise."

Creevy nodded. "At present, your daughter's presence here is an inconvenience, given that her investigation is likely to cause her to run afoul of our experiment here."

"I'm aware, Seamus. I'm aware," Donal said, sighing in exasperation. "If I know my daughter, she will be focused on saving the human and the banshee involved in the incident. It is unlikely that she will interfere in our experiment. Even if she did, I doubt she has the strength and power to banish that Saturnian elemental."

Seamus chuckled. "Aye, then it's a fortunate accident old man Crowley shot the boy. What, Donal? Didn't you know he's a Duilearga cell archivist? The moment she learns that," he paused and smirked.

"She'll turn her rage onto him," Donal finished Seamus' thought. He sighed and added, "He will become her target, and that will buy us time to bind and control that thing and send it forward against the people of Chełm and their precious guardian." Then, with a dismissive snort, he added, "Weak magic."

Chapter 5

A cool, gentle breeze carried the fresh scent of a morning rain topped with notes from peonies and tulips to our noses as the rowboat approached the sea foam sand beach ahead of us. Though we had been traveling north in a straight line, the air grew progressively warmer. The sky's blue resembled stained glass that refracted the light from the sun alongside tiny dancing orbs of light. Oddly, no matter where I looked, I couldn't see the sun on this cloudless day. As we approached the beach, Flann Mac Maghnus, my leprechaun guide, hopped from the boat and pulled us onto the shore. Aside from the faint warbling and whistling of birds, it was quiet. It would have been a perfect spring day if everything didn't feel about six degrees askew.

As I stepped onto the beach, I reached down and ran my fingers through the sand. I jerked my hand back as a dozen needles pricked my skin. I winced as blood dripped onto the sand. I applied pressure with my other hand and exclaimed, "Fuck! That's sharp."

Flann's head turned just enough to see my bleeding hand. "Well, it is the Glass Shore," he replied as he continued walking toward the grassland ahead of us.

"And you were going to tell me this when?" I asked as I

followed him.

"I didn't think you'd be daft enough to run your hands through the sand shards," he replied.

I glared at his messy red hair. "You're right. After all, sea foam glass shards that look like sand are so common. And how is the air so warm? We've been heading north for like half an hour. Where are we?"

He continued walking, hopping over a large rock in his path. "Isn't it obvious? We're in the Vernal Court. Come on."

"Hold your silver-buckled shoes," I said as I stopped at the edge of the field where viridian-scaled blades of grass swayed like rolling fingers in the breeze. I continued, "Faerie? I don't have time to be in Faerie. I've got an investigation to complete."

Flann spun around, hopped onto the rock, and placed his hands on his hips. His forehead wrinkled as he stared directly into my eyes. "That's why you don't have time to not be in Faerie, Miss Hain." He sighed. "I promised I would take you to someone who could help you, so this way."

He jerked his head toward, what I assumed to be, the east, hopped off the rock, and continued walking. The scaly grass rose to his chest, making it a challenge to follow him. I chuckled and shook my head as I started to understand all those legends about mortals getting lost in Faerie while chasing after these little shits. The part of me that remained the heart-filled-with-wonder twenty-year-old wanted to touch everything and explore every acre of the Spring Court, but the jaded, experienced P.I. knew that getting lost here could lead to spending a decade or more wandering around this place. That worried me.

We continued walking for what felt like an hour, and I turned around to see that we had only moved about one hundred yards from the beach. I reached into my purse to check the time on my phone. This was not the time to have a dead battery. I don't know what I expected. I started to realize that all those "a year and a day" legends and those damned Narnia books made more sense than I believed. The last thing I needed was to lose time to some magical, inter-planar travel bullshit.

After another ten minutes or two hours of walking, we moved through a garden of massive tulips, peonies, and roses whose buds rose above my head. Tiny lights flickered from within their translucent petals. The bulbs were almost as large as my head, and the stems and leaves resembled the viridian scales of the grass blades, allowing these flowers to slither and sway in the breeze. A handful of orange and blue bees buzzed, pollinating the flowers as they went about their honey-making duties. I leaned over, inhaling the tulip's scent of freshly cut grass with hints of ginger; my nose wrinkled, and I blinked rapidly as a massive, and ever-so-ladylike, sneeze erupted from my nostrils. Flann shook his head as we continued onward.

We continued through the flower field, and it wasn't long before the birdsong I heard while we neared the shore returned. Only it wasn't warbling and chirping like I thought. I could discern pitch variation and rhythm. It was clearly a language, a familiar one sung by a strangely familiar voice. A woman's voice, gentle but passionate. I couldn't stop myself from listening; her song was so melodic. I blinked a few times; tiny lights danced in my vision as my head grew fuzzy. Flann said something to me, but I was so engrossed by that beautiful voice that he sounded like an adult in a Peanuts cartoon speaking to me from a distance as I followed that voice.

As I moved through the field of giant flowers whose leaves sparkled like Christmas light-illuminated cellophane toward

101

the voice, I soon realized that whoever was singing was singing in German, another language in which I can hold amazing conversations with small children. I waded through the sea of giant scaled plants, and the song grew louder and more beautiful. I knew the voice, damn it, but I couldn't place the singer. Something snapped under my feet as I pushed my way through two thick bushes covered in red roses. I moaned as I breathed in the thick scent of musk and clove that emanated from their petals. My eyes went hazy as I stepped into the small clearing beyond where the singer sat.

When my vision cleared, I stood in a clearing before a pool of clear water that refracted the light like a mosaic of stained-glass shards. At the center of the pool, emerging from within a giant crimson rose bloom, singing, stood Countess Carmilla Karnstein in all her naked glory. I inhaled sharply and bit my lip as I struggled to maintain eye contact as her pale, full breasts were as perfect as I'd drunkenly imagined. She extended her slender arms and beckoned me to approach as her song gained a pleading, passionate tone. My breath rate increased as I forced my eyes to meet hers, and as I gazed into her eyes, I stepped into the pool.

The stained-glass shard water resisted my first few steps. I thought I would get to walk on water, but my feet eventually sank to the bottom of the knee-deep pool. A breeze pushed me forward, and the rich citrusy, herbal, and earthy aroma of her perfume guided me into her cool, soft arms. I inhaled sharply as she wrapped her arms around me, smiling as I blushed, my eyes taking in the sight of this beautiful vampire. My hands shook as they explored her body, my fingertips brushing her soft skin before kneading her ass. Her hand cupped my chin. My breath became raspy and rapid. My lips parted instinctively, and my eyes closed as 'Milla kissed and nibbled her way up my neck.

My eyes shot open as something hard thunked the back of my head. A large, reptilian face, covered in dew-glistening green scales, emerged from the giant rosebud and stared at me with hungry yellow eyes. Spittle oozed from its finger-long fangs as its forked tongue darted from its mouth to lick my cheek. I pulled away and found its long, scaly tentacles had wrapped around my waist and arms; their thorns digging into my skin. Its grip tightened as I pushed and twisted against it. Sweat beaded on my brow, and I breathed like a kid in middle school gym who just ran their first mile.

It lunged forward, pulling back only when a small spear pierced its right eye, causing a thin chartreuse liquid to ooze onto its snout. I winced at its screech of pain, but kicked against its scaly stem as hard as I could. Another tiny spear poked its shoulder, and I repeated my kick, this time pushing myself from its grasp. I looked over and saw Flann, another little spear in his hand, shouting, "Run, you daft lass. Get away from it!"

I scrambled to the edge of the small island and fished around in my purse until I grabbed my Walther. I flipped off the safety and fired three rounds into that lizard plant's skull between its blood to splatter on the grass and my boots as it crashed to the ground. I exhaled deeply and wiped my brow. I walked over to Flann and asked, "So who forgot to feed Audrey II?"

He threw his hat onto the ground and stamped his feet. He wagged his finger as he spoke, "You got to be careful here. That's an amhránaí bláthanna, and if I hadn't noticed you weren't following me, you'd be flower food and potting soil by now."

"A what?" I asked, grabbing my holster from my purse and attaching my gun to my belt.

Flann wiped his hat clean and returned it to his head. With his eyes narrowed, he spoke deliberately. "An amhránaí bláthanna. You would probably call it something like a flower siren. Its song and scent cause its prey to hallucinate, seeing a person they desire greatly. Lures them in, kills them, and then uses what it doesn't eat to provide nourishment for its seeds."

I snorted and shook my head. "I suppose no Faeries have heard of consent," I replied.

"We have," he said, glaring at me. "These amhránaithe are more like animals, not smart enough to do nothing but act on instinct."

I nodded. "So, they're like my father. Great," I added.

Flann shrugged. "Well, keep your weapons on you, lass. Spring and Summer are dangerous, but Autumn and Winter are worse."

I opened the map case and slipped my rapier onto my belt and attached the map case to my purse. Flann started walking, and I followed. After a few moments, I asked, "Let me guess. You're taking me to the heart of the Winter Court, right?"

He shivered and quickened his pace. His head shaking rapidly, he answered, "No. No. No. Not if I can help it. I won't set foot in that place. You go there; you're on your own."

* * *

Flann Mac Maghnus led Sam into a thick forest of trees whose caramel and ash trunks resembled carved marble; six-bladed emerald leaves with amber veins swayed in the warm eastern wind. Birds resembling hawks and eagles with pink, purple, and orange plumage warbled from the branches. A pink and lavender hawk dove from the canopy and snatched a mouse scurrying about the underbrush that, in contrast to the field they left, rose no higher than the middle of Sam's calf. The air smelled of grass freshly cut on the morning after a rain. Flann slapped Sam's hand as she tried to pluck one chrysanthemum with red, pink, and white petals.

"I don't suppose if I sing to these animals, they'll follow me home and clean my apartment?" Sam asked as she watched a handful of squirrels flit about the thick roots, searching for acorns.

Flann laughed from deep within his core. "Oh, I needed that, lass. You think any here would think you a princess."

Sam growled as he continued laughing. She ran her middle finger over her gun and eyed the back of his head, smirking. She shook her head and relaxed. "Well," she said, "if I see a white rabbit with a pocket watch running while whining about being late, I'm following him."

Flann spun around and glowered at Sam. He pointed his finger at her chest and said, "You'll do no such thing, lassie. A lot of people are depending on you to fix this. A lot more than usually rest their hopes on your skills. So, you're going to follow and stay out of trouble."

Sam stopped. Her eyes narrowed. Her skin flushed. "Hold the fuck up," she said. "I keep hearing so many people say that something big is going on and that it's somehow connected to whatever is happening here. However, no one, not Dagh Mobh, Nick Scratch, my asshole of a father, or anyone else. No one has thought that maybe, just maybe, it might be important to fucking tell me what the fuck I'm involved in."

Without turning, Flann said, "From what I hear, it's best to not ask those questions. Let's keep going."

"No." Sam replied flatly.

The leprechaun spun around. His eyes grew wide as he asked, "What do you mean, 'No'?"

Sam folded her arms across her chest and stared Flann down. "I mean that unless someone starts being honest with me about what the fucking hell is going on. I walk. I go my own way. I'll solve this on my own. It won't be the first time."

"I can't let you do that," Flann said. "The Prince'll pluck out my beard."

"I've always wanted to know what a leprechaun looked like after a waxing." Sam remained motionless.

Flann's eyes blinked rapidly. The beating of his heart quickened, and his skin reddened. With wide eyes, he shook his head and replied, "You've got to trust me, Miss Hain. Just, please, come on. Let's go see the Prince."

"Ha!" Sam snorted as she laughed. "Trust you? The last time I met you, you lied about your identity, you cheated at cards, and you blackmailed county officials. You're not exactly a beacon of virtue, Flann. Talk."

"I don't – it's just that – look," he stammered, "I don't know what you don't know, and I don't know what you do. I just think you should come and let the Prince explain."

Sam drew her gun and fired a quick shot that knocked the leprechaun's hat off his head. He curled on the ground in fear as she cocked an eyebrow. "I don't want to shoot you, but if somebody, and right now, that would be you, doesn't start talking, I may change my mind."

Flann fanned out his fingers so he could see Sam's flushed cheeks and withering glare. Sweat fell from his brow as he panted. His entire body trembled, but he slowly stood, donned his hat, and said, "I don't think I'm really the best to talk. No, no no no no! Wait! Put that gun down, please. I don't know much. I've heard rumors from people who heard rumors from important people. That's why the Prince sent me. You know me, and I don't know enough to be a danger if something happens. So, please, can we please keep walking?"

"And these rumors that you've heard are?" Sam asked.

He threw up his hands and sighed. "Some ancient evil is rising that was in the area near Bannagh before. The Brownie Court seems to think some order is working with that evil to bring the dead back to life. I really don't know what's going on or how it's all connected. That's all I know?"

Flann's widened eyes became glassy as he removed his hat, holding it beneath his chin. He inhaled, holding the breath as he watched Sam contemplate her next move. She sighed and asked, "That's all you know?"

He nodded. "Aye."

"Well," she said. "Then I'm done here." She spun on her heels and walked off toward the north.

The birds, squirrels, hares, and other woodland creatures raced in various directions as Sam stalked through the forest, her fists clenched and trembling as she spewed a profanity-laden tirade. The grass crunched beneath her feet. A sudden southern wind picked up speed to match her breathing; its dry heat whipped a storm of dirt and small pebbles that battered everything in its path. As Sam stormed away, Flann followed, his hand shielding his eyes from the wind's assault as he begged her to turn back. Sam did not respond. Flann panted as he chased after her, sweat matting his red curls to his face as his cheeks flushed to match the color of his hair, but he could not reach her. And then, when a golden mist with flashes of lapis, orchid, wisteria, and emerald rose from the earth, Flann lost sight of Sam.

After an hour of walking, the mist dissipated, and Sam found herself alone in a dense part of the forest with thorny underbrush that rose to her waist. Thick, black clouds hovered in the sky above the canopy. The hot air smelled of bitter earth as a wind, whose direction changed constantly, hurled a stinging rain at the landscape. Sam raised her hand to shield her eyes from the rain; she squinted as the raindrops pelted her. She found a towering fern whose fronds provided a modicum of shelter, allowing her a respite to breathe deeply. She surveyed the landscape in which only flora surrounded her. Her shoulders slumped, and she slammed her elbow against the fern, saying "Fuck!"

She rubbed her temples with the thumb and index fingers of her right hand and then leaned back against the fern. Tears fell as she clenched her jaw and punched the ground. She hissed out a cracking, whispered voice, "You fucked it up, Samantha Blake. You fucked it up, and now how many are going to die? I don't know how I'm going to get home, and no one will know. Who's going to take care of Sandy Paws? And Destiny." Her voice trailed off as her tears fell harder than the rain.

She rubbed the back of her neck and sighed. "Destiny was right. Rachel was right. Mom was right. Carmilla was right. Fuck! Even – no, he doesn't get to be right. Mom. I just want to spend more time with you. There's so much I need that I can't get in a few hours on my birthday, and there's only one way to guarantee we'd be in the same place for eternity. I just don't know if I can do it."

Her index finger traced the exposed parts of her handgun. Her muscles tensed as she hesitatingly gripped and then released it. Mascara mixed with her tears that fell down her cheeks. Her chest heaved, and her hands shook. The rain swirled around her, pelting her with bitter droplets and matting her hair to her face. She opened her glassy eyes and stared at the gun she drew from its holster. She whispered, "I don't know. I don't – wait," and then she called out, "Who's there?"

Sam blinked as several orbs of light danced through her vision as the storm ended. When they disappeared, a hunched woman shuffled through the underbrush, her eyes searching the ground so that Sam only glimpsed her curved nose and wrinkled, pointy chin from the dirt and twig matted mess of tarnished silver hair that hung from her head. Her gnarled hands tore through the underbrush, ripping grass, flowers, and bushes from the soil. Jagged, warbling shrieks trembled in the air as they left her throat between rapid, raspy breathing and guttural snarls. Sam stood, curled her fingers around her Walther's grip, and approached her.

She inhaled and said, "Are you okay?"

The old woman's neck snapped up as she studied Sam's approach with the one cloudy eye that remained in its socket. Though missing several broken, yellowed teeth, she smiled a hungry smile as she replied in a raspy alto voice, "Come closer, dear, and let me see you through the clouds."

Sam held her breath for a brief moment and inched forward, her hand still holding the grip. She flexed her stomach and stood erect. Her free hand trembled as she extended an open palm toward the old woman. She raised an eyebrow as she took in the woman's shriveled but lithe appearance. She asked, "Who are you? Are you lost?"

The old woman laughed and shook her head. "Oh no, dearie,"

she replied. "I know perfectly well where I am, but what I see says that you can't say the same."

Sam pursed her lips and glared. "What I saw," she said, "was someone frantically searching for something."

The old woman held up her bent index finger and said, "To search for something implies that it is lost not that I am lost. For I know precisely where I am." She tilted her head to the side, thrust it forward, and added, "Do you?"

"No," Sam answered quietly.

The old woman chuckled and sat cross-legged on the grass. She patted the ground beside her and looked toward Sam's eyes. "Don't mind the wet grass, dearie. Come and sit beside Mama Ty and tell her all about it." Sam hesitated, so Mama Ty added, "How about an exchange? I will tell you what I've lost, and you can tell me an equally valuable bit of why you're here. Does that sound fair?"

Sam scratched her neck and sighed. She shrugged her shoulders, sat beside the older woman, and said, "What the hell do I have to lose? Alright, Mama Ty, what did you lose?"

She cackled and shoved her skeletal right index finger up her nose so that the dirt-crusted fingernail poked through the empty eye socket. Waving the nail at Sam, she said, "Isn't it obvious? My crystal eye is gone."

"And it fell onto the forest floor?" Sam asked.

Mama Ty shook her head. "No, child," she answered, "the aderyn trawiadol swooped down and plucked it out of my socket while I ate my lunch."

Sam tilted her head to the side and asked, "So why did I just watch you scouring the ground? You were ripping up bushes."

Mama Ty slid her finger out through her nose, slipped into her mouth, and sucked it clean. Sam recoiled. Mama Ty

110

laughed and said, "The aderyn drops tail feathers near the cave where it nests, child. If I can find the orange and purple plumage, I can find the bird. Of course," she chuckled and pointed to her cloudy eye, "my one eye is so darkened that I can only see shades of gray. So, what of you, dearie?"

They sat in silence for a moment before Sam exhaled. Nodding, she recounted select portions of her investigation. She focused on her search for Mabd Donovan and meeting Niamh O'Cuinn's banshee. She mentioned her confusion over what "Liam's doom" was supposed to be. She then mentioned how she chased a leprechaun into Faerie, because he promised to take her to a prince who could give her answers. They had an argument, because she grew tired of being told to trust people who seemed to know something important but refused to tell her. She stormed off and then found herself in an unknown part of the forest during a storm. Mama Ty listened, nodding at appropriate places.

"I see," the old woman said, "Lost your temper and walked into a passion storm. Best be careful, dearie."

"Passion storm?" Sam asked.

"You're in Faerie, child. You know that," she chuckled. "The land and weather here reflect the moods of the rulers of the court. You're in the Vernal Court, and so either the Prince or Princess has been a bit moody lately – angry, terrified, sad. And so, the weather changed as their moods changed." Sam nodded. Mama Ty grinned, "Why don't we help each other? You help me find my eye, and I will take you to the Prince myself."

Sam sighed and closed her eyes. With a shrug, she said, "What have I got to lose? Let's go."

* * *

They searched the forest for an orange and purple feather dropped by the aderyn trawiadol. While Mama Ty began digging through the underbrush recklessly, Sam's help calmed her so that her movements, while still unnatural in their angles, became less frantic. The air became hot and dry; Sam felt it crack and crumble around her as she walked. Her nose wrinkled as the fetid stench of moss and rot permeated the forest. The bark on the trees turned black with jagged obsidian protrusions; Mama Ty warned Sam not to touch the bladed bark oaks unless she wanted her spilled blood to alert the predatory cnacogfiafuil whose head-sized crimson fangs could crush a mortal's skeleton in a single bite. After hours of searching, they came to a small pond filled with brackish green water where Mama Ty knelt, scooped up the feather which was as long as Sam's forearm, and said, "Ah, child. Here's the place. The Dead of Spring, fitting."

"The Dead of Spring?" Sam asked.

"Yes, child," she replied. "That place where winter is not yet done, and summer is not yet come. A place where the darkness that lurks beneath beauty and the fear that shackles new hope resides. And there," she extended her arm and pointed her long middle finger toward a small hill, "is the aderyn trawiadol's cavern."

"Well," Sam said, "in we go."

Mama Ty laughed. Sam turned to see her shaking her head as she replied, "No, dearie, this is for you to do alone. I found the feather, so you go and get my crystal eye."

Sam shot Mama Ty a glare and asked, "I suppose that the only thing in there is what I bring with me?"

112

The old woman cackled. "You're a funny one, child," she said. "Beyond darkness and a nesting bird, I do not know."

"Great," Sam said. "I suppose it's at least an interesting way to die."

Sam stepped forward into the cavern's mouth and squinted as loose dirt fell into her eyes. The rancid air reeked of moss, mushrooms, and rot. The cavern walls felt damp to the touch. Pebbles crumbled and twigs snapped as Sam slowly moved along the floor; otherwise, all was quiet. After a few moments of feeling the wall to guide herself, Sam stopped and dug through her purse. She found and activated the flashlight from the previous night. Scanning the cavern, Sam saw the thick patches of purple, orange, and green mushrooms sprouting from the black dirt of the cavern's floor. Patches of violet moss clung to the walls; when the light touched them, they emitted a faint glow, providing additional soft light. She exhaled and said, "I never gave this back to Frank. Well, buddy, maybe this can be my wish that you'll recover."

The cavern spiraled down in a counterclockwise direction. With each spiral, the moss color changed along the visible spectrum. As she traversed from the indigo layer into the blue layer, the cavern's air grew humid. Sweat beads slid down Sam's face as she fanned herself. The green layer, filled with thick patches of tall mushrooms, reeked of ammonia and feces. As the moss on the walls turned from green to yellow, the ground solidified into rock; a lone, dried violet lay on the charcoal gray floor. The reek of waste and rot intensified as Sam continued along the spiral.

Orange light washed over the broken remains of human and animal skeletons. Sam knelt to examine the bones; the indentations, shatter points, and dime-sized holes suggested a large bird had killed and eaten them; however, the gnawing suggested teeth, which puzzled Sam. Rummaging through the ripped and bloodied clothing, purses, and backpacks revealed that these were humans whose arrival here seemed unconnected, but none of them ever returned home. Sam sighed, turning her head back toward the ascending spiral. She massaged her neck before placing the remains in as respectful an arrangement as she could. Drawing both her Walther and her rapier, she continued along the path.

Sam squinted as salty sweat drops, caused by the surge of heat in the air, which smelled of smoke and sulfur, stung her eyes. Her body felt weak as she trudged the last spiral, staggering as the heat threw off her balance. The moss patches glowed red, and their brightness intensified as she descended; she switched off her flashlight. Her ears perked as she heard a sonorous warble emanating from the distance. The sound's pitch raised steadily as she reached the mouth of a larger chamber from which the crackling of fire danced around the warble's rhythm.

The aderyn trawiadol, curled into a ball like a sleeping cat, lay in a nest of bone and branch built inside a large bowl held in the outstretched arms of a moss-covered statue of a woman that stood in the center of a large dome-shaped chamber. Fires raged from seven piles of leaves, clothing, and corpses, adding their stench to that of the cavern. The aderyn appeared to be the size of an enormous crocodile and had a wide beak with a long, pointed bill like a hummingbird and radiant red and orange scales covering most of its body. The orange and purple feathers grew from its slender tail. The warble she heard seemed to be its snoring; Sam sheathed her rapier and holstered her gun.

"Well," she whispered, "now I know what happens when a parrot fucks a lizard. Now to find that eye."

Sam began searching the stony ground around the first pile of burning refuse, forcing down the bile that rose in her throat from the stench of fire and flesh. Using her rapier, she picked through knee-high pile of gray ash that continually fell as the fires atop the pile raged. Sweat matted her hair to her face and the sides of her head; her mascara washed away, and her shoulders melted into her ribs as she quickened the pace of her breathing. She moved to the second pile and then to the third. As she finished searching that pile, every hair on her body stood upright as the aderyn trawiadol screeched a warbling yawn. She stiffened and drew a deep breath as the creature raised its head and sniffed the air in its lair. Unblinking and motionless, she watched the creature's head move as its yellow eyes remained narrow slits. When its eyes closed and its head returned to its previous curled position, Sam exhaled and moved to the next pile.

As she thrust her rapier into the pile, a shrill voice called out, "Well, what have we here? A little field mouse digging through my refuse?"

Sam spun around and threatened the aderyn trawiadol whose neck snaked toward her and its yellow eyes bored into her core. She swallowed hard and said, "Could you drop the volume? I like my nails trimmed – not long enough to scratch on a chalkboard."

The aderyn squawked a cackling laugh as it replied. "The mouse has pluck. Tell me, little mouse, what can you say that will prevent me from making a snack of you?"

The creature thrust its head forward, spewing flames toward Sam, who lunged to the left, tripped, and avoided the worst of the fire; she patted the flames that danced on her sweater. "Fuck! I just bought that sweater," she said, drawing her Walther. She fired a single round into the creature's shoulder, wincing as its shrill cry of pain shook the chamber. She continued, "I'll tell you what, lizard bird, I've got enough cold iron rounds to blow you from here all the way to the lowest level of hell. I didn't come here to kill, but I have no intention of becoming a snack. The way I see it, we can avoid mutually assured destruction if you just hand over the crystal eye you plucked from Mama Ty. Then I'll be on my way."

The aderyn trawiadol growled as it searched Sam. "Courage and purpose," it purred, "the little mouse even came prepared."

Sam smiled and shrugged. "I learned more in scouts than peddling cookies. So what do you say? You give me the eye. I leave. We both live. Seems like a good deal to me."

"A deal," the creature replied, "where you leave with my shiny and your life, but I retain only my life. Why should I not fight for all I desire?"

Sam nodded. "You could. You could fight and win, but if you lose, you get nothing. Take the offer."

As she folded her arms across her chest, the aderyn trawiadol raised itself up to its full, towering height and looked down upon Sam. "I respect the mouse's boldness, but I propose a contest. I have a riddle, and if you become the first to answer it, I will grant you what you seek. If you fail, as did all those whose bones you see here, you become my next snack."

Sam breathed deeply. Riddle contests have long been known for their serious, and sometimes deadly, nature. The goal was not merely to provide an answer, but to provide the answer the riddler had in mind. She searched the bird, trying to glean any bit of information that might help her if she chose this path. Violence remained an option, and this would not be her first otherworldly kill; however, a voice spoke from the back of her head and reminded her she made the choice to help those whom no one else would. A tear formed in the corner of her closed right eye as she sighed and said, "Very well, bird, ask your riddle."

The aderyn trawiadol buffeted Sam with a burst of air from its massive draconic wings, dropping her to one knee. It screeched a cackle before saying, "Beneath the moon, I cause you to sing songs of lasting love. In the fields of valor, my sweet song arouses the raven's feeding knife. I raise others' voices but speak not on my own; although love is birthed by my honeyed words, they dull the mind and summon strife. What am I?"

A string of profanities thundered through Sam's mind as the creature finished speaking its riddle. A handful of answers flashed in her mind, and she found a logical argument for each one – no matter how serious, silly, or crass the answer was. The creature breathed flames onto the piles; Sam fanned herself as sweat stung her eyes. Her eyes darted from pile to pile, hoping to spy the crystal eye. The aderyn trawiadol cackled and clicked its beak as its eyes bored through Sam. And then it said, its long green tongue darting forth to lick its beak, "Well, little mouse, what is your answer?"

Sam breathed deeply and then spun around as the sound of rapid footfalls drew her attention. The aderyn trawiadol shifted its focus toward the cavern's mouth as a heavy brogue called out from the distance to wait. As they stared into the passage, illuminated by red moss, Flann Mac Maghnus, his face redder than the curly hair that hung limply from his head, burst into the chamber, tripped on a skull, and fell on his face.

He leapt to his feet, thrust his index finger toward the aderyn trawiadol, and said, "Halt! This mortal is summoned by the Prince of the Vernal Court. As such, she is under his protection and may not be harmed!"

The creature's screeching laughter rattled the cavern's walls as it answered, "Oh, little dove, we have entered into a sacred contest of riddles. None, even the Queen of Air and Summer, may halt such a battle." It then turned to Sam and asked, "Now, little mouse, what is your answer?"

As Sam opened her mouth, Flann shouted, "I demand to know the riddle you asked her. I will answer in her place."

"The fuck you will," Sam replied, glaring at him. "I agreed to help Mama Ty, and I'm not going back on my word. The answer is–"

Flann spun around and thrust his hand toward Sam's face. Oblivious to her narrowed eyes and flushed face, he interrupted her, saying, "Listen, little lass, I know more about these than you do. I've got a few centuries more experience, so be quiet and let me handle this."

Sam pushed him to the ground and stepped over him. She glared into the aderyn's yellow eyes, repeated the riddle, and then said, "The answer, obviously, is mead."

The aderyn trawiadol growled, narrowing its eyes at Sam. She and Flann inhaled deeply; their muscled tensed. The room shook with its screech, as it reached into its nest, grasped something shiny in its beak, and presented it to Sam. She exhaled as she saw the grape-sized quartz crystal with a rose-pink sphere in its center. The creature nodded and said, "You have answered correctly, little mouse. Take your prize and the little dove and depart."

As it curled and returned to slumber, Sam grabbed Flann by

the back of his collar and dragged him out of the cavern. As they reached the level illuminated by violet moss, she slapped him awake and asked, "What the fuck was that about?"

"Ouch," Flann replied, rubbing his neck, "You didn't have to hit so hard, lass. I was just trying to help you."

"Help me?" She scoffed. "The last thing I remember is you refusing to provide me with any information after intimating that you know something about what the fuck is going on. Now, you burst in here and try to be some big damned hero, but you seem to have forgotten your sword. And just so we're clear, I'm no damsel in need of saving by someone who treats me like I'm incapable of acting for myself."

"I did no such thing, lass," Flann countered. His fists clenched and trembled. "I have more experience dealing with the creatures here than you do, so I was offering my expertise."

"By forcing your way into our conversation and contest," Sam hissed.

Flann sighed. "Maybe I came across a bit strong," he said. "In my defense, how was I supposed to know that you knew the answer?"

"Faith," she replied. "I had no clue how to get your ass out of that jam in Cork, but I did."

"I get that," he sighed. "Don't look at me like that. I do! It's just that His Excellency and Her Majesty think something big is connected to what you're doing right now. This isn't about faith; it's about hedging your bets. That's something I know a thing or two about."

"Then why not tell me that, Flann?" She growled. "I'm fucking tired of everyone treating me like a child who needs their guidance instead of an adult who can be trusted to make a decision if you give her the information she needs. And you know how I act when I get angry."

He nodded. "Aye, my hat still has that hole you shot just above my head."

She saw he spoke the truth. With a sigh, she said, "Look, I'm sorry. This case has been a struggle since Dagh Mobh hired me to handle this case. I've had people treat me like a child. A friend got shot. And I don't have the faintest idea where Mabd Donovan is or how I'll fix this."

The leprechaun nodded. "I get that, lassie. So, how'd'you know the answer?"

She shrugged. "I didn't. If I were asking, the answer would've been pussy. I wagered the flaming lizard bird didn't think like me, so I assumed it would be some kind of alcohol. I then figured that wasn't specific enough and hoped the references to sweetness and honey were meant to help me narrow the choices down. And since mead is made from honey, I figured that was my best option."

Flann laughed. "A good guess. Now, let's get the eye back to that old crone and head to the Prince."

* * *

Mama Ty sat on a moss-covered stone near the small pond by the cave's entrance. Sam and Flann emerged from the cavern to see her slurping the skin and meat from the bones of a frog-like creature. She then snapped off its left leg and used the bones to clean her ears. When her remaining eye spotted them, her neck twisted as she watched them approach. As they reached her seat, she cackled, "So, your little friend found you, eh?"

Sam tossed her the crystal eye and said, "Yeah, and you

could've informed me that damned bird could breathe fire. It singed my new sweater."

The old woman licked the crystal eye and then placed it into the eye socket, sliding the index finger of her other hand into her nose to help position the eye. Sam shivered. Mama Ty blinked rapidly, causing the eye to glow with a pale pink light. She turned her crystal eye on Sam and said, "Ah, now I see the truth."

Sam cocked an eyebrow and searched Mama Ty's inscrutable face. She shook her head and replied, "That's great. Can you also see the way to the Vernal Court? I'm on a time crunch here."

"If you're in such a hurry," Flann interjected, "you could've just followed me."

Sam rolled her eyes and asked Mama Ty, "Anyway, can you direct me to the Vernal Court?"

Mama Ty cackled again. "Oh, dear child," she said, "are you ready to learn what the Prince has to tell you?"

"If someone will actually tell me what the fuck is going on," Sam said, "yes, I'm fucking ready."

With an amused laugh that flitted like wind chimes, Mama Ty grasped Sam's left hand and led her onward; Flann Mac Maghnus hurried after them. They departed the Death of Spring and reentered a verdant landscape filled with flowers, mushrooms, and leaf-covered trees. Butterflies flitted from flower to flower. Rabbits with pastel fur and singular horns hopped and frolicked in the fields. A grove of dryads danced naked, their barky skin rich and healthy, near a pool. Sam searched her purse, but she left her emergency makeup kit elsewhere; she cursed under her breath.

After traveling for some way, a castle appeared atop a hill

in the distance. Its general structure resembled the classic medieval castle in Hollywood movies, but the specifics of its construction strained imagination. Surrounded by a deep moat of crystalline water, the castle island proved accessible only by a bridge of giant brown mushrooms. Tall rosebushes with foot-long thorns formed the palisade. The main keep appeared to a series of trees intertwined with gigantic, leafy vines. White and yellow tulips formed the minarets atop the four corner towers. As they crossed the bridge, they saw the oak and thorn portcullis, flanked by two armored guards, before them.

Sam spun to her left as the sound of tinkling bells and a gentle white light surrounded Mama Ty, spiraling clockwise as it descended from her head. Youth, beauty, and human proportion returned to her figure. Her hair became a lustrous pale blonde. Her ears elongated and ended in gentle points. A crown of tulips and peonies sat on her head. Her eyes – one ice blue and the other absinthe green – held Sam's gaze as Mama Ty reached forward, cupped Sam's chin in her soft, pale hand, and raised it. With a gasp, Flann dropped to one knee and doffed his hat. He failed to pull Sam down to one knee but whispered, "Bow down, lassie! That's the Vernal Princess, Mora Nangle, Mother of the Tylwyth Teg."

"Wait! What?" Sam sputtered in reply.

Princess Mora giggled at the confusion carved into Sam's face. She said, "You, Samantha Hain, Daughter of Donal, should know that we give not our secret knowledge to just any."

Sam snorted. "Well," she said, "he hasn't exactly spent much time with me, and I don't exactly listen to him when he does. So, this entire thing has been a test of my resolve or worthiness or some other bullshit? Even Flann showing up to guide me?"

"No," Flann said, "the Prince did send me to get you. Everything that happened after you stormed off, I had nothing to do with until I found you again."

"Your abrupt departure concerned us," the Vernal Princess added. "As such, we decreed that a trial of worthiness was required of you. That trial, I administered alone. This leprechaun's unsummoned appearance," she glared at Flann, who shrank toward the soil, "could have endangered the assessment of your readiness to learn that which you seek."

"No one told me," Flann blurted out. "They haven't trusted me since that little indiscretion in Cork."

Sam rolled her eyes. "Well," she said, "I gather that I passed, so let's go see what this Vernal Prince has to say."

The Princess of the Vernal Court led them to the portcullis; the guards opened the gate and bowed as she strode past them. Faerie rings dotted the bailey that surrounded the giant rosebud that served as the main keep. She led them through the floral-and-earth scented halls to the throne room. Iridescent pansies growing from vine sconces illuminated the chamber; several backlit the meticulously arranged rosebuds that functioned as stained-glass windows. At the chamber's far end, atop a raised dais of oak planks, sat two blue tulip chairs. Seated in the chair on Sam's right-hand side, a short male with red hair and green eyes, wearing a crown and robe of roses and thorns and holding a tulip scepter, stood to greet the trio.

Sam's eyes widened, and she exclaimed, "You have got to be fucking shitting me!"

Chapter 6

Dagh fucking Mobh! That fucking redcap who bitched about my fee when he hired me was the fucking Prince of the Vernal Court. I knew that lying little bastard still had a few secrets he refused to share with me. What is it with this fucking case? Everyone kept information from me while saying that I don't know what's going on. I half-expected this from the damned Fae, but then Nick Scratch and my fucking father both articulated a vague warning about ancient evils. I haven't set foot in a damned cathedral since Mom passed, and, as sure as the Nine Hells, I do not remember praying for patience and understanding.

The Prince of the Vernal Court bowed toward Mora and said, "Welcome home, our darling sister." He rose and glanced at Flann and me, adding, "And to our esteemed guest, Miss Samantha Hain and my loyal, if incompetent, servant, Flann Mac Maghnus, we bid you welcome."

Flann rushed forward and prostrated himself before the dais. His top hat flopped onto the floor as his body trembled as he said, "Your Excellency, Most Noble Prince of the Vernal Court, I beg your forgiveness for my incompetence and submit to the aforementioned punishment of beard plucking."

My eyes rolled. Dagh snapped his fingers, and two armed

guards emerged from the rosebud windows, grabbed Flann, and dragged him away. I rushed forward and screamed, "Wait!" I turned toward Dagh and said, "Look, Flann is an idiot. I think you and I both agree on that. He bungles his way through things and somehow gets lucky that people bail him out. And while I'm curious to know what a beardless leprechaun looks like, show him a little bit of mercy and leave his ginger glory intact."

That damned redcap stared at me for a moment, turned to Flann, and then focused his attention on Mora. I glanced toward her and saw her nod. He waved his left hand, and the guards dropped Flann, who crashed with a thud onto the floor. He rose to his feet, keeping his eyes downcast, and shuffled to stand at my side. The Vernal Prince said, "Flann Mac Magnus. Though your incompetence has once pierced the Veil and now endangered us all, we recognize the authority of Samantha Hain. As such, we grant her request that you be shown mercy in our punishments. Your beard shall remain where it is." He turned toward me and said, "And now, Miss Hain, I believe we have much to discuss."

Dagh snapped both of his fingers, and the dais slid forward and became a vine-supported table. Two tulip chairs, one red and one yellow, emerged from the ground. The Vernal Princess sauntered forward to sit beside him. They kissed, and I realized the origin of certain European monarchical traditions. He gracefully extended his arm to the side, and she placed her hand in his. It would be sickeningly romantic if he didn't identify her as his sister. He gestured for us to sit, and we did; I chose the red tulip chair while Flann chose the yellow one. Servants brought plates loaded with plant-based dishes and chalices filled with what smelled like elderflower wine. I knew how the stories went, so I declined to partake.

I nodded toward my host and said, "That we do, Mister Dagh Mobh, Prince of the Vernal Court, who, I would assume, still hasn't told me his true name; although, he still likely has many secrets he could have told me when he hired me." I crossed my arms and cocked an eyebrow at the Prince.

He chuckled, sipped his wine, and said, "If you knew what we knew, you would understand our secrecy. However, the wheels of the war engines have turned so many revolutions toward their inevitable fate that we can no longer afford such secrecy."

As they ate and drank, I nodded and said, "Well, I would like to know where Mabd Donovan is, if you happen to know that."

He waved his hand dismissively; I cocked an eyebrow. He said, "In due time. First, we will discuss the movement that brings ancient evils into play. We are certain that you have some knowledge of this, no?"

My sigh came out as more of a growl than intended as I replied, "You could say that. I know that Liam O'Cuinn made a pact with some entity centuries ago, promising his thirteenth female heir in exchange for winning the hand of Niamh Connacht, and apparently that heir is about to be born. I can't make out the sigil the spirit used to sign the contract, so I'm guessing that's what everyone's worried about."

The Prince and Princess ate from the herbal dishes on their plates before they nodded in unison like those creepy little dolls in the Small World ride. "That is true," Dagh said, "but there is more. The spirit's name is Zozo, and it is an ancient spirit of malicious will. We are uncertain of its origins, for it was Liam O'Cuinn's summoning of that creature that first introduced it unto us and our brethren."

Zozo. I grabbed my phone from my purse. I still had a quarter battery life, but I would be able to view my photos. There it was, carved on the inside of the capstone of O'Cuinn-Gaell Portal, four letters: Z-O-Z-O. Frank didn't recognize the name when I showed him. Maybe I should have asked – no, let's not go there, Sam. Asking Donal would've opened more cans of shit and brought out his asshole "watch me be a good father a few decades too late" routine. I nodded and asked, "What do you know of this Zozo?"

"Very little," Princess Mora answered. After dabbing her napkin on her chin, she continued, "We know it is a spirit of pestilence and plague. We know it delights in deceit and bringing about the destruction of mortals. We know neither its origin nor its allegiance."

"Nor the ends it seeks," Dagh added as he massaged Mora's shoulder. "Were the situation normal, we would encourage you to ignore this spirit and focus on protecting those who unknowingly pierced the Veil."

"But shit hasn't been normal for a few years, so I'll have to deal with it. Is that the whole story?" I asked.

Dagh shook his head. "Were that the stream ended there; however, there are other rivers that merge into this one."

"And they are?" I asked with a sigh.

"In the autumn twilight," he said, "A single silver star shines as the red dragon rises in the east. They plan to wage war to subjugate all in Faerie and on Earth."

Another Faerie riddle. Great. I guessed that silver star referred to the Astrum Argentum, but the red dragon and autumn twilight stumped me. I really didn't need this right now. I just wanted to find Mabd, keep her safe, and, if I were lucky, keep Niamh safe as well. And then I wanted to spend

127

time with my mother on my birthday. I neither wanted nor needed to be dragged into whatever secret little game the damned Astrum Argentum felt like playing this time around. My shoulders slumped, and I sighed. "So, I have to stop this too?"

The Prince and Princess looked into each other's eyes for a moment before responding in unison, "Perhaps you will. Perhaps you will not. The winds have not decided their course. These adversaries may seek to hamper your investigation. Be wary."

The situation was bad enough, but this creepy tandem shit they did made it worse. I sighed, "Well, that covers the ancient forces not respecting the Treaty shit I've heard so little about so frequently," I snarked as I crossed my arms over my chest. "But, Your Redcap Majesty, you hired me to help Niamh O'Cuinn and Mabd Donovan. I can't do that without knowing where Mabd is and if she's still alive. So, could someone just tell me where she is, because time is running out for them both."

The Prince of the Vernal Court leaned forward and rested his pointy chin in his left hand. Red flecks of light sparkled in his eyes as their focus danced between Flann and me. He leaned back in his chair, drumming the fingers of his right hand on the armrest. Flann's eyes widened; his breathing quickened, and his knees shook. I rolled my eyes while I clenched my fists. The Prince smirked. Laughter bellowed through the throne room before he replied, "You have not dined as we have, Miss Hain. Is our food not appealing to you?"

I rolled my eyes at this cheap attempt at ducking the issue. I leaned forward and answered, "I'm sure this food is lovely, good Vernal Prince. However, I'm familiar with numerous faerie stories where eating and drinking along with your people leads mortals to fall into a deep, sometimes decades long, slumber. I can't afford to have my last name changed to Van Winkle, so why don't you just tell me what you know about Mabd Donovan's disappearance from Bannagh a week ago."

The rulers of the Vernal Court laughed in harmony. The Prince toasted me with his glass as he said, "That is wisdom, Miss Hain."

I shook my head and smirked. "Wisdom," I replied, "comes to us after it can no longer be any good. And since I know I can't control that whole time dilation thing that happens here, I'm taking as few chances as I can. So what do you know?"

"What we told you then," Dagh said, "was true. Oh, do not give us that look in our throne room, Miss Hain. We may possess centuries of wisdom, but we do not have perfect knowledge. Since the time of your hiring, it has come to our attention that the young mortal you seek was kidnapped and taken to the dungeon of Count Bha'esi in the Court of Autumn."

"Do you think this Bha'esi is involved with whatever is going on?" I asked.

Princess Mora nodded and replied, "We have our suspicions, yes."

"However," Prince Dagh interjected, "our spies have yet to provide confirmation of that assumption."

"And how do I get to his castle? I doubt it's as simple as clicking my heels together and wishing I were there," I asked.

Princess Mora smiled. "Simply cross through the Center of the Year, traverse the Sea of Grass, and travel through the Wailing Woods beyond the Forlorn Cavern until you reach the Swamp of Sighs. Avoid the Leshy Grove as you move toward

Winter, and you will find Count Bha'esi's castle atop a crooked hill."

I couldn't say without sarcasm that none of that sounded ominous and foreboding. I grabbed my pen and notepad from my purse and scribbled down these directions, such as they were, while thinking that I would have had an easier time with a backwards-talking white knight. I sighed and asked, "Alright, out of the many fucking questions that we don't have time for, I will ask one. How the hell do I cross the Center of the Year?"

Dagh laughed and said, "Walk backward from whence you came. Flann will show you the path. Now go. Time is blood money."

* * *

A cool autumnal breeze blew through the streets of Butcher's Bend on a sunny afternoon on the twenty-ninth day of October. Destiny Grimm sat on a wooden bench beside the pond at the north edge of the running track in Murphy Park, feeding the ducks some rye bread from her Reuben. The air smelled of pretzels, spiced hot cider, and chicken and waffles sold by the street vendors who walked through the park. Elderly and collegiate joggers passed as they made their way around the track. She checked her phone every five minutes. Her heart pounded against her chest, and she held her breath each time she did so. She had not heard from Sam since the morning Frank was shot, which was early yesterday morning. She left two voicemails and five text messages, but none of them had received either a read notification or a reply. She sighed and finished her lunch.

As she walked to the parking lot, she stopped by a food cart to buy an ice cream sandwich. The wind blew her hair first into the ice cream and then into her mouth. She smiled as the sweet, creamy vanilla ice cream reached her tongue; she failed to notice the same ice cream drip onto her blue scarf and mint blouse. She tossed the wrapper in one of the garbage cans before checking her phone again. Sam still had not replied to her. She continued checking her phone for nonexistent messages, failing to notice the footsteps approaching from behind her.

An Isotoner-gloved hand grabbed her green and gray plaid crossbody bag while another slid around her neck. Destiny inhaled sharply. As the hand slid over her mouth, she bit hard, slammed her right heel onto the assailant's toes, and elbowed his stomach. He groaned and released his hold, allowing her to spin around, hook her arm under his shoulder, and toss him onto his back. The assailant blinked and found Destiny's knee on his throat and her staring into his dull green eyes with her right hand raised and her keys between her fingers ready to strike. A squeal came from behind the black mask that covered the lower half of his trembling face, allowing Destiny to see his tanned skin and heavily gelled auburn hair. His eyes saw emptiness in hers, and he begged her not to kill him. Destiny blinked and noticed what was happening. Her hand holding the keys trembled, and her breathing quickened. She stood quickly, backed away trembling, and then raced to her car.

After spending her afternoon drumming her fingers on her desk as she repeatedly checked her phone, Destiny left the office and drove to Sal's Pastas and Pies. Located at the corner of Harry and Main, Sal Fuero's red brick and white awning restaurant had served pizza, Italian American favorites, and authentic Sicilian dishes to the residents of Butcher's

Bend since Sal and his wife Donna immigrated in 1957. The recent remodeling, with its gray wood flooring, mahogany tables and booths punctuated with red velvet cushions, red tile door frames, and two Pac-Man table arcade games, created an elegant reminder that evoked nostalgia for 1990s Pizza Hut. Soft R&B played from the jukebox beside the restroom doors, and the homey scents of herbaceous tomato and cream sauces, roasting garlic, and fresh bread filled the air. Half-past six o'clock was early, but there were a handful of individuals, couples, and families dining as Destiny entered.

The hostess, a young woman with a black bob and brown eyes named Lucy Nguyen, smiled and greeted Destiny, "Hi, Miss Grimm! Welcome to Sal's Pastas and Pies. Dining alone tonight or picking up a carryout?"

"Hi, Lucy, how's school? No, I'm going to place a carryout order for my usual, but I really need to see Donna. Is she in?"

Lucy thought for a second and shrugged. "I'll check for you," she said, "and school is school. Do you mind waiting in the bar? That way you can have a drink while waiting for your Quattro and garlic knots."

"Sure thing. A drink sounds good," Destiny replied.

Lucy led Destiny to a stool at the far end of the bar, near the window to the pizza dough tossing station. Sal, an olive-skinned man with curly charcoal hair, smiled at Destiny as he tossed the dough into the air. As the dough dangled from his fists, he called to the bartender, his son, Junior, to pay attention to his customers. Junior, who strongly resembled a younger, more physically fit version of his father, sauntered over to her and greeted Destiny with a warm smile and open arms. Within seconds, he handed her a glass filled with a rich and complex Chianti. After a few minutes, Lucy returned and escorted Destiny to a room in the back where Donna Fuera would speak to her.

Donna Fuera sat in a small, dark room next to the restaurant's business office. The scents of lavender flowers and rose petals danced in the air alongside two white taper candles whose wax dripped onto her desk. Though she was only two years younger than Sal, looked to be in her mid-forties; her thick black hair cascaded in thick curls over her shoulders. Her entrancing green eyes sparkled in the candlelight as she leaned back in her mahogany throne, rolling a Mercury dime between the fingers of her left hand while holding a lit cigarette in her right. Lucy directed Destiny to sit in the empty mahogany chair opposite Donna Fuera. Lucy poured Donna a drink from one of the crystal decanters filled with amber spirits before taking her leave.

Donna Fuera sipped her drink and searched Destiny with her eyes for several minutes before saying, "I remember a time, just over six years ago, when a young werewolf named Ludo Caresi, a good boy who never so much as pilfered gum sticks from babies, was vacationing in Berlin and lost control of himself for the first time in years. Now, he only scared a few dozen discotheque patrons; however, the Grimms sent a junior agent who broke both of his legs and his left wrist before firing a silver bullet between his eyes at point blank range. Just following orders."

Destiny shuffled in her seat and looked at the floor. She nodded and replied, "I remember that night."

Donna Fuera leaned forward and said, "That werewolf was my sister's son." She leaned back in her chair, smirked, and resumed rolling the Mercury dollar between her fingers before continuing, "And now, you have come to me in your hour of need. Tell me, little Grimm, is it a draught of love, communion with a grandparent who has died, or a cleansing of your honor? What do you desire?"

Destiny continued staring at the floor as she fidgeted with her hands. "I – I'm sorry. I didn't know – I thought – I didn't think – I just." She fell silent. Her body began shaking. Her breaths and heartbeats came rapidly. Her palms sweated. Through her trembling voice, she continued, "I came to ask if you could locate a friend who's gone missing in Ireland."

"Ireland," Donna Fuera asked, taking a drag from her cigarette and expelling its pungent odor, "If that's the case, then why not contact the polizia on the island?"

Destiny shook her head, replying, "I don't think it's something they could handle. She went after a banshee, and I haven't heard from her in over a day, which is unusual for her."

"Ah," Donna Fuera replied with a raised eyebrow. "So, your friend has willingly pierced the Veil. That can be dangerous." She laughed and added, "Now I see why you came to me."

She slid open a drawer and produced a wooden box with the phases of the moon burned into it. From inside the box, she took a palm-sized obsidian mirror, its stand, and a single candle. She lit the candle with her cigarette and then blew its smoke in front of the mirror. She chanted in Sicilian, and the smoke plumes curled and danced, creating shadowy images in the mirror. Donna Fuera raised an eyebrow and smirked as the images told their tale. When the smoke dissipated, she snuffed the candle and returned the mirror, stand, and candle to its box.

Donna Fuera sat in silence for a few moments. Destiny's breathing returned to normal, but her heart hammered against her ribcage. She leaned forward and gripped the edge of the desk, asking, "Well? What did you see?"

The old woman's hollow laughter caused Destiny to jump back with widened eyes. Donna flipped the Mercury dime and caught it in her hand. She smiled and said, "When the dragon rises beneath the great star, the twin eagles must choose their action. I will tell you no more. Now, your meal should be ready." Her laughter rang in Destiny's ears as she left the office, the restaurant with her food, and returned to Sam's apartment to feed Sandy.

Destiny learned a hard truth at Sam's apartment; when living alone with a cat, eating a meal on the couch is a futile endeavor. Even though she fed Sandy Paws before she sat to eat, the spoiled calico cat made regular attempts to eat both pizza and garlic knots. After finishing, Destiny played with Sandy for an hour and then sent her older brother a text message, "Sam may be in trouble on a case in Bannagh, Ireland. If you can spare an agent or two to find her, please do so. Thanks. Love."

* * *

Guided by Flann Mac Maghnus, Sam Hain left the palace of the Vernal Prince and Princess, beginning her journey to the Court of Autumn to rescue Mabd Donovan. While traveling through the field surrounding Flann guided Sam to a languid river that they followed as it crept through the field and split a range of rolling, clover-covered hills. The air smelled of freshly cut grass and warm rain; dandelion seeds floated through the air. A lone corvid cawed in the distance. Sam saw a circle of standing stones rising beyond a field of mushrooms at the edge of her vision.

While walking, Flann looked up at Sam and asked, "I'm not

ungrateful, but why did you stick your neck out to save my beard?"

Sam shrugged and answered, "It was the right thing to do. Sure, you could've avoided that by just telling me things earlier, but my temper has been a known problem for a few years. It wasn't entirely your fault."

He nodded and said, "Still, rules are rules. You spared my life, so I must grant you a wish. What do you desire?"

Sam stopped walking and closed her eyes. A pair of tears fell. She sighed and said, "I would like to find a sealed bag containing my weight in fresh Lucky Charms marshmallows in my apartment when I return home."

Flann cocked his head and scratched his chin. When Sam continued walking, he followed her and asked, "You could have anything. Your bills could be paid. True love could find you. Your worst enemy could be made to croak like a frog for the rest of their life. Why that?"

Sam exhaled slowly. "Well," she said, "they are magically fucking delicious, but more importantly, when I was a kid, my mom would buy a box of Lucky Charms every year the day before my birthday and then pick out all the marshmallows to serve me for breakfast on my birthday. I just want that moment one more time."

When they reached the mushrooms, Sam learned it was a circle of tall, brown mushrooms wide enough to surround and tower over Stonehenge. The eight standing stones formed a ring inside the mushroom circle. The air fell silent and still. Sam smelled nothing. The sky above was black, like the color behind closed eyes. She touched one of the stones that towered over her and then recoiled as her hand felt a powerful dry heat. She touched the next one, and while still warm, its heat was less painful to the touch.

"Stop touching things," Flann yelled. "Give it a rest, and we'll touch the one we need."

"What is this place?" Sam asked as she turned in place, surveying the area.

"The Center of the Year, of course," Flann replied. "Why are you looking at me like – oh, you've never been here before? The Center of the Year is sort of like what your wizards would call a portal, but what your scientists would call an escalator? No, an elevator. No, a revolving door. It's a thing that lets you go between different areas that are connected but separated. Look, I don't do all this theory stuff. Anyway, while in the circle, we are in a nowhere place between the Courts. What you have to do is touch certain stones and then leave the circle to travel to that Court."

"How do you know which stones to touch?" Sam asked.

"You feel them," he replied. "Warm paired with wetness is the Vernal Court. Hot paired with dryness is the Summer Court. Cool paired with dryness is the Autumnal Court. And Cold paired with wetness is the Winter Court. What did the two you touched feel like?"

Sam said, "They were hot and pretty dry, so I guess they were the Summer Court stones."

"Aye, they were," Flann said. He walked over to the first stone she touched, sighed, and said, "Okay, so if this is Summer Court, then moving to Autumn means going with the sun. So that's a step to the right." He moved to the larger of the two stones immediately to that stone's right, held his hand up to the stone without touching it, and then added, "That's it. Get ready."

Flann touched the stone and waited. A cool wind blew from

the northwest. He turned to Sam and nodded. He then walked between the two Autumnal Court stones and left the circle, vanishing from Sam's field of vision. She followed.

They emerged in a sea of blue-green crystalline grass with a cool north wind blowing behind them. The wind carried the scents of spiced apples and warm pretzels as it moved. The purple, orange, and red sky resembled a sunset. A range of mountain-sized trees adorned with red, orange, and yellow leaves stood behind them. A single Victorian lamppost, unlit, stood mournfully at the forest's edge. A purple and red hawk flew overhead as a robin egg blue rabbit with a golden horn hopped across their path. Sam snickered and said, "Well, he doesn't have a pocket watch, so I guess I won't chase him into Wonderland."

"There is no Wonderland," Flann said as he started walking.

"And let me guess," Sam asked, "that lamppost back there doesn't mean we're in Narnia?"

Flann glowered as he continued walking. After a few minutes, he said, "If you see a talking lion here, it'll likely eat your face off instead of saving you from a winter hag."

Their journey continued. After some time, they reached a forest of hill-sized oak and mahogany trees with vivid autumnal plumage. The air felt dry and heavy. It was quiet. As Flann led Sam through the trees, they passed by several cats, bats, weasels, owls, hawks, and a small creature whose veiny, spherical body held only its toothy maw and a giant eye with ten eyestalks protruding from its purple and green flesh. All sat with their eyes downcast. They continued on, and she saw a one-eyed raven with a blue and green plaid bowtie perched on a branch, looking to the north. She walked over and nuzzled him. He responded by rubbing his head against her and allowing her to see a tear fall from his eye.

Flann grabbed her and dragged her away, asking, "What are you doing that for? Do you know where we are?"

"No," she replied, "but I recognize that bird. It's Jake, Mister Fingal's familiar. When my father convinced me to learn a few basic rituals, Jake would keep me company while I was sitting around in the library reading those boring theory books. I haven't seen him since Mister Fingal died."

Flann nodded. "That's why he's here. This is the Grove of Lost Familiars. It's where familiar spirits go after their witch or wizard dies. They come here and wait for another to summon them. We need to keep moving."

The density of the familiar spirits thinned steadily as they continued through the forest. The sky remained in a state of constant sunset. The wind blew harder, grew colder, and carried with it the humid heaviness of rot and sorrow. Flann's top hat and his eyes alone remained visible above the piles of brown, red, and orange leaves that covered the ground and crunched beneath their feet; the trees steadily contorted into gnarled, twisted, gray husks of their former glory. As they walked, the sounds of crying tugged at Sam's left ear. The more they walked, the more she felt like she recognized that specific sorrow.

The trees thinned as they continued their journey, and a small hill rose to their left. The crying grew louder and more plaintive; its sorrow weighed on Sam's heart. The stench from the rot and decay grew more pungent. The leaf-covered ground was softer underfoot, and the humid air intensified the cold wind's bite. Thorny brambles covered the hill to their left, and a cavern, like a rough and uneven maw, opened in the side facing them. The crying clearly emanated from within the cave. It sounded like a woman. Sam closed her eyes as she walked, focusing on the familiar sound of the crying. As her steps drifted toward the cave, Flann failed to notice that she was no longer behind him.

"Steady now," he said, "this is the Forlorn Cavern. I've heard the monster within calls to those without hope, drawing them to it so it can devour them." He continued walking for a few minutes before adding, "You're being quiet for once. No mouthy little retort?"

He turned to see her reaction. His eyes widened, and his jaw dropped when he saw that Sam was no longer behind him. His heart raced as he jumped to get a better view over the piles of fallen leaves. When he spotted her, he raced toward her, screaming her name and begging her to stop. Sam walked toward the cavern, oblivious to his words. He raced toward her and reached her as the cavern's mouth closed behind her. He clenched his fists, kicked the hill, and said, "Fuck! My beard may be all that's left of me if the Prince hears about this."

Sam turned to watch Flann rush toward her as the cavern's mouth closed around her. As she fished the flashlight from her purse, she said, "Well, that's fucking normal."

She banged on the newly formed wall. The impact's heavy thud resembled the sound of punching packed sand. It was dry and gritty. Sorrow and fear weighed heavily on the cold, dry air. Sam licked her lips, tasting an acidic tang. The crying grew louder. Sam spun around and listened as the crier shrieked and sobbed; the sound echoed throughout the cave. She turned at the waist, her eyes darting to each circle formed by the flashlight. Her heart pounded in her chest. Her hands grew cold, and her jaw trembled. As the sound bounced off the walls, it acquired a brittle, almost mocking tone. As the hand

140

holding the flashlight shook, Sam whispered, "Hell. Mom, are you here?"

Her footsteps sounded those of someone walking along on a dry beach. The crying intensified as she moved through the cavernous passage, each echo adding a distorted voicing of the original until a mocking, sardonic chorus cackled its morose laughter into her ears. Sweat beaded on her forehead. Her shallow breaths rasped from her throat. Her eyes fluttered like the wings of a moth as it kisses the flame. As the laughter, her breathing, and her heart rate joined for their atonal crescendo, all fell silent, and the flashlight died.

The crying returned, but this time, only a single vocal strain emerged and did not echo throughout the cavern. Her fingertips touching the dry, sandy wall, Sam raced the source of the sound. The crying's volume increased and decreased in waves. It gripped Sam and pulled her onward. She released the wall from her touch. Her heart strained to pump fast enough, and her lungs struggled to produce enough air to support her frantic pace. Sam's eyes adjusted, and she found herself able to smell the gritty dirt of the walls and to see minute changes in tone as the passages snaked. After rushing through what felt like a quarter of a mile, her eyes regained the ability to see shape, color, and detail amidst the darkness. And then Sam saw the source of the crying.

A weeping woman knelt on the cavern's floor, cradling the head of another woman in her lap. Her back was to Sam. Her soaked, graying brown hair twisted around her neck like a noose. Her skin had the same greenish discoloration of old bronze. Wrinkles pulled at her skin, most prominently on her hands and bare feet. Her waterlogged clothing, a burgundy cardigan and black jeans, clung to her skin. Sam sucked in air

141

before cautiously approaching the woman. Sam covered her mouth with her hand; her eyes shot wide as she saw the face of the woman being cradled. Her face. As she searched her reflection, she saw it was her; blood covered her neck and the shattered remains of her lower jaw.

Sam's stomach plummeted. Her jaw trembled. Her words hung low in the air as she said, "Mom?"

The weeping woman turned, and Sam recoiled at the glassy, colorless eyes that should have had the rich coloration of tiger's eye stones. The woman searched the area, appearing to be unable to either see or focus her sight, as she replied, "Who – who's there?"

Sam found her words clung to her throat as she forced the sounds into the air. "Mom, it's me. Samantha."

The woman shook her head as she stroked the hair of the Sam in her lap. She said, "You sound like her, but my Samantha is here. I can't believe she did this. Why?"

Sam bit her lip. Her eyes glassed over. She whispered, "I just – she just wanted to spend more time with you. This was the only way. She missed you." She drew a quick breath and then asked in her normal voice, "What happened?"

The woman hugged her Sam tightly and rocked back and forth. She sang, "Great darling of the world's people, they spilt your blood yesterday, and they put your head on an oaken stake near where your body lay."

She continued singing. Sam knew the song, "*Griogal Cridhe*," as the lullaby her mother always sang to her. Sam knelt and wrapped her arms around her mother. Sam felt the wetness and weight of the body. Tears fell. Sam laid her head on her mother's shoulder and joined her in singing the lullaby to its conclusion. The woman's empty eyes looked toward Sam. Sam closed her own eyes and said, "I'm so sorry. What happened?"

The woman slumped forward, stroking her Sam's head gently. She sighed. Her voice trembled as she answered, "She tried to fight a demon to protect me. She was so good at that, but this one, he got inside her head. And then, and then she – it had to be him, because she would never do this – she turned her gun on herself."

Sam tilted her head as she rasped her next question, "To protect you? When did this happen?"

"A few minutes ago," she said. "If you had been here, maybe you could have helped her." Her voice trailed off as she said, "I couldn't. I'm so sorry, Samantha. I failed you again."

"It's not your fault, Mom," Sam whispered as she tightened her hug. "It hurt more to lose you than to learn why. One day a year isn't enough. I just want to spend more time with you."

The woman cupped Sam's cheek in her right hand and smiled through tears as she said, "That sounds like something my Samantha would say. Would you do a grieving mother a big favor?"

Sam wept and nodded. "Of course, mom. What do you need?"

The woman kissed Sam's cheek and said, "My Samantha has a talent for fixing the problems of others. No one can fix this. But the demon retreated into the cave. I heard its footsteps and its laughter. Would you – could you – do what she couldn't do and kill it?"

Sam nodded. "Of course, Mom. Anything for you."

Sam stood, drew her rapier, and unholstered her gun. She took a deep breath and walked forward into the darkness that seemed to spiral around her. After a few steps, all fell silent. She turned back and saw the darkness swallow her mother and her mother's Sam. She bowed her head, allowing a tear to fall to the ground. She steeled herself and nodded. The cave sloped down and grew colder and more damp as Sam continued along the dark path. The wall felt wet and sticky; the air smelled of iron. The only sounds echoing through the cave were Sam's footsteps, her breathing, and her heart beating. The passage leveled, and then her sight returned.

Hunched in the corner, ripping bloody flesh from the bones of its prey, was the demon who caused the death of the other Sam Hain. Even hunched on its furry legs, it stood taller than Sam. Four obsidian horns sprouted from its goat-like head: two extended vertically, and one spiraled from each side. Four wings, two bat-like and two birdlike, grew from its back. Its forearms, which ended in six-finger claws, were almost twice the length of its upper arms. Its legs, which began with thighs covered in the same auburn fur that covered its body, ended in large talons. Flies buzzed in the surrounding air. Sam swallowed hard as she saw blood covering the hand with which she touched the wall.

Attempting to prevent herself from vomiting, Sam coughed. The demon turned its head, and Sam saw the pale green fire that burned in its eyes and the blood dripping from its mouth. It dropped the limb it was eating, baring its rotting yellow fangs and growling. It charged her, and Sam fired. It snarled as the blessed cold iron bullet pierced its shoulder. Blood gushed from the wound. It leapt with claws extended. Sam thrust her rapier through its chest. It gargled, its tongue extended, as it slid down the blade toward her. When it reached the crossguard, it smirked. Its form shifted, and Sam stared at her own face, hollow and lifeless, with a brittle, mocking grin. It disappeared.

Sam blinked. Shallow, rapid breaths escaped her lungs. She sat on the cavern's floor. Darkness and solitude were her only companions. A cool wind brushed against her back. She turned and saw the cavern's mouth had once again opened, and Flann Mac Maghnus stared from the outside, his head tilted to the side in confusion. Sam stood, sheathed her rapier, and holstered her handgun. She sighed and walked past the leprechaun who spun around and followed after her, calling out, "Hey! What happened in there? You okay?"

Sam replied flatly, "I don't want to talk about it. Let's just keep going."

Chapter 7

What the fuck just happened? I don't even know where to begin processing that. I mean, the last thing I remember was seeing Jake, Mister Fingal's old familiar, sitting alone in a tree. The next thing I knew, I was following the sound of crying into a cave that swallowed me and, I guess, spit me back out. It was Mom's crying. I heard it so often right before her accident – before she drowned – that I'll never forget the sound. And her body looked just like it did when I went to the police station to identify her. I'd just finished taking the final for English Lit 2710. Shakespearean Tragedies. Fitting. But when we talked on my birthday last year, she looked more like her old self – like she was healing. But why was I there with what was clearly a gunshot wound to the jaw?

"Hey! Hold up, lassie!" Flann's voice shook me back to the weird reality of Faerie. He stretched his arms forward, motioning for me to stop walking.

"What, Flann?" I asked. "I figured we needed to hurry along."

"We do," he replied, "but no one's ever come out of the Forlorn Cavern before. When the mouth opened back up, you were just sitting there alone. What happened?"

"What do you mean?" I replied. "I heard crying; specifically, I heard my mom crying like she did most nights during the month leading up to her death. I followed the sound into the cave and found her crying over my dead body."

Flann stroked his ginger beard thoughtfully and then shook his head. "That makes little sense," he said. "There's supposed to be a monster in that cave that devours the hope of all who go in. No one has ever come back. Did you see anything besides that?"

I shrugged and sighed. "I thought I did, but when I stabbed it with my rapier, it transformed into me. Then everything vanished, and the mouth opened up again. I don't know."

Flann looked back in the direction we were heading. I think it was east, but given that the sky has remained at the same level of near-twilight sunset that I saw when we entered the Court of Autumn, I have no clue what direction we're going or how long we've been traveling. He turned back to me and said, "Well, don't run off in the Swamp of Sighs. Between the ancient Leshy that guards its grove and the deep-water pockets, you may not have that luck that's gotten you out of the last few scrapes here."

"So noted," I replied and followed as he trod toward the Crooked Hill and Count Bha'esi's castle.

Flann continued pressing me for details about what happened in the cave, and I had to forcefully decline answering to get him to lay off. He really did not understand how little I wanted to discuss what happened in there with anyone except for my mom. It's been hard not having her with me, going from being able to call her daily – sometimes two or three times a day – to only getting a few hours with her each year on my birthday. And even getting that approved wasn't free. I still owed Nick for that one. Worse than a car note, but easier to repay than student loans. As he always says in that wannabe

Downton Abbey accent of his, "I'm evil, but I'm not cruel." I'm sure some in Hell would argue the point, but he's not too terrible if you know how to work within his system.

I just want to spend more time with my mom, but that's not possible, given the specifics of the situation. The ancient magical texts were wrong; the shades of those who died as she did cannot be summoned, cannot cross the Veil of their own accord, and cannot communicate via spirit boards or other such means. Dante understood the matter; once judgment has been passed, the only way to communicate with souls who died like mom is to either visit them or join them. In the Seventh Circle of Hell. Otherwise, you have to hope that the Eternal Powers haven't passed judgment on them, allowing them to remain on our world for a time, but even that comes with risks, as their unsettled emotions can lead to copycats among the living and can draw Veil Watcher attention.

She's missed so much since she's been gone. I've had ups and downs that I wanted to share with her. Hell, I almost got married after it became legal, and I really wanted her to walk me down the aisle and not my jackass father. But Celeste broke off our engagement after accusing me of cheating on her with a dryad I helped escape the Moustoxydes after she unleashed her powers during a protest in the Kesariani Forest. I came clean with her about what I do for a living, but she didn't believe me. What a shock. Destiny, 'Milla, Kina, Laura, and Jose Cuervo were there for me during that time. I also quit smoking last year and only gained ten pounds. I don't have the occult knowledge to travel to Hell, so there's only one way I know that will let me spend more time with Mom. I'd have to die like she did. I'd have to take my own life.

As I admitted that to myself, my eyes flooded with tears.

My knees shook, and I sank to the ground. Flann jolted to attention, spun around, and, with wide eyes, asked, "What did I say? I didn't mean to make you cry?"

I shook my head and whispered, "No. I made me cry. I told myself the truth."

He nodded and replied, "That'll do it. I always say, 'If you're going to lie to anyone well, best lie to yourself well.' Makes things easier."

I smiled weakly and nodded, brushing my hair behind my left ear. "Yeah, it did for almost a decade. Just give me a minute, okay?"

He nodded, sat on the ground, and smoked his pipe while I cried. I still wasn't sure why my mom couldn't see the version of me she held in her arms, but I knew why that version of me looked like its jaw had been shot off. I've kept a bullet in my purse with my initials engraved on the casing for almost two months now. Business has been sporadic, and I know I haven't helped matters by doing as much pro bono work as I have, but I just couldn't let those women go through that alone. Mom always taught me to value helping others above profit. That hasn't been quite so easy the last few years, but Destiny and I made it work. It's just that I miss my mom, and it wasn't fair to lose all that time with her.

I wiped my eyes, stood, and said, "Alright, let's go."

Flann leapt up, nodded, and led the way forward. I started seeing my breath as we continued through the forest, which was now filled with leafless trees. The air grew still and silent. No bird flew in the sky; no animals scurried across the barren, rocky ground. After we finally left the forest, my eyes blinked, and my stomach churned worse than it did that night I stepped onto the Emberheath Bog. My first thought was, "That's a supernatural stench," and then I slapped my wrist for sounding like my fucking father. My feet sloshed through the soggy ground as we moved from forest to swamp. Gas bubbles about the size of cat heads rose to the surface and popped, spewing their rancid stench that hung in the still air with a sound that mimicked a despondent sigh. Gnarled, leafless trees rose from the sludge as if they were hands grasping for one last display of hope and kindness that failed to arrive before darkness pulled someone under.

Flann's movements became erratic as we moved through the swamp. At first, I thought he was just searching for dry, solid ground, but then I noticed it wasn't just leaping from side to side while finding ground or avoiding the large snapping tortoises. Then I noticed his hands trembled faster than his eyes darted. He crouched low, almost crawling, as he led me along a series of dried logs that formed a makeshift bridge across a series of water pockets. I've seen him like that before, but he wasn't – we weren't – being chased by anyone. I looked behind us to confirm, and I was right.

"Expecting the Duilearga?" I asked, hopping from the log onto a patch of mossy ground.

He stiffened, spun around, and asked, "No. Why do you ask?"

I held my hands up and tried to soothe him with my reply, "It's okay. I haven't seen you this jumpy since Michael Cormack was chasing you through Cork. What gives?"

"What gives what? I'm not giving anything. Why would you ask that?" He sputtered while slipping his hands behind his back.

Now I was curious. His behavior mirrored mine when, as a kid, I snuck into my father's library and found his secret ritual chamber. I thought his Three Kings incense was just funny smelling Nerds candy, and I ate a handful of it, got dizzy, and then knocked over a pedestal with his personal grimoire on it. I don't remember much else, but when he found me, he claimed I was halfway through reciting a Goetic invocation. I thought the words looked funny. It took him an hour of yelling and threatening to lock me in my room for a month to get me to tell him exactly what I did.

I raised a disbelieving eyebrow – my left eyebrow – and asked, "Flann, what's got you freaked? I need to know what threats we're going to face, since no one in this entire damned plane of existence seems to enjoy being open and honest about who they are and about what's going on. You are trembling, and you are avoiding answering my questions. What's going on?"

The sky darkened even more than it already was, and a gust of wind hurled me forward a few steps before I regained my balance. My gaze shot skyward to see the bronze underbelly of a massive red-scaled dragon flying overhead. Fuck, those things are easily the size of 747s. Gorgeous and terrifying. As my jaw hung open in awe of this majestic creature, I heard Flann say, "That's why I'm skittish. Bye!"

I looked toward Flann to see him vanish, leaving me alone in this fucking swamp. I growled, kicked the ground, muttered a "fuck this shit," and walked on toward Count Bha'esi's castle atop the crooked hill – wherever that was.

* * *

"*Amhrán na bhFiann*" sounded from the phone on the dining table, causing George Crowley to rise from his oversized brown armchair with an orange, gold, and green floral upholstery; gently set his book on the right armrest; and walk to the mahogany table while muttering a string of curses about age, old joints, and forgetfulness. As the choir sang, "Soldiers are we whose lives are pledged to Ireland," George reached the table and saw the name Werther Grimm on the Caller ID. He pursed his lips and furrowed his brow. George answered with, "*Cén chaoi a bhfuil tú?*"

A deep bass voice with a German accent replied, "Why so formal, George? I thought we were friends."

George sat at his table and said, "It's been a while since you called me, Werther. I assumed you needed something from our library."

Werther Grimm chuckled into his phone. "Were it that simple, old friend. I am calling at the request of my youngest daughter, Destiny."

As he paused, George interjected, "Has she returned to the fold then?"

Werther sighed and said, "It saddens me to say that she has not. She continues to work for Donal Hain's daughter, Samantha."

"Samantha? Well, this will be interesting. I happened to see the young lass the other night while hunting for Order of the Dragon scum."

"So, you are saying she is safe?" Werther asked.

George shrugged. "I assume she is," he replied. "That was the night before last when I accidentally shot the young man she was with while he danced in a faerie ring and blocked my shot. Dragon bastard walked away with her while the Garda questioned me. Has anything happened?"

Werther replied, "My daughter has not heard from her friend

in over twenty-four hours. She is worried. If the Order of the Dragon has operations in Bannagh, perhaps her fear is justified."

George sighed. "They might be. We're dispatching an agent on All Hallows' to handle the banshee situation, which I assume Miss Hain is there to handle as well."

"It is," Werther confirmed. "My daughter provided no other details than that Samantha believes a Duilearga agent is already investigating."

George shook his head and ran his fingers through what remained of his hair. "Not yet, Werther. Given the clarity of the video recording, no investigation is necessary. Michael Cormack will be dispatched to handle the situation per our usual protocols. It should be a simple operation. Is that all you needed?"

"I am afraid I have one small favor to ask, old friend," Werther said. "Would you be able to watch out for Samantha while she is there? I know she and Mister Cormack have a history, and that alongside the appearance of a Dragon could become volatile."

"Aye, I can do that for you, Werther." George said. "She seemed like a nice girl from our brief interaction. I could try to keep Michael from engaging with her, but I'll be honest, I'm more worried about the Dragon's presence."

"You have a name for their agent?" Werther asked.

"Seamus Creevy," George replied. "He's a Professor of History at Trinity. Don't know his rank in the Order. Seems that he knows a family friend of Miss Hain's. Bannagh's a sleepy little village, so I wonder why he's here."

Werther stroked his chin. "Destiny made no mention of his presence, which leads me to assume she is unaware of it," he answered. "Given the recent uproar over the banshee sighting, one would surmise that to be the reason; however, I can see no obvious alignment between their known interests and a, forgive me, small town's banshee."

"No offense taken." George said. "And you're right about that. I don't know what the fuck's going on, but with Samhain right around the corner, this bloody year we may have a real blood moon on our hands."

"And I think we would all prefer if that did not transpire," Werther replied. "If you discover any information that I should pass along to Destiny, please contact me. And come to Hanau next month. It has been far too long since we have dined together."

"If I survive this, I just may," he replied before ending the call.

He scratched his head and sighed. He set the phone on the table again, walked into his kitchen, and filled the kettle with water. He lit the gas burner and set the kettle atop its blue flame. As he walked to the five glass jars where he kept his teas, he paused and looked up at a faded wedding photograph above the door; a soft, sad smile crossed his face as he stared at the happy memory. His late wife radiated resplendent joy and happiness in her gown, and he, in his tailcoat, held back happy tears as he held her hand. As he spooned the rose petal black tea into the green ceramic tea pot decorated with hand-painted pink and white tulips, he recalled handing her a bouquet of tulips when he proposed; she chose a single pink tulip instead of a wedding bouquet. His eyes glassed over as he recalled those days. He was still at university, studying philology and anthropology – two subjects that served him well as a Duilearga archivist. He grabbed matching cups and

154

then put one back on the shelf as he sat at the table, poured a cup of tea, and swirled a teaspoon of honey into the steaming liquid as he inhaled the strong, floral aroma. He sighed. As he returned to his reading chair, he sipped his tea and said, "Just like you always made it, Margaret. I hope you're enjoying heaven. These last few years have brought hell onto earth."

* * *

Sam continued her way through the rancid swamp beneath the twilight sky of the Court of Autumn, searching for anything that might resemble the two markers the Vernal Prince mentioned: the Leshy Grove and the Crooked Hill. Her pace slowed as she trudged, guideless, through the grayish brown muck. Her eyes watered as she breathed through her mouth, trying to avoid smelling the fetid odors emerging from the exploding gas pockets around her. Bile rose in her throat. She dropped to her knees and vomited. She wiped her mouth on a handkerchief she kept in her purse, placed it in a side pocket, and sat on the least hollow stump she could find. She sighed and wiped the sweat from her forehead.

As her foundation coated her sweater's sleeve, she shook her head and laughed. She had not dressed for an adventurous trek through multiple Faerie courts. The possibility of traveling to Faerie had not even entered her mind. Her initial fear was being unable to think of a way to fix the issue that protected Mabd, the banshee, and the ghost hunters from being killed by the Duilearga. Returning home alive had ascended to its place. Peering into the twilight, Sam shrugged her shoulders and unholstered her Walther. As she continued walking in what she hoped was the right direction, she whispered, "Mabd goes home, or I don't. That's the deal now. Let's do this, Samantha."

She continued her journey through the desolate, windless landscape of the Swamp of Sighs. Her feet sloshed through the muddy soil, and the gas pockets sighed; otherwise, no sounds reached Sam's ears. The air was heavy; the humidity of ancient sorrow blended the general stench wafting from the swamp, forming a fetid and foul brew through which Sam trudged. As the cold air shot needles into her body, Sam watched her breath float over cracked, brittle ground. The gnarled, leafless trees developed twisted, bulging trunk protrusions. No animals wandered, and no plants, save for the gnarled trees whose bark became progressively whiter, grew in this wasteland at the edge of the swamp.

After what felt like hours of walking, Sam heard the beating of a single pair of wings behind her. She spun around, gun ready, but she saw nothing. She turned back and continued walking. Her feet sloshed as she trudged through a patch of muddy ground. As patches of murky water rose to the surface, Sam tested her steps before committing to a path. The reek of decay returned, and several brittle, skeletal arms rose and sank in the waters as the gas pockets belched their foul odors into the air. Sam coughed as she tasted the stench when she inhaled. She plodded through the renewed swamp for a time before, at the edge of her vision, Sam saw a thick patch of the lifeless trees, and a guttural, droning warble rattled the air.

Inhaling, Sam crept toward the patch of trees, her eyes searching for both the source of the warble and the crooked hill. Corpse flowers rose from the drier patches of soil; a single plant bloomed, filling the air with a noxious odor resembling rotting meat. Sam blinked rapidly and held her breath. Her eyes watered from the stench. She coughed. The sonorous warble rose in pitch. The flapping of the wings returned. Sam spun around toward the sound of the wings; again, she saw nothing. Tensing her muscles, she exhaled and crept forward. Something snapped beneath her feet. Sam's gaze darted toward the soil; the broken remains of a brittle femur, surrounded by rotten and tattered clothing, lay at her feet. The warble grew louder, faster, and inquisitive; whatever creature uttered that cry was searching for something. Sam's heart rate and breathing accelerated.

When Sam reached the edge of the tree patch, the strange protrusions she noticed on other trees became faces contorted in pain and grief. Brittle bones and leathered body parts floated to the surface as gas bubbles exploded, filling the cold, heavy air with their foul stench. Sam took a step forward, her breathing rapid and shallow. The wings fluttered behind her. The thunderous creak of something twisting sounded before her. She saw something rustling amidst the thick curve of white, leafless, gnarled trees. She crouched and inhaled sharply. After a few moments, she crept forward a few more steps. Her heart pushed its way into her throat as a thunderous pounding shook the ground as something from within the clump of trees moved. Sam tensed, exhaled, and crept a few more steps around the edge, hoping to get a better view of what caused the thunderous pounding and the deep, sonorous warble.

Peering through the gnarled, leafless, bone-white trees, Sam saw a towering, bipedal creature made of rotting wood with the skull of a sixteen-point deer poking through the bark-hood of its body. Pale green fires blazed from its searching eyes. Human skulls hung from the vine belt around its waist. Its gnarled, gangling arms ended in oversized, branch-claws that dusted the tips of the brown grass as it stalked about the open space bounded by the lifeless trees. A twig snapped beneath her boot; She winced and cursed silently as the creature turned its glowing eyes in her direction. She gasped as it stalked toward her, its thunderous footsteps flattening the grass beneath its trunk-sized feet. A wooden altar, adorned with animal skulls and horns, stood behind the creature; its tattered altar cloth hung limp at its sides.

Sam moved to run, but the force of the creature's thunderous strides knocked her on her behind. Her heart raced. She crawled backward a few paces; her eyes wide and unblinking. The creature's roar sounded like tree trunks breaking in a hurricane. Her rapid, shallow breaths flew through her open mouth. She scrambled to her feet and bolted to her left. The creature pushed trees to the side, snapping several trunks as it bounded after her. She raced through the swamp; the brown grass crunched beneath her feet. Her eyes darted from side to side, scanning the barren landscape for anywhere she could hide. The strange beating of wings returned from behind her; Sam darted to the left, cursing as she looked over her shoulder and saw that the creature had exited the grove and gained on her.

Brackish water splashed up to Sam's knees as she raced through a watery patch of swamp. She grimaced; her left calf tensed, and a sharp pain shot through her leg. She cursed in pain. The creature roared. Its thunderous footsteps threw off Sam's balance. With a squeak and a splash, she fell into a shallow pool of brackish water. She spied a half-submerged log that appeared partially hollow. She held her breath and crawled inside. She felt and saw insects crawling on and around her. She shivered. The cold water soaked her clothing.

She tensed her muscles and held her breath as the creature's roar and footsteps grew louder.

The ground shook. Sam heard the creature's feet splash through the water. From her vantage point, Sam saw one of its legs, and its size dwarfed her waist. Her hands arms shook. Her thoughts raced faster than her heartbeats. The creature uttered a low, guttural growl as Sam watched its shadow swing back and forth. Its arboreal body creaked as it turned from side to side, searching. She swallowed, feeling her stomach sink as she waited for the creature's next move. Sam held her breath for a count of twenty before gently exhaling. She heard the creature growl again; its body creaked as it turned. Sam tensed every muscle in her body, hoping to stop any movement, no matter how small, that could make a sound. After another twenty count, Sam heard the thunderous footsteps again, this time becoming more distant. She sighed.

After silence returned to the swamp, Sam crawled from her hiding spot. Mud caked the front of her clothing. Her wet, muddy hair hung limp against her face and neck. She sat atop the log where she hid, removed each of her boots, and drained the water from them. She cleaned her rapier and checked her handgun, which remained dry. Running her fingers through her muck-drenched hair, Sam grumbled, "Fuck. No guide. No clean clothes. No idea. At least I have an overabundance of stubbornness." She flicked her hand, flinging mud forward as she stood. "Well, onward and…forward, I guess."

* * *

Nine tarot cards lay upturned on a mahogany-framed, gray marble desk in Donal Hain's study. The angry, beady eyes

159

of the ninth card, The Devil, stared at the Arch Magus. He frowned. His right hand floated over the next card in his worn deck before he slid the card onto the table and turned it over. His index finger traced the card's image: a regal woman in a white gown with a cloak of clouds seated atop a throne high in the sky with an unsheathed sword in her right hand. He leaned back in his gray leather and mahogany armchair and sipped his peaty, single-malt Scotch. He held his chin in his thumb and index finger as he scanned the drawn cards again. The Queen of Swords. Whenever he drew this card over the past thirty years, it referenced his daughter: quick-witted, fiercely individualistic, and principled but spiteful and unforgiving. And here, the queen stared into the distance in the Outcome position of his reading.

It appeared the outcome of his endeavor hinged on Samantha's choices. Paired with the Devil's wildness and chaos as his fears, he knew that she would prove problematic. After all, wildness and chaos were the motivating reasons behind both this alliance and this ritual. Born in Bangor, he grew up during the height of fighting in The Troubles. His father, a member of the Royal Ulster Constabulary, died in a pipe bomb explosion, and he joined the Ulster Volunteer Force to protect his mother and younger siblings. He left Ireland at seventeen and studied at King's College, Cambridge where, in his final year, he learned of and received his first initiation into the mysteries of the Hermetic Order of the Astrum Argentum. Five years later, he met and married Amelia Burnside, who was studying abroad for her senior year. She convinced him to move to Greenville, South Carolina, and, less than a year later, she gave birth to their only child, Samantha Blake. As he ascended through the ranks in both his profession, law, and in the Order, his recurring and extended absences led to the couple's divorce.

"Samantha, Samantha, Samantha," he mused, "why do you have to be so stubborn and so blind? Can't you see we both want a world at peace? No one wants the fear of riots, bigotry, incompetent national leadership, wars fought over money and childish displays of honor, and pandemics spread due to arrogant fools refusing to follow expert advice. For centuries, we have waited in the shadows, patiently hoping that the Vulgar would come to us and allow enlightenment to guide them. What fools we were. It is both our right and our responsibility to lead, to stand at the helm and guide these children into becoming proper, enlightened adults. With the world brought to heel, you won't have to worry about your little private investigations, and you can get a real job."

He checked his cell phone notifications. His daughter had yet to respond. He called her once more; the voicemail answered, "You have reached Sam Hain, Private Investigator. At the sound of the tone, please leave a message, and I'll get back to you soon. Thank you."

He sighed. Shaking his head, he replied, "Samantha, it's your father. Stop ignoring my messages. If you do not call me by noon on the twenty-ninth of October, I will not be able to protect you. I will explain in person." He ended the call, sank into his chair, and said, "This will either be the greatest or the worst birthday present I have ever given you, Samantha Blake."

Donal leaned forward and took the old, brown leather book on his desk. Sipping his scotch, he opened the tome whose title page bore the words Volkhardt Brauner's Cyclopedia of Mesopotamian Fiends. Knowing that Brauner arranged the entries alphabetically, Donal flipped to the last few entries, stopping on the entry labeled Zozo. Next to the ornately decorate drop cap entry name sat a black and white illustration of the demon: a tall humanoid with a four-horned goat's head, furry legs, and four wings. From the entry, it appeared that little was known of this demon's origins, but Brauner believed it to be of Sumerian origin, citing sources naming Zozo as a warrior serving under Pazuzu. Brauner stated that he was tasked with deceiving enemies, often masquerading as a scared child; infiltrating their minds to cause them to commit acts of violence against themselves and others; and playing upon their insecurities by mimicking the voices of the dead. He closed the book and returned it to his desk before draining his glass.

The Arch Magus rose from his chair and walked to his workbench and opened the mahogany cabinet behind it. His eyes scanned the glass jars filled with resins, barks, saps, bones, nails, and other reagents. Grabbing several jars, he measured the proper amounts of olibanum, frankincense, cedarwood, copal, and myrrh before placing them in a lead tin. He placed the tin inside a black leather doctor's bag along with a censor, charcoal, his ritual sword, his wand, two black and two red candles, a small amber jar of anointing oil, a mixture of purified salt and ground dragon bone, and a cigarette lighter. He walked over to the ornate French armoire behind his desk, unlocked it, and took his faceless mask and a portal stone, which stores a prepared ritual that would allow him to open a return portal to his study. He placed them in his bag. He picked up his cell phone and called Shirley Dorrington, who confirmed that his package had been shipped to Sam's office. With his bag in hand, he left his study to return to Bannagh.

* * *

162

Hours had passed, and Sam Hain continued wandering through the Swamp of Sighs, her clothing and body slowly drying after hiding in a half-submerged hollow log. Though it no longer nauseated her, she still mentally, and sometimes audibly, complained about the swamp's reek. She coughed and sneezed in the cold air that felt like a midwinter's night. A few strands of hair, matted down by mud and sweat, dangled over her nose as the wind blew. She had avoided that bark creature and had spent the last few hours running from the unseen creature whose beating wings followed her. Stretching her sore back, she winced and then yawned; she shook her eyes rapidly and then shook her head. She stumbled as tiredness slowed her pace.

Not that it would have been of any use, but the battery on Sam's phone died some time ago. She yawned and rubbed her eyes. She wanted a full night's sleep, but she would have accepted a good nap followed by a cup of hot coffee. She tried pushing that desire from her mind, knowing that falling asleep in Faerie could result in her waking up decades later. She had a young, likely terrified, woman to help. She staggered through the dry soil, her soaked, muddied boots slurped and sloshed as she moved. Her eyes unfocused as she yawned again; she slapped her face and blinked to focus her eyes on the lone, gnarled tree from which a single yellow leaf clung to its brittle, white branch. Sam sank into the dirt beneath the tree and sighed.

Sam rubbed her temples and said, "Fuck. If there's anyone I know who would know what to do now, it's my fucking father. He may have been fucking right about me going home. Have I been too stubborn? I mean, I am his daughter. I should give him a chance. I mean, I'm not a teenager anymore. Time to drop the angst, forgive, and ask for forgiveness for the bitch I've been.

"That's why when I agreed to learn a few protective rites. But I was such a bitch to him when he tried that he had Mister Fingal teach me. And I enjoyed spending time with him and Jake. He told some amazing stories about his time working at the Embassy in Bucharest, right around the time when the Iron Curtain crashed. I wish I had my grimoire with me. Fuck, I should've memorized the damned things. But no, 'I don't need to memorize these rites, Mister Fingal; I'll never be without them when I need them. I do my research and prepare for every case.'" She shook her head and chuckled before continuing, "Twenty-three. I was as cute as I was cocky. Dumb bitch. I've learned a lot since then, but fuck if I listened to any of those lessons this time around."

She lowered her head into her hands and cried, cursing her own arrogance and stupidity. The beating of strange wings returned; Sam waved to it without looking to the twilight sky. She ground her teeth, something she only did when upset, and clenched her fists. She wracked her brain attempting to remember the simple divination rite Mister Fingal taught her, but her thoughts raced from failure to failure; she recalled when she accidentally shot a bystander on a case in New Orleans during Mardi Gras, when she dropped out of college, when she failed to fix an issue where a kitsune living in San Francisco got caught running a con on the mob bosses, when she lost her first post-college job and had to return home, and when she forgot to return her mother's call the night before her death.

Holding her head in her right hand, she sighed and said, "Fucking thoughts. What was it Mister Fingal always said about thoughts? Fuck. I know this. Shit. Yeah, 'Thoughts contain a subtle power, Samantha, a subtle energy that wells up from the darkened parts of our souls and gently directs the movements of our psyches. The unenlightened, and even many of the enlightened, allow them to direct these movements unchecked, wreaking havoc on our intentions, our words, and our actions. However, when we become conscious of our thoughts, pruning away those mental branches that bear either no fruit or rotten fruit, we gain the clarity of mental form that allows us to harness the energy of true, focused, and directed thoughts to manifest that which we desire in our lives.' I wonder."

Her voice trailed into a whisper as she crossed her legs and moved into a lotus position. She closed her eyes and inhaled deeply, focusing on her breath. She had not meditated in almost two years. Thoughts came, and for the first quarter of an hour, Sam entertained them. Slowly, she regained the confidence and strength first to push them from her mind and then to let them come and depart with little notice from her consciousness. As her mind emptied, she focused on the Crooked Hill, which she imagined as looking like something from a Dr. Seuss book with elongated curves and spirals but without the bright primary colors. She laughed at the mental image but kept it centered in her mind as she envisioned herself approaching it. Ignoring a single flap of those invisible wings, she continued focusing on her arrival at the Crooked Hill. The wings flapped in a slow, deliberate rhythm. Something dry brushed across Sam's nose. Her eyes opened, and she saw the tree's single leaf floating in a spiral to her left.

The leaf dipped low, and then the wings flapped once more, causing the leaf to rise and spiral once more in its gentle dance.

She extended her hand; the wings flapped again, and the leaf slipped beyond her reach. As it continued its journey onward, Sam stood and followed. No wind carried the leaf, and so with each mysterious flapping of the invisible wings, Sam's eyes scanned the area for their source. She saw nothing in the dim light of the Court of Autumn. After a few moments of walking, Sam watched the leaf drift to the ground. The wings fell silent. She raised her right eyebrow, shrugged, and raised her head.

A castle stood atop a hill at the edge of her vision. The hill resembled the upside-down shoe of a giant Christmas Elf, complete with the elongated toe that curls into a bell-shaped shrub. Shadowed in the darkness of the Court of Autumn twilight, the castle perched above the sole near the beginning of the curl. From Sam's vantage point, the castle appeared to be made of mud and bark, with leaf-shaped tiles forming the roofs. She took a deep breath, unholstered her handgun, and to the darkened castle, she walked.

Chapter 8

One thought has been running through my head for the past however long I've been wandering through this damned swamp: I want a bath. I decided that my birthday present to myself would involve using some of the money from this fix to take the girls on a spa day. After trudging through this cold, wet, rancid-smelling swamp, covered in mud and my own sweat, I needed a spa day. And they're better with friends. Before I get to do that, I still had to rescue Mabd and figure out how to keep her, Niamh, and all the ghost hunters safe from the fucking Duilearga.

I saw the crooked hill and Count Bha'esi's castle before me in the distance; it appeared to be about half a mile away. It wasn't what I pictured in my mind when Dagh Mobh the Vernal Prince gave directions for finding this place. This upside-down shoe of a hill looked like one of Santa's elves got drunk and fell off the sleigh in flight, landing ankle deep in brown snow. I had envisioned something like a twisted version of the mountain the Grinch lived on in the old cartoon. Yet here I stood, amidst the shadows of the Court of Autumn's perpetual twilight, before this hill that rose at a strange angle, causing the castle to sit precariously near the thinnest edge where the hill curls under into a dirt spiral. Still, the path that spiraled up the hill meant the ascent would be easy. I ensured my Walther had a full clip of blessed cold iron rounds; with that, I started walking the path toward the castle.

The Count's castle wasn't exactly my idea of a villain's lair either. As I stood at the far edge of the summit, I saw a building that blended seamlessly with the natural – or, in this case, supernatural – surroundings. I had wanted something foreboding made of dark stone with a portcullis shaped like a skull's mouth, rows of rotting bodies impaled on stakes or nailed to crosses lining the path towards it, and battalions of faceless armored soldiers creating thunder as they marched. Instead, Count Bha'esi's castle resembled a large, rectangular, wood-framed adobe hut about three stories tall with two towers branching off the main keep at the second story and rising about another two stories above the keep's thatch roof. There wasn't even a moat or a palisade, but at least a few trees rose from the hilltop. I saw a pair of guards flanking the door, but from this distance, I couldn't tell if they had faces or faceless helmets.

Crouching low, I stalked toward the gate, using the few gnarled trees as cover. I froze as I reached the second tree from the far edge. My heart rate and breathing slowly returned to normal before I bit my lip and peered around the bone white bark. Two guards flanked the white double doors to the keep. Shorter than me, I could see they had my father's bulbous nose and a snaggle-toothed overbite. Their olive skin had red and orange undertones; their black eyes had white pupils, and they wore bark armor. They carried wooden spears with leaf blades; the hafts appeared to have been carved from twisted roots.

Fuck! I kicked the dirt as that strange wing-flapping sound

returned and flew toward the keep. I looked up when I heard a repeated cawing in the sky. The black outline of a large crow, barely visible, flew through the purple twilight sky and landed on the tree nearest the keep. Its continuous and rhythmic cawing drew the guards' attention. They nodded, and the guard on the left walked toward the bird. I held my breath. An invisibility spell would have been great, but, as my father always droned, "The true purpose of magic is the ascension toward true enlightenment. While using one's focused will for protection against psychic threats is an unfortunate necessity, using one's power for such base and easily abusable ends will neither be taught nor tolerated." I decided that my father and I would revisit that conversation soon.

The guard searched the area around the tree where that damned crow screamed. I remained motionless, crouched on the ground with only the right side of my face peering around the gnarled tree I used for cover. My heart pounded. Sweat beaded on my mud-covered forehead. The guard turned toward his partner and shrugged. I exhaled in relief. He shouted that there was nothing and started walking back. I froze. My heart sank. The other guard barked something to him that I assumed to mean, "search the area," but my grasp of the fae language allowed me to differentiate its presence from the sounds of local fauna. It's never been a problem, since most fae, like angels and demons, use a minor form of telepathy when communicating with humans.

With my back against the tree, I stayed motionless and quiet. My breathing raced against my heartbeat. Both sounded so loud that I trembled in fear, knowing that this guard heard them. Whatever plans I had almost formed disappeared. My eyes darted from left to right as I followed the sound of the guard's footsteps as they grew louder. The guard moved closer. I accepted that I would have to fight my way through this castle; I tensed my muscles as I visualized myself spinning out from my cover to fire at the approaching guard. All fell silent; the crow ceased cawing, and the guard halted. After a minute, the crow flew away to my left. It perched somewhere nearby, and its cawing became frantic and insistent. The guard turned when his partner yelled something in a language that sounded like a mixture of animal sounds inflected like speech.

One set of footprints raced away, but the guard closer to me walked toward the door. A new plan formed in my mind. I took a deep breath and crept forward a few steps at a time, pausing at the slightest movement the guard made. I shifted my grip on my Walther slightly, hoping that a faerie's anatomy proved similar enough to a human's. I crept behind him, stopping when he stopped. It must've looked like a bad spy comedy. When he stopped, I raised my gun high and drove the barrel down into his temple; he slumped onto the ground. The other guard appeared busy searching the crow's new roost. I searched the guard and grabbed his key ring, hoping they would prove useful. Then I walked to the keep's gate and unlocked the door with the key.

I saw my breath as I walked through Count Bha'esi's castle. For a noble faerie involved in kidnapping a young girl, this guy needed help with interior decorating in his castle. The wide halls, the bright bioluminescent flora and fungi, and the fresh scent worked against that whole evil overlord aesthetic. There were no faceless guards patrolling the halls. Sure, the gray stone flooring, the bone-white wooden walls, and the cold helped, but when compared to the Vernal Prince's palace, this place lacked both the sense of otherworldly wonder and aesthetic coherence with the realm in which it was set. Granted that Bha'esi isn't the Prince of Autumn, but I expected more from a castle in a place named the Swamp of Sighs.

I avoided two patrols as I searched the keep for Mabd Donovan. Logic dictated that she would be kept in either one of the towers – likely in the highest room – or in a dungeon in the basement. I figured he wasn't creative enough to do anything interesting. Honestly, I doubted this place had a basement, given the weird shape of the hill it sat on, so I started by searching the towers. The first tower contained a large library and an observatory. The doors in the second tower were locked, but the keys on the guard's key ring allowed me to open and see three bedrooms. The canopy bed in the room on the highest floor had ornate carvings of autumnal scenes on the posts, the headboard, and the footboard that were masterfully done. Otherwise, the room looked plain and almost spartan. Shrugging my shoulders, I started looking for a staircase to the keep's basement, hoping that perhaps space worked as uniquely as time did in Faerie.

A stone staircase spiraled down to the keep's dungeon, and to my surprise, I found brick walls and floors, likely adobe from their appearance and texture, and thick roots pushing through the ceiling. The warm, humid air smelled rich and earthy like the garden section of Livingston Hardware on an August afternoon. No guards sat around a table playing cards or patrolled the dungeon's entrance, but, like any lazy villain's build-by-numbers dungeon, this one consisted of a long corridor lined with individual cells, each featuring a stone door with a barred viewing hole. Small bioluminescent fungi jutted from the walls, allowing me to see far enough ahead to not run into anything as I crept through the passage. Other than my footsteps and the faint echoes of voices in the distance, it was quiet. I chuckled. Mabd's prison wasn't at the highest room of the tallest tower, but it was in the darkest cell of the deepest dungeon.

The guards outside her cell had similar features to the ones guarding the keep. I stopped as soon as I could hear them as they bickered. From the rhythm and the handful of words I had learned, I guessed the conversation centered on how many cycles they had to guard the human. I caught a stray word about a battle that I shrugged aside. I scratched the side of my head, my eyes darting around the passage. Voices did not echo well in this passage, and it appeared that the sounds of my footsteps did not travel far ahead of me; therefore, if I had to resort to force, gunshots would likely not draw unwanted attention. I planned to try negotiating first, but it comforted me to know that if I had to fight, the odds might not be stacked so high against me.

I approached the guards and stopped when they drew their curved wooden blades. One of them narrowed his eyes and telepathically demanded, "Halt, why are you here?"

"That's a good question," I replied, "I'm here to negotiate for the release of a human girl named Mabd Donovan. From what I overheard while I walked down this corridor, you two fine fae are tired of guarding her. So, I'll make you a deal. You let me take her back to earth, and you won't have to guard her any longer."

I flashed my best, most sincere smile as I watched them exchange glances and whisper to each other. That same guard turned back to me and said, "His Excellency, Count Bha'esi of the Court of Autumn has decreed that the human is to remain a prisoner until such a time as he decrees she may either be released, enslaved, or executed."

I shook my head and sighed. "I thought you might say that, but those really aren't good options. See, she was accidentally involved in a Veil Piercing incident, which has drawn the attention of the Duilearga, who, as everyone knows, have a 'shoot lots of people first, and create a narrative later' policy. And their body counts go deep on both sides, so the two of you might end up dead. Now, I've got a reputation for fixing situations like this with little, and often no, bloodshed. We can do things my way, and we all walk away alive. We can do thing your Count's way, and there's a good chance the two of you will end up dead." I cocked an eyebrow in challenge.

The guards extended their swords and took one step toward me. One asked, "If all of this is true, why don't you tell us your name?"

I laughed and winked before replying, "I've dealt with enough of your kind to know better than to tell you my name. Notice how I didn't ask yours? The less we know about each other, the more even footing we'll be on."

The talkative guard took another step forward. His eyes searched me. I smiled. "How do we know," he asked, "that you're not the Duilearga agent sent to contain the matter?"

I turned the back of my left hand toward him. In an even voice, I said, "Duilearga agents wear a distinctive signet ring on their left hand. As you can see, I have no rings on my left hand. And if that doesn't convince you, I have a scar on my left shoulder from a Duilearga agent's bullet that I got while saving a leprechaun a few years ago. I'm on your side."

The guard stroked his pointy chin with his free hand while nodding. After a moment of silence, he narrowed his eyes and said, "You seem to know an awful lot of the goings on around the Veil – maybe too much. I think we're going to have to keep you here and let His Excellency decide what to do with you."

Both guards advanced, so I shifted and fired. The shot echoed louder than I had hoped it would, but the closer guard screamed and froze as the bullet pierced his left kneecap. Dropping his blade, he grabbed his knee and pulled to no effect. Confusion covered his face; he gargled and gasped for air as he looked at me, struggling but unable to move. The other guard pointed and shrieked, his arm and jaw trembling. As the other guard coughed and wheezed, a midnight blue color spread from the knee toward the extremities.

As both guards trembled, I smirked, raised my Walther, and said, "Blessed cold iron rounds. I always knew they protected against your kind, but judging by that spreading discoloration and coughing, it seems that they have other effects as well." I pointed my handgun at the other guard and said, "I don't know if you can save your friend, but if you unlock that cell and run away, telling no one about this, I won't shoot you."

The guard looked genuinely terrified as his eyes darted from my gun to his friend, whose skin grew increasingly black as he struggled to breathe. I clicked my tongue against my mouth, mimicking the ticking of a clock, watching the sweat bead on his trembling forehead. He sheathed his sword and lowered his head. His partner's gasps for air weakened. He removed the key chain from his belt and faced the cell they were guarding. With his back toward me, he kept nervously looking over his shoulder. I showed him my finger wasn't on the trigger. A final rattling rasp crawled from his partner's lips the moment he unlocked the cell door. He dropped the keys on the floor, turned, and walked past me. I turned and watched as he left my field of vision and then waited a few minutes before walking toward the cell.

I opened the heavy door and saw a lone human woman chained to the back wall of a cell that looked to be about half the size of my freshman dorm. Her brown hair was a matted mess of tangled curls, and her clothes were tattered and stained. The cell reeked of ammonia and shit. The shattered remains of an empty bowl lay against the wall opposite her. Her skin looked dry. I holstered my gun and said, "Mabd Donovan, I'm Samantha Hain. I'm here to take you home."

* * *

A team of six paranormal investigators, the Hoosier Haunters, talked excitedly in the sitting room at The Slouching Giant on the morning of October 29th. As Mister O'Gill stoked the hearth's fire, tossing in sachets of cinnamon, coriander, and clove, they laughed and cheered. He refilled their ciders, and they toasted each other on a successful investigation. As three o'clock neared, the investigators returned to their rooms until only one of them, a middle-aged man with a ruddy tan; short, dirty blond hair that thinned at the crown of his head; brown eyes; and a small beer belly. He sat at a table by the hearth, sipping his cider and finishing up the investigation report. After his teammates retired for the evening, Mister O'Gill informed his guest that he would not be available for a few minutes, as he had to check on a guest whom he had not seen in almost two days. A few minutes after Mister O'Gill left, a man approached him.

The man was tall and fair-skinned with dirty blond hair cut short and neat; in the emerald button-down shirt, gray wool cardigan, and gray trousers he wore, a casual observer

175

might have mistaken him for either a young professor or a young physician. From behind his wire-rimmed glasses, the firelight danced in his hazel eyes. He set his brown leather knapsack on the floor beside an empty chair near the other man and said in a light, melodic brogue, "Good morning, sir. I'm Michael O'Donald, a journalist for the Spectral Inquirer, and my editor sent me here to research the reports we're getting of this Bannagh Banshee. It seems you're part of a team who's had some luck spotting the old girl. That so?"

He extended a hand, and the man shook it and replied, "Hello there, I'm Bart Morris, founder of Hoosier Haunters, a paranormal investigation group based in the city of Great Bend, Indiana, in the great country of the U.S. of A. It's a pleasure to meet you, and no, I don't mind answering a few questions."

"Good," Michael said, sitting in the chair opposite Bart. He rummaged through his knapsack and kicked it. "Shite, I forgot my recorder in my room. I apologize. I was on a case tracking down a werewolf in Budapest and flew straight here." He yawned. "It's been a long day. I'll trade you a story for a story."

Bart thought it over and said, "I don't see why that'd be a problem." He downed his cider and then said, "This cider is delicious, but you wouldn't happen to have something stronger, would you?"

Michael smiled and nodded. "I do indeed," he said, rising and leading the way to his room.

Michael's room had more rustic charm than Sam's had. His bed had a barn door headboard, and the varnished wooden chairs had cushions made of the same fabric as the quilt atop the bed. Michael's brown leather duffel bag sat unopened on the floor beside the bed. After Bart entered, Michael slipped the "Do Not Disturb" sign on the door, closed it, and walked toward the round table between the two chairs where he pocketed his recorder. He turned to Bart and said, "Take a seat, and I'll pour us each a glass of whiskey."

Bart sat in the chair facing the door. Michael poured Teeling Single Grain into the ceramic mugs. He placed them both on the table, removed the recorder from his pocket, and sat down. Raising his mug to Bart, he said, "*Sláinte.*" He switched on the recorder, pressed the record button, and then added, "This is Michael O'Donald at The Slouching Giant in Bannagh, County Sligo. It is 29 October and too damned early in the morning to be awake. So, Bart, for the record, would you state your name and where you're from?"

Bart nodded and said, "My name is Bart Morris, and I'm from Great Bend, Indiana, in the USA."

"Thank you," Michael said. "And from what I understand, you are part of an organization that has definitive evidence of a banshee. Correct?"

Bart sipped his whiskey and coughed as it went down. "That's good stuff, but it burns," he said. They chuckled, and he added, "Yes, I am the founder of Hoosier Haunters, and we have captured first-hand evidence of a banshee in the moors outside of Bannagh."

Michael smiled in a way that accentuated the angular features of his face. Scratching the two-day stubble on his chin with his left hand, he said, "That's fantastic. Can you tell me what you obtained?"

Bart scratched his right ear and nodded. "We obtained both video and audio recordings of the banshee singing on the moors outside Castle Gaelladgh." His face and body grew animated as he spoke. "She was an old woman with long, wispy hair. She was probably gorgeous in her youth. None of us speak Irish, so we really haven't been able to figure out what she was saying. The only thing we think we recognize is the name Liam. Our plan is to get some sleep and then do some research, ask around town, see who this Liam is."

Michael nodded. "That's a solid plan," he said. "I know our readers will want to hear about what you find. But let us humanize this story for them. Tell me a bit about yourself. You a family man? Is investigating ghosts in other countries a full-time job? How'd you get started?"

Bart reclined in his chair and looked wistfully toward the ceiling. "I've got a family. Married ten years to the love of my life, Angela. We've got three kids. Aaron is 8. Stephanie is 6. Chad is 5. I'm a financial planner by day, and I own my own firm, which gives me the chance to do more travel for pleasure. I wish paranormal investigations paid the bills, but they don't." He sighed. "I never believed in ghosts or spirits. Or much of anything, really. I was a troubled kid, a punk rebel without a cause – and without a clue. Had lots of run-ins with the cops, been in and out of jail through my twenties, and been shot and pronounced dead twice. But through it all, my grandma believed in me and prayed for me. She's the reason I do this."

Michael tilted his head and asked, "How did she inspire you?"

Bart's eyes glassed over, and he revealed an old rosary of red and white beads that he wore around his neck. "This was my grandma's rosary," he said. "I'd bet my life she said a hundred 'Hail Mary's' a day for me with this thing. Anyway, I was in jail on an assault and battery charge when she died." His voice grew hoarse as he spoke. "She left me her house in the will so that I'd always have a place to stay. So, when I got out, I moved into her home. Nothing was out of the ordinary for the first few nights, but then, on the first Sunday – Easter – I woke up early and, I know this sounds crazy to most people, but I swear I saw her in the kitchen pouring, well, pouring Lucky Charms cereal into a mixing bowl and picking all the marshmallows out so I could have more marshmallows than would normally fall into a bowl. And this kept happening, every Sunday."

Michael nodded and replied, "That's fascinating. She must've, er must have, loved you to stay on after passing and care for you like that. Did you ever communicate with her?"

Bart nodded. "I tried," he said. "Well, I tried the way a kid who doesn't know no better tried. I just talked to her. All I ever got in response was her smile. Not that that was a bad thing. She made me feel like a million bucks, ya know?"

Michael nodded and smiled a genuine smile. "Aye," he said, stroking his ear, "a gran's love is always the purest."

"Well, then I got stupid," Bart said. "I bought a Ouija board, a dozen white candles, a bottle of Jack, some good weed, and got some friends over to have a séance." He made air quotes as he said séance. "That went about as well as you'd imagine. Anyway, a couple of months later, I happened to see an episode of Maury Povich where he had some ghost hunters on. They talked about EVPs and thermal imaging and other stuff I'd never heard of. So, I bought myself a tape recorder, talked to my grandma, and things moved on from there. What about you? I know this is your interview, but you did promise me a story."

Michael smiled and put his knapsack on the table, allowing the flap to fall open before him. "I did, and so I shall," he said. He held up his left hand and continued, "You see, most of this land is haunted in some fashion or another. The veils between our world, Faerie, and the Otherworld have always been a bit thin here. Add to that all the massacres amongst the clans and then what the bloody English have done, and you've got a spiritual volcano ready to erupt on a finger snap. I grew up with ghost stories and faerie stories. The 'everyone knows' what path you don't take in the woods, what hill you don't climb at night, and why you don't ever sit in mushroom circles. You don't have to believe, because you see people who flaunt the old lore and end up with misfortune. It's part of who we are, and we accept that.

"However, when I was in college studying literature, I made some friends with a group of men who told me they were in a society dedicated to preserving our customs and stories – the Duilearga they called it. I joined up with them and learned a lot. For one thing, I learned that the Veil is both a real thing and a metaphor for the mystical force that prevents most humans from seeing the spirits and monsters that live alongside us. And like the rest of my new colleagues, I dedicated myself to preserving that secret. A few years ago, there was an incident in Berlin that led to a few laws being passed."

He paused and reached into his knapsack and produced a Beretta M9A3 with a silencer attached to the barrel. Bart's eyes widened. He gasped. He pushed away from the table and fell backwards onto the floor. As he scrambled to his feet, Michael slid back, blocking access to the room's only door. Bart put his hands in the air and begged, "Don't shoot. Please, I thought we were getting along. I've got a wife and kids at home. Please. What do you want? Credit? I'll give you all our stuff, and we'll say nothing. I swear to God."

Michael flipped the safety off and said, "Credit? No, Bart, you see, I've already got your audio and video on a flash drive.

I spoke to Billy about an hour before speaking to you. And this isn't personal, no; this is simply business. You see, when the young girl spotted the banshee and posted her video to the TikTok, that created an incident called a Veil Piercing, which is a crime now. And those laws I mentioned, well they empower people like me to ensure that such a crime is punished so that the secrecy is maintained. This isn't personal, you see. It's for the good of humanity as a whole."

He fired two rounds into Bart's chest, and Bart fell to the floor. Michael removed his cardigan, exchanging it for a black and gold argyle sweater he kept in the knapsack. He then removed the dirty blond wig and allowed his curly black hair to flow freely. He shoved it into the knapsack before removing the colored lenses that transformed his brown eyes into hazel ones and flushing them down the toilet. He then returned to the table, picked up the recorder, and said, "This is agent Michael Cormack. Having dispatched the escaped leprechaun who fled to Budapest two days earlier than planned, I flew to Bannagh to begin operations sooner than expected. I have neutralized ten individuals who have claimed to have seen the banshee and confiscated some of their evidence. I have destroyed the rest in order to mislead police into investigating any and all amateur investigators. Cell Archivist Crowley has informed me that another American named Samantha Hain is investigating as well, and while I have not seen her, I will follow orders not to engage. But I might scare her into going home. I will now return to the local cell base to examine the evidence and plan further moves."

Michael Cormack slung the knapsack over his shoulder and picked up his duffel bag. He walked over and stared down at the lifeless body of Bart Morris. He made the sign of the cross and said, "I'll say a prayer for you and send flowers to your wife. It wasn't your fault, Bart, but we can't just let the entire world know that faeries, ghosts, demons, and monsters are real and that they walk among us. There would be chaos and panic. Rest well."

* * *

Mabd Donovan's head inched upward to look at the unfamiliar voice calling to her. She squinted and shook her head. "No," she said in a resigned voice, "you're just a faerie in disguise here to mock my suffering for your own amusement."

Sam narrowed her eyes and scrunched her mouth. She sighed and said, "Really? If I were a disguised faerie, wouldn't I show up with perfect hair and clean clothes? No, I sailed north from Bannagh, trekked through the Vernal Court, met with the Vernal Prince, had a fucked up experience in a strange cave in the Court of Autumn, fled from a strange tree monster, and hid under gross water in the Swamp of Sighs. If I'm not dead yet, I'm still very much a human – a bitch in need of a bath and a spa day – but still a human." She held out her hand and added, "Come on, Lady O'Cuinn misses you."

The young woman perked up at the mention of her employer. She scrambled forward, stopping when she reached the end of her chain. Her eyes pleaded with Sam as she said, "You spoke to her? She hasn't replaced me after all this time?"

Sam approached Mabd and knelt to be on her level. She smiled knowingly and said, "Oh sweetie, you've only been gone a week by my estimation. At least that's what I hope. Time is a bit wibbly wobbly in Faerie. It should be October 28th, and Great-Grandbaby O'Cuinn hasn't been born yet.

She thinks of you as a granddaughter, and given all the shit going on around town with the banshee and the ghost hunters, she's worried something bad might have happened to you. I don't think this is what she thought."

Mabd sighed and looked at the floor. "That's just it," she sighed, "I saw the banshee, and I heard it sing. I'm dead anyway."

"Not if I can help it," Sam muttered under her breath before gently cupping Mabd's chin in her hand and adding, "I don't know much Irish, but with what I do know, I understood the banshee – her name's Niamh O'Cuinn, by the way – to be lamenting the coming of Liam's doom. Based on what I've been able to uncover, that's not you. Neither of us are out of the woods yet, but there is comfort in knowing that the banshee isn't targeting you."

Sam slid toward her and unlocked the shackles. Mabd blinked and rubbed her ankles. A smile crept onto her face as the realization set in that she was going home. Sam smiled and helped her to her feet. Mabd hugged Sam and cried into her shoulder, thanking her profusely. Sam nodded and held her tightly. Suddenly, this endeavor felt no different from the mundane cases she took on a regular basis. It had the same heart, helping a woman in trouble; the situational specifics alone gave it a different surface dressing. Sam cried as well.

As they started to leave, Mabd asked, "How did you get the guards to give you the key?"

Sam smirked and said, "I can be very persuasive when I need to be."

As they exited the cell, Mabd gasped when she saw the lifeless, blackened body of the guard on the dungeon floor. His limbs had shriveled and contorted, and his discolored skin clung to his bones like stretched leather. With a trembling finger, she pointed to the guard and asked, "Is that?"

"That," Sam interjected, "is how I persuaded the other guard to unlock your cell. It seems blessed cold iron rounds do more damage to fae than I knew. Look, I've dealt with them before, but I didn't have to shoot anyone. Good thing, seeing as I didn't have these bullets at that time."

"What?" Mabd asked, pinching her nose to avoid any death-related odors.

"Long story," Sam said, waving her hand dismissively. "The gist of it is that, yeah, all the legends are true, but creatures like fae, djinn, angels, demons, vampires, and lycanthropes tend to hide in plain sight, because, well, we humans have a history of being shitty to anyone who's the slightest bit different. I mean, if we can't handle pigment variations on humans, what makes you think we could handle knowing our neighbor is a vampire or a werewolf? When the secret gets out, as is the case of you recording the banshee, there are groups of people who act to maintain that secret at all costs. Body counts tend to happen. So, someone close to those involved tends to make a habit of contacting me to fix the situation, and my goal is to avoid bloodshed. Do you smell that?"

The scents of lavender, patchouli, and sulfur wafted into the dungeon corridor. The air grew heavy. As Sam finished her question, the bioluminescent fungi on the walls flared. Both Sam and Mabd closed their eyes and shielded them with an arm. As they blinked rapidly, they heard a darkly melodic but dangerous voice say, "If you wish to avoid bloodshed, we advise you to surrender and return to that open cell."

When their eyes adjusted, Sam and Mabd saw Count Bha'esi, lavender bows in their black ringlets, dressed in a sheer mint silk duster over a flouncy white shirt and fitted plum trousers. Standing beside and towering over the Fae noble was a furry bipedal goat with four obsidian horns, two pairs of wings, and eye that glowed with green fire. Mabd cowered behind Sam, and Sam switched her handgun into her other hand and then drew her rapier. Ignoring the salut, Sam moved into the en garde position. As Mabd panted nervously behind her, Sam kept her breathing even as her eyes shifted between the two beings who oppose their progress.

Mabd whispered, "Maybe you could talk to them?"

Sam smirked and said, "I knew this would happen if I stayed in Faerie too long. I'd run into a D-grade gothic lolita Jareth and his hench-sheep Bah-ah-ah-ahgle. Look, we don't want any trouble, so why don't you just step aside and let us pass?"

The fiend growled, baring its rotting yellow fangs as the fae noble bowed and said, "Greetings, Samantha Hain, daughter of Arch Magus Donal Hain. Allow us to introduce ourselves." He placed his right hand upon his chest and said, "We are Fosiri Bha'esi, Count of Autumn's Twilight and Thane to the Queen of Earth and Winter. We welcome you unto our domain." He then motioned toward the demonic entity and said, "And this is our associate Zozo."

Sam jerked to attention at the mention of the demon's name. Her eyes focused on it as she asked, "How do you know my name? I haven't stated it."

The Count giggled, causing Sam to shoot them a side eyed glance. "We well know you and your abilities beyond The Veil, Miss Hain. We had hoped to meet with you earlier, but it appears that you had another engagement."

Sam snorted in disbelief before replying, "See, I don't normally accept invitations to meet with kidnappers, but I have been known to pick a few locks and break a few innocent people out of their clutches." She smiled.

Bha'esi glared at her. "And yet," he said, "when you enter our keep, you draw first blood and kill one of our soldiers. Why do you show us such disrespect?"

Sam laughed. "Disrespect? Oh, that's hilarious." She then shifted her gaze to Count Bha'esi, waved her handgun twice, and said, "A kidnapper demands respect. Too funny. And yeah, I killed a guard down here. I knew blessed cold iron would stop your kind, but I didn't realize it would seriously fuck you up. If you were wise, O noble Count, you would take it as a warning and not as disrespect. I like my violent body count to be zero, but I'm here to bring this young lady home. And I will not let you stop me. Stand aside."

Zozo growled and started to advance, but Bha'esi extended an arm to stop him. They smiled and bowed to Sam. "Your point is made," they said. "We will stand aside as we have pressing business elsewhere. Zozo, apprehend or execute them. The choice is yours." Bha'esi then turned and walked away.

"Stay back," Sam said to Mabd as she and Zozo advanced toward each other. The air grew hot; it reeked of sulfur. Zozo, who towered over Sam by at least two feet, growled a vile laugh as black claws extended from the ends of the six fingers on his hands. Sam noticed Zozo's had two pair of wings; one pair resembled giant falcon wings, and the other resembled giant bat wings. Recognizing that this was the demon she fought in the cave, she smirked, confident that this would be an easy victory.

The two opponents closed in on each other. Zozo slashed downward. Mabd hid her face in her hands. Sam ducked the strike; she shifted to his left. Sam pointed with her rapier. She lunged toward Zozo's kidney. The fiend spun left, grabbed the silver-edged blade in its giant right hand, and twisted his wrist. The blade snapped, and Sam's jaw dropped. Her heart pounded in her chest, and her mind blanked. She failed to notice the back of Zozo's left-hand slam into the side of her head, hurling her into the dungeon's wall.

Sam scurried to her feet. Zozo uttered a guttural growl that stopped Sam's movement. A voice entered her head, mocking her with a hollow, brittle laugh as it said, "You want to kill. I know you do. Admit it."

Raspy breaths punctuated Sam's response, "Yes, I want to kill you, you fucking monster."

The voice laughed again. "What about the young girl? If you kill her, you can go free."

"Nice fucking try, goat boy," Sam replied. "I'm not killing her. I'm going to kill you."

"Wait, what?" Mabd asked. Her eyes widened as she ran to Sam. Her jaw trembled, and her eyes glassed. She shook Sam's arm and begged, "Please snap out of whatever is happening. Please don't kill me."

Sam dropped to her knees and covered her ears with her hands. She screamed in pain as the voice in her head became her mother's voice, "Samantha, I miss you. Don't you want to spend time with me? Please, Samantha, I miss you. I love you so much."

Sam's body shook. She rocked back and forth on her knees. Tears streamed down her cheeks. "Mom," she whispered, "Mom, I miss you so much. I – I want nothing more than to spend time with you, but I – we can't – just a few more days. Nick will give us a few hours."

The voice that sounded like Sam's mother cried. Sam winced at the sound. The voice pleaded, "It's not enough, darling. And if this thing kills you, we'll never see each other again. There's only one way. Go ahead, mommy will give you the strength to do it." And then the voice whispered, "I love you."

Sam closed her eyes and nodded. She whispered an apology to Mabd as she ran her fingers along the barrel of her Walther. Mabd pleaded with her not to do whatever she had planned to do; she shook Sam, begging her to open her eyes. Mabd's pleading abruptly stopped when she heard Zozo's laughter in her own mind as the fiend needled her fear of never truly belonging to a family. She collapsed on the stone floor and cried. Sam held the gun and nodded. She placed it under her chin, pointing the barrel slightly inward. Every muscle tensed as she took one long, deep breath. And then she heard a baby cry, and her eyes shot open. The voice in her head growled and said, "Damn. Another's life is mine to claim. I'm sure we'll meet again soon."

Zozo's laughter filled both their minds. They looked up to see him disappear in a flash of flame the color of lapis lazuli. Sam engaged the gun's safety and holstered it as she sank. Mabd wiped the tears from her eyes. She and Sam looked at each other. Sam offered a weak smile as the realization of exactly what saved them dawned on her. She slammed her fist on the floor and screamed, "Fuck!"

Chapter 9

"What – what just happened?" Mabd asked, her brown eyes reddened from tears.

I lowered my head into my hands and sighed. "It's a long story," I said, "and I'll tell you the whole thing after we're back in Ireland, and I've had a bath. For now, let me just say that the demon who just royally kicked my ass is named Zozo. According to a contract I found buried beneath Old Tom's Hill, Liam O'Cuinn made a deal with Zozo – promising the life of the thirteenth firstborn girl born in Castle Gaelladgh in exchange for permission to marry Niamh O'Cuinn. She is the banshee you saw. And her song was a warning that Liam's doom is coming. By filming her, you committed what is called a 'Veil Piercing,' where a human sees one of the supernatural creatures with whom we share a world. Most people can't handle that knowledge, so it's a carefully guarded secret."

"So am I going to go to jail?" She asked.

I shook my head and took a deep breath before replying, "There are this group of people who protect the secret called Veil Watchers. In Ireland, they're called the Duilearga. And they have a habit of enforcing it," I paused and exhaled before continuing, "through a body count. That's why I was hired – to fix this matter before they get involved. And my track record is pretty damned strong."

Mabd smiled weakly, which was understandable after being told that her life was in danger. She clutched at her chest, opening and closing her hand as if searching for something that wasn't there. She gasped. Her eyes widened as she said, "I can't find my St. William Rochester medal! Damn. But why did the demon spare us? It's clearly working with the faeries who abducted me."

I exhaled in frustration, shaking my head. I looked into her eyes and asked, "Did you hear the sound of a baby crying before he disappeared?"

"Yeah. That didn't make any sense to me," she said.

I rose to my feet and punched the wall. My arms shook with frustration as I said, "I can't say from this side of the Veil, but given that Liam O'Cuinn promised Zozo the life of the thirteenth firstborn daughter, I would assume that Great Grandbaby O'Cuinn has been born."

Mabd's body trembled as she broke down. She folded her hands over her nose as she cried. Tears flowed down her cheeks. She raised her eyes to meet mine; her jaw trembled. Her rapid breaths punctuated her reply as she said, "Poor Angelica. After half a dozen scares and another half a dozen miscarriages, she was so excited. I mean, given her condition, I can't blame her. Lady O'Cuinn was excited, if concerned for scandal since Angelica and Matthew haven't married after eight years of faithful coupling. And I helped Angelica through the pregnancy, and I helped her decorate the nursery. I was going to be her nanny. It's not fair."

She collapsed into tears again. I nodded but then turned my head to face the exit. We needed to get moving, but I knew from working normal cases this had to be a lot to process. And that would've been without the whole being kidnapped and imprisoned by the faeries thing. I knelt beside her and put my arm around her shoulder. "No," I said, "it's not fair. It's never fair when we have to suffer for the failures and sins of previous generations. And it fucking sucks when the burden falls on us to fix shit we didn't cause. It's hard. Sometimes we can't fix everything." My voice cracked, and my eyes welled up as I continued, "Sometimes, the only thing – the best thing – that we can do for others is to be at their side when things get dark. We don't have to offer advice. We don't have to provide light. We just have to be there for them."

I winced as Mabd sucked snot back into her nose. I've always hated that sound the way so many people seem to hate hearing someone say the word moist. I would have offered her a handkerchief, but mine were covered in swamp mud. We remained silent for a few minutes before Mabd nodded. She stood up and asked, "Can I go home now?"

I smiled and nodded. I gathered the broken pieces of my sword. I knew better than to leave anything connected to me in the hands of the Fae. I switched the safety on my Walther to the off position and said, "Be careful. I snuck in here, so there may be a fight or two on the way out. Stay behind me."

As we crept along the dungeon's corridor to the stairs, I stifled a giggle at the thought that no one would believe that I was a private investigator helping to free a kidnapping victim. I extended my arm, directing Mabd to stop, as I reached the top of the stairs. I scanned the hallway, maintaining slow and even breathing as I searched for any signs of movement. All was clear. I gave the signal, and we continued our way through the halls. We turned a corner and ran into a patrol, which I dispatched with three rounds that echoed farther down the hallways than I would have liked.

I turned to Mabd and said, "Now we run."

Breaking into a sprint, we raced toward the keep's main entrance. My heart raced, and I heard Mabd's breathing quicken. Two more guards emerged. Two shots dropped them to the floor. We reached the main entrance, and Mabd screamed. I spun around to see two patrols emerge from side hallways. I shot the one farthest on the left. I shot the one farthest on the right. I aimed again and heard the distinctive click of an empty magazine. Knowing I was taller than the guards, I charged one, shoulder checking him, and kicking the other. Knocking them back gave me a few seconds to reload and fire two more rounds, dropping the last two guards here.

I noticed Mabd trembling in fear, her wide and unblinking eyes staring at the blackening corpses. Poor girl probably hasn't been this close to this much violence. I still haven't gotten used to it, and I've seen vampire and lycranthrope violence. I slid to the left, and said, "Okay, we're almost out. This is the main door. When I count to three, I want you to open it and hide behind it while I take care of the guards outside. Then, we book it down the hill and go from there. Got it?"

She nodded. I readied myself and counted to three. Mabd tensed and closed her eyes as she opened the door, keeping herself hidden behind it. As soon as the guard came into view, I fired, pegging the shoulder of his sword arm. I shoulder checked him as I raced outside, turned on my heel, and shot the final guard in the head. Mabd nervously peeked outside. I nodded, and we raced along the spiral path that led down the hill.

We ran for what felt like fifteen minutes before Mabd begged through her tears for a break. I nodded, and she sat on the cold, muddy ground and breathed deeply and rapidly. Only a few gnarled trees stood in this open field near the edge of the swamp. We were exposed. I didn't like that. I kept my finger on the trigger and my eyes watching our path for any pursuers. As my own breathing and heart rate crept toward normal, I pinched the bridge of my nose and exhaled in frustration as I wracked my brain for a way to get us home.

"Now where do we go?" Mabd asked. Her breathing punctuated her words.

"If we head back the way I came, we should reach this strange place called the Center of the Year. From there, we can quickly get to the Vernal Court, and then we can get home easily." I lied when I spoke. That plan should have worked in theory, but I didn't know for certain if it would work. If I had my grimoire, I could have created a portal with the rituals that Mister Fingal and my father taught me. Fuck! Nick was right; I should have brought that damned book. I had no choice but to move forward until I figured out a real solution.

Mabd pointed to the tree to our left and said, "That's a strange little bird there."

"It's just a…" My voice trailed to silence as I looked at the bird. This crow had a patch of gray feathers on its head that looked like a cloak's hood. It's black feathers had a translucence to them, but other than that, it looked like a normal crow, which made it stand out here. I tilted my head and scratched my nose before adding, "It's probably the bird that chased me through the Court of Autumn and distracted the guards so I could sneak in Bha'esi's keep."

Mabd stood and walked toward the crow. She turned to me with a smile and said, "Well, if it distracted the guards, it can't be all bad, right?" She then turned to the bird and said, "Hello, little friend. Thank you for your part in helping me escape. Is there something you need?"

If she would have started singing like a damned Disney princess, I would have just given up, drank some Fae wine, and let fate go as it must. However, Mabd maintained as much normalcy as could be expected in this situation, holding her finger out for the crow to perch on. The bird hopped from the twisted branch on which it sat, spiraled around Mabd, and landed on the ground. There, the bird transformed into the translucent burial shroud and gray cloaked form of Niamh O'Cuinn. Mabd gasped and hid behind me.

I nodded toward Niamh, and in my broken Irish said, "Greetings, Niamh. What news bring you to us?"

Mabd whispered, "Your Irish isn't that good. It's like this." She stood beside me and said, "Greetings, Lady O'Cuinn. What news do you bring us?"

I rolled my eyes. But it made communicating with Niamh's banshee easier – even if everything I learned had to be filtered through both my own limited understanding of Irish and Mabd's translations. Niamh nodded to Mabd and said, "The time of Liam's doom is upon House O'Cuinn. Your return to the human world is needed. I will guide you."

Mabd and I shrugged at each other, but we agreed to follow Niamh. She led us through the Court of Autumn, walking in counterclockwise circles. It was like doing some strange waltz, but Niamh glided through the twilight landscape with purpose, which was more than I could say for my half-assed plan. We danced around the edge of the swamp and continued our spiraling journey until we arrived at the mouth of a cave in the depths of a range of tall tree-covered mountains. She pointed to the cave and told us that it would lead us to Old Tom's Hill. We thanked her, and we walked into the darkness.

* * *

Sam and Mabd emerged from the cave at the foot of Old Tom's Hill near the broken faerie ring. Both squinted and shielded their eyes as the midday sun's light stabbed their eyes. The woodsy, earthy smells of the forest beyond the hill caused them to smile, its freshness a reminder that they had returned to Ireland. Sheep bleated as they grazed in the fields. A cold breeze blew from behind them. When their eyes adjusted to daylight, Sam turned and examined the hill, which felt solid to her touch; she kicked the ground, which felt solid as well. Shaking her head, she made a mental note to ask her father for information on methods of traveling to and from Faerie.

Mabd, with tears in her eyes, beamed at Sam. "Thank you," she said, "I never thought I'd see home again. Can we go see Lady O'Cuinn to let her know I'm back?"

Sam shook her head as she replied, "Not yet, sweetie. I think both of us could use a shower first. Maybe wipe the soles of our shoes so we don't track mud into the castle. And since The Slouching Giant is on the way, let's head there first. I promise you'll be having tea with the O'Cuinns today. Okay?"

She nodded and agreed. A violent buzzing in her muddied and torn purse shook Sam. Rummaging through the contents caked with mud and stained by the brackish water, Sam saw her cell phone had regained power; although, the power indicator flashed red. She sighed in relief at seeing the date read October twenty-nine. She had lost over a day, but she felt relief knowing that she still had time before the Duilearga swept in to "handle" the matter. She scanned her messages and voicemail and saw a pair of messages from her father, nearly a dozen panicked voice and text messages from Destiny, and a single voice message from Carmilla. She shot Destiny a quick text to let her know she was safe and that her phone was almost dead before returning the phone to her purse and heading into Bannagh.

A white car with the distinctive blue and yellow markings of the Garda drove away from The Slouching Giant as the two women approached. Mabd mused that there might have been a robbery. Sam scanned the area around the building's doors, but she found nothing unusual. The air inside was cold and heavy, made heavier by the thick silence that filled it. Two men, on opposite sides of the room, sat in silence, drinking coffee. As they reached the desk, Mister O'Gill called her name, rushed over, and hugged her tightly.

"Miss Hain, I'm so glad you're safe," he said as he released her. "When we didn't see you return last night, and after all that happened this morning, we feared the worst. You, uh, you look like you rolled around in the bog. What happened? Is that Mabd Donovan with you?"

Sam wanted to chuckle and smile, but her body released all the tension within, causing her to weep in his arms as she said, "I'm sorry to worry you, Mister O'Gill. And yeah, it's a long story, but I followed a hunch and found Mabd. And it was my own clumsiness that got me looking like this. I figured we'd come and have a shower before she heads back to the O'Cuinns. What do you mean by that? What happened this morning?"

He smiled and wiped her eyes. Looking away, he crossed himself. With a sigh, and a sorrow-darkened face, he said, "A few of the ghost hunters – mostly ones from your country but a few from Britain and Germany – were found in their rooms. All were shot. Seems the killer also took any evidence they had of seeing the banshee."

Sam's jaw fell, and she and Mabd shared a quick, worried glance. Sam swallowed, her eyes downcast, as the realization dawned. The Duilearga had arrived earlier than she had been told they would. She nodded and asked, "But some of them are alive, right?"

Mister O'Gill nodded. "Only those who arrived after three this morning, and most of them, "he glanced at the two men drinking coffee, "have already changed their departure dates."

"Fuck," Sam said. "I'm sorry, Mister O'Gill. I wish I knew what to say."

He nodded. "I wish I did too," he said. He sighed and then smiled at the two women, adding, "But you're safe, and you've brought young Mabd back safe and sound just in time to see the newborn, Abigail Madeline O'Cuinn-Runciman, born this morning. Well, you girls go shower, and I'll have Margaret wash those clothes for you."

As they entered her room, Sam locked the door and closed the curtains. She told Mabd to shower first while she charged her cell phone. Mrs. O'Gill knocked on the door and collected our filthy clothing; Sam thanked her. Sitting on her bed in one of the two soft, pale blue bathrobes Mrs. O'Gill provided them, Sam waited a few moments before calling Destiny. The phone rang twice. She knew it would be early for her, but she hoped Destiny would be awake. It rang a third time. Perhaps Destiny was in the shower. On the fourth ring, Destiny's voice burst through the phone, "Sam! Oh my god, you're still alive. What happened? Where were you? I was so worried? Did any of father's agents meet you? What's going on?"

Sam laughed before replying, "Hey, Des, it's good to hear your voice too. It's a long story, but I ended up in Faerie where I found Mabd Donovan who had been kidnapped by a count in the Court of Autumn. Apparently, this guy, some D-grade Jareth the Goblin King, who is in league with this demon named Zozo – don't know shit about him – who's connected to the event that led to the banshee's appearance. Also, the fucking Duilearga have already started cleaning house. How was your date?"

Destiny pursed her lips and growled before responding, "There was food. There was conversation. There was no personality. So, let's talk about something else. Like what the hell did you go through? Oh, and you may want to plan a trip to Austria soon."

I tilted my head and released my jaw. I asked, "Wait. What? Austria? Why?"

Destiny's voice leapt an octave as she said, "When I went to ask Mister Scratch for some help for you, he wanted information. You know how he is. Well, I didn't have anything that he felt was equal, so I excused myself to the ladies' room where Countess Karnstein offered me information about the Order of the Dragon obtaining Dracula's signet ring in exchange for you considering visiting her at her castle in Austria. No pressure. No obligation. Your choice."

Sam bit her lower lip and smiled sheepishly. She drew a sharp breath, exhaled slowly, and replied, "Order of the Dragon, I wonder if that has anything to do with the dragon rising prophecy or warning thing the Vernal Prince – oh! Get this. Dagh fucking Mobh – that redcap happens to be the fucking Vernal Prince himself."

"No way!" Destiny squeaked into the phone. "You were right about him hiding the truth. But I know you're on a time crunch," she yawned, "so what's the plan now?"

Sam shook her head and sighed. "I don't know," she said. "The situation's gotten far more complex than I thought. Look, I have one favor to ask you, Des. If you do this, take the day off."

"You know I'll do it, Sam." Destiny responded.

Sam sighed. "Alright," she said, "I want you – when you go feed Sandy this morning – to go into my office and send me pics of that mind shielding spell I have in my grimoire."

Destiny nodded as she said, "Sure thing. Just let me chug a Red Bull, so I'm not a driving zombie, and I'll take care of it for you within an hour."

Sam thanked her, and they ended the call. She paused; her eyes locked on the list of unanswered voicemail messages. She deleted the ones from Destiny. She knew she would have to call him eventually, but as she stretched her aching muscles, she knew she was too tired to hear her father chastise her for missing lunch the other day. With the sun still in the sky, Carmilla would be asleep, so that call would have to wait. Still, she took a deep breath. Her heartbeat quickened as she set the phone on speaker and played the message.

"Samantha," Carmilla's normally confident Austrian voice trembled as she spoke. Sam's muscles tensed, and she closed her eyes as the message continued, "Samantha, is this working? I need to hear your voice right now. My associates tell me there were several foreigners found dead in that little Irish village where you are working. Are you safe? Please call me, dear. Be safe."

"Is that your girlfriend?" Mabd teased as she, covering

herself in a pale blue towel, walked from the bathroom. Sam's startled face caused her to gasp and add, "I don't mean it in a judgmental way. It's just there seemed to be a longing on your face as you listened."

Sam set her phone on the nightstand to continue charging and answered, "No, she's just a friend." She sighed, forcing her fingers through her matted, mud-caked hair. "It's complicated. It wouldn't work. I'm going to shower. Mrs. O'Gill said she'd bring our clothes back soon."

Sam ran the water hotter than usual as she enjoyed a long, steamy shower. Mabd cocked an eyebrow a handful of times as she heard Sam moaning; the young girl giggled and shook her head. Before Sam finished, Mrs. O'Gill returned their clothes, which she repaired to the best of her ability, and brought them leftover shepherd's pie from last night. After lunch, Sam quickly did her makeup before dressing. She filled her Walther's magazine, placed the broken pieces of her rapier in the map case in which she carried it, and, along with Mabd, headed for Castle Gaelladgh.

* * *

Donal Hain walked through the harvest golden halls of Sligo University Hospital. His gray tweed suit and black turtleneck gave him a professorial air. The air was cold, sterile, and heavy with the vibrations of a myriad of strong emotions. A family cried in a hospital room as a beloved grandfather's life came to an end. A newborn cried as it entered the world. A young man paced the floor in a room, his partner asleep in the bed, as he awaited test results. Donal passed a busy nurse's station where three nurses updated physicians on patient responses to treatment. He stood for a moment outside a patient's room, watching as Frank Caldwell ate his lunch.

After a few moments, Donal knocked on the partially open door before entering. Frank set his fork on the tray where the remainder of his white chicken breast, broccoli, and mashed potatoes. He turned to offer the Arch Magus a smile and greeting amidst the IV tube and the ECG leads connected to his body. The pale blue hospital robe hung loosely on his body as he sat up, pushing the thin gray blanket down. He muted the television channel showing the football game between Chelsea and Manchester United.

"Arch Magus," he said, "to what do I owe this visit?"

Donal Hain closed the door behind him as he entered. Sitting in the faux leather armchair beside the bed, he leaned forward and said, "I have Order business in the area, so I thought I would see how you're recovering."

Frank winced as he rolled his shoulder before raising his hand to massage it gently. "Well," he said, "I'm in a lot of pain. I've only got about thirty percent mobility in my shoulder right now. Doc said I have some nerve damage that might require a surgery or two. All in all, I missed death by two centimeters, so I suppose I'm doing good."

Donal noticed the suitcases in the corner. All of Frank's travel supplies had been brought to the hospital as well. "How much longer before you can return home," he asked.

"Next week," Frank replied. "My mum and dad are flying over in a couple of days to check up on me. Speaking of, Mister Hain, how's Sam doing?"

Donal stood and looked out the window as storm clouds darkened the early afternoon sky. He checked his cell phone and saw he had neither any unread text messages nor missed calls. Shaking his head, he said, "She is home. I spoke to her the morning after your accident. Although we had a heated argument over my desire for both her safety and her involvement in tonight's working. And though we could not come to an agreement on the latter, she agreed to return to the States."

Frank nodded and sighed. He said, "I wish I could have at least told her goodbye. But I guess with the work that has to be done, it's for the best that she's safe."

Donal Hain nodded. "It is," he said, glancing toward the closed door. "And that needs discussing."

Frank nodded. "I'm honored, Arch Magus, that you selected me to participate in such a great working," he said.

"From the moment you petitioned to join the Astrum Argentum, you showed potential. Of course, given your condition, your role in tonight's working in Bannagh will need to be altered." The Arch Magus said. Frank nodded in agreement, and Donal Hain continued, "I had hoped that you would be able to serve as a torch bearer as well as open the Watch Towers before we call our special guests into our plane of existence; however, due to unfortunate circumstances, I believe it best if you perform the role I had hoped to convince my daughter to perform."

His business concluded, Donal Hain purchased a condolences card from the hospital's gift shop before leaving Sligo University Hospital. His cell phone pulsed and beeped from the interior pocket of his tweed blazer. Destiny Grimm confirmed that the package he sent for Sam's birthday had arrived. There was still no communication from his daughter. He growled. After lunch at Embassy Steakhouse, Donal Hain headed for Bannagh by train.

Upon reaching the train station outside of town, Donal Hain overheard several people talking about the killer who targeted guests at The Slouching Giant; apparently this murderer had yet to be apprehended. He again checked his phone, finding that Sam had yet to message him through any channel. Pinching the bridge of his nose and sighing, he sent her a quick text message to say he worried for her safety and that she needed to call him as soon as possible.

Donal Hain surveyed the area north of Old Tom's Hill where, centuries ago, Liam O'Cuinn struck a bargain with the demonic entity known as Zozo to obtain the hand of his beloved. Now, on behalf of the Hermetic Order of the Astrum Argentum, Donal Hain prepared to strike a similar bargain with the same entity for his order's ends. The cool autumnal air hung still as he searched the ground. Apart from his deliberate movements, a single goat's bleating was the only sound that pierced the still silence. He knelt by the broken mushroom circle, his eyes focusing on the hastily excavated chest, which had been emptied of its contents. He cursed and called Seamus Creevy.

The professor answered after three rings, "Donal, I'm nearing Bannagh. What news have you?"

"Concern, Seamus," he said. "I'm at the site, and it appears that Liam O'Cuinn's contract has been found and taken."

"It was my understanding that the contract was not necessary for tonight's working," Seamus said. "Am I not correct?"

Donal Hain shook his head as he scanned the forest beyond the village. "It's not needed," he replied, "strictly speaking. Its presence would have provided a sense of continuance and made the evocation easier. That said, I can certainly perform the working without it. It just concerns me."

"What concerns you, old friend?" Seamus asked.

Donal Hain jerked his head to the left and focused his eyes on the landscape. After a moment of silence, Seamus' voice snapped his attention. He sighed and said, "Sorry, I thought I heard something in one of the hedges at the edge of the field where goats are grazing. No, I'm concerned that either the person killing the guests at the Giant, all of whom have been ghost hunters searching for the banshee, may have grown bold enough to find the contract to whatever those ends may be or else my daughter has found it and may get herself in trouble during her own investigation."

Seamus Creevy pursed his lips and hummed. "So," he asked, "you still have not heard from her?"

Donal shook his head, saying, "No. I've left numerous messages and even called her office. No response from her, and Destiny has not heard from her either. And now, there's this killer…"

"And that concerns you more," Seamus finished the sentence. "I understand, old friend, but we have a duty to our orders and to the world to guide it into peace, prosperity, and safety. I trust everything is prepared?"

Donal nodded. "It is. I have secured a replacement for her role. I hope that Samantha appreciates what I am doing to protect her and everyone else. Well, let me prepare mentally for our midnight working. I'll be in my room at the Giant when you arrive."

Donal ended the call and walked back into Bannagh. After a few moments, George Crowley's camel and gray deerstalker hat rose above the bushes. He watched Donal Hain's form disappear as it moved through Bannagh's streets before he walked over to the mushroom circle north of Old Tom's Hill.

He pursed his lips as he examined the empty box where Liam O'Cuinn placed the contract. He sighed, saying, "That's not what I expected to hear. Well, I need to brief Michael and the High Bard on this development."

* * *

"So," Lady O'Cuinn said, sipping her afternoon tea while sitting across from a suited man with curly black hair, "you are Miss Hain's assistant? Is what Jameson told me correct, Mister Cormack?"

He smirked and nodded, saying, "Not exactly, Lady O'Cuinn. I told your butler I was her Irish liaison. While her father is Irish, she hasn't lived here since she was a small child. When she has cases here, and sometimes in England, I help her with travel arrangements, translation, and investigation. And since she hasn't checked in with me in almost two days, I felt it appropriate to seek information on her whereabouts."

Lady O'Cuinn smiled. "It was yesterday morning, early, that I met with her. I was impressed that her desire was to find our dear Mabd and not to obtain proof of the banshee she saw."

Michael Cormack shifted in his chair before asking, "The banshee the girl Mabd saw? Or did you mean that Samantha saw it as well?"

Lady O'Cuinn sipped her tea and chuckled. "Both, I suppose," she replied. "Mabd's little video started this mess, and Miss Hain mentioned that she spoke with the banshee."

"Oh," Michael said. "Did she happen to mention what she thought it said? She speaks Irish like a toddler."

They laughed. Lady O'Cuinn said, "Well, my grasp isn't much better for communication. I learned to pronounce the words so I could sing the language. She did mention something the banshee said. Now what was it?" She paused and scratched her right ear. "Yes, yes, she said the banshee said that Liam's doom was coming. I didn't know then – and I don't know now – what it meant. I'm sorry."

Both turned their heads toward the sound of a newborn's cries. Lady O'Cuinn smiled. Michael raised an eyebrow and asked, "Grandchild?"

She laughed and smiled, sighing wistfully. "No, Mister Cormack," she answered, "my first, and likely only, great-granddaughter, Abigail Madeline, born at midnight."

Michael Cormack shook his head and smiled. "A birth is a beautiful thing," he said, "Oh, to be born at such a time as this. I pray all the excitement surrounding her birth never harms her soul."

Lady O'Cuinn set her empty teacup on the lace doily atop the mahogany table beside her chair. She leaned forward slightly, her face searching Michael Cormack's. She stroked her chin as she scanned his face for any twitching muscle, any flickering glint in his eyes, or any changing breath rate. His face lacked both emotion and movement. She leaned back, nodded, and said, "I don't see why it should. Are you implying her birth is connected to the banshee or these dreadful murders?"

"Oh, I meant nothing by it, Lady O'Cuinn," Michael said as he pulled his backpack into his lap. "However, I can't help but wonder if the appearance of a banshee that the family seems to know about, a banshee seen to a serving girl, and a series of deaths of those who claim t have seen it, I can't help but wonder if that tragedy will follow her through her life. It's not unheard of in the old stories. And with Miss Hain hastily arriving shortly before the thirty-first, so many coincidences seem to be lining up, given who she fears may come."

Lady O'Cuinn pursed her lips and raised her left eyebrow purposefully. "Do you refer," she asked, "to this Duilearga organization? I know they were her rivals before in Cork. They seem a bit overzealous in their duties from what I've heard."

Michael Cormack's lip twitched slightly at her words. He slid his hand inside his backpack and said, "Samantha's opinion may be a little biased by her own experiences. Sure, some may be a little zealous, but like Samantha, we seek to keep humanity safe regardless of the costs."

Lady O'Cuinn's eyes shot wide as he produced his handgun. His bag fell to the floor as he stood. A single shot broke the silence. Lady O'Cuinn shrieked and fell to her knees. Michael Cormack howled in pain, dropped his handgun, and grabbed his bleeding hand. Both turned toward the hallway to see Mabd Donovan rush to Lady O'Cuinn and embrace her as Samantha Hain sauntered forward, a smoking gun in her hand and a triumphant smirk on her face.

"Michael fucking Cormack," she jeered as she approached him. "You should have stayed home, playing with your tin soldiers, and left this to the professionals."

"You bloody shot me, you bitch!" He said as he breathed heavily, wincing as electric bolts of pain pulsed from his wound.

"You'll live," she said. She glared at him and kicked his gun against the wall. "You'll have a scar like mine, but I gave you a much better chance of walking away alive."

"I was following protocols," he spat at her. "You're just spiteful."

Sam turned toward the butler who hid in an alcove in the

hallway and said, "Jameson, please be a dear and bandage Mister Cormack's wound and call him an ambulance. Let them know he was in a – what was it again, Michael, that you told them in Cork? – oh yes! Let them know he was in a hunting accident."

During this exchange, Mabd helped Lady O'Cuinn to her seat. Her breathing heavy and ragged, Mabd raced to bring her a glass of water. Lady O'Cuinn turned to Sam and asked, "Miss Hain, thank you for stopping him, but what is the meaning of this?"

"I'm sorry about the violence, Lady O'Cuinn," Sam said as she sat in one of the chairs, her eyes focused on Michael Cormack as Jameson arrived and began cleaning and bandaging the wound in his hand. She continued, "This Duilearga slime and I have a history, and after all I've been through lately, I'm a bit on edge. That said, Michael and I are going to have a nice little talk as I negotiate the end of Duilearga involvement here."

"You won't get a bloody word out of me," he growled.

"I honestly don't care if you talk, Michael," Sam replied. "All you have to do is nod your head, leave town, and inform your superiors that all is taken care of. That's all I want."

Jameson finished bandaging the wound. Michael Cormack laughed and said, "Oh, you're a right funny one, little lass. If I leave, the High Bard will send another. We'll keep the secret, regardless of who has to be killed or slandered in the process."

"No, another will not come," a voice from the hallway said.

Michael Cormack stiffened, wincing in pain. All turned to face the hallway where two men entered. One was George Crowley. The other looked to be of a similar age, but thick curls of white hair covered his head. His icy sapphire eyes focused on Sam. He smiled weakly from behind his neatly groomed beard. Sam shot glares at him, Crowley, and Cormack. Lady O'Cuinn stood, causing the older gentleman to bow as she said, "And who are our new guests?"

"Forgive me, Lady O'Cuinn," the old man said. "My name is Eric Murphy, High Bard of the Duilearga Bardic College. And this man is George Crowley, one of our archivists."

"And the fucking asshole who shot Frank Caldwell two nights ago," Sam interjected as she focused her glare on him. "So, this has all been a setup."

George Crowley sighed and looked at the floor. "That was an unfortunate accident," he said before looking directly into Sam's eyes and adding, "And he wasn't my target, Miss Hain. Seamus Creevy was my target."

"The fuck?" Sam asked. "Why should I believe you wanted to shoot an old history professor?"

Crowley nodded and said, "Given your history with us, you have no reason to believe me. But I ask you to believe Werther Grimm."

Sam narrowed her eyes and growled. "You didn't answer my question. And how dare you drag Mister Werther into this?"

Crowley took a deep breath and said, "Seamus Creevy is a ranking member of the Order of the Dragon, and we've been watching them ever since they obtained Tepes' signet ring. To your other concern, Werther is an old friend of mine, and he contacted me when you went missing. Seems his daughter was worried."

"Destiny would reach out," Sam mused, relaxing her shoulders for the first time since she entered the castle. "But you still have a lot of talking to do, so get to it."

"We've known for some time that the Order of the Dragon has been planning something since they obtained the Tepes signet ring, likely trying to resurrect the Impaler. But why Creevy came to Bannagh had us hitting walls until this morning when I happened upon the Arch Magus of the Astrum Argentum searching around Old Tom's Hill and confirming a joint working tonight at midnight."

Sam's arm fell to her side, and her jaw fell to her chest. Shaking her head, she said, "No. My father's an arrogant, neglectful, and unfaithful jackass, but he would never." She paused for a moment and said in a voice just above a whisper, "Fuck! He's part of those forces who don't respect the Treaty. He tried to get me to leave before I found Mabd. Seems now I know why."

"And that is why we came," Eric Murphy said. "Miss Hain, you have no reason to trust us, but we are here asking for your help."

"What?" Sam Hain and Michael Cormack asked simultaneously.

"High Bard," Michael said, "with all due respect, Sir, you cannot be serious. This bitch is a loose cannon and a wild card. We have other agents who are more discreet and more talented than she is."

"More talented, my ass," Sam shot back. "I've got a track record of keeping things secret without a body count. None of your 'discreet and talented' agents can say that. But I also question why you need me."

High Bard Murphy sighed. He stroked his chin thrice before saying, "Honestly, we hope you know more of what's going on than we do. Archivist Crowley informed me that your father was searching for Liam O'Cuinn's contract, long thought to be buried beneath Old Tom's Hill."

"Miss Hain," Lady O'Cuinn asked, "Was that what you sought

as well?"

Sam sighed and said, "Unfortunately, it was."

A scream from another room interrupted Sam's response. Jameson raced into the room, his eyes frantic and his hands trembling more than usual. Rapid, shallow breathing punctuated his speech as he said, "Madame, I've called Kingsbridge already, but young Miss Abigail has stopped breathing."

Lady O'Cuinn and Mabd raced toward Angelica's room. The Duilearga and Sam remained in the sitting room. Sam sank to the floor, covering her face with her hands. Silence loomed heavy in the air. Sam cried. "He took her. I failed. Liam's doom is come."

High Bard Murphy knelt beside her, placing his hand on her shoulder as he asked, "Who took her? What do you know that we don't?"

Sam looked at him through the haze of teary eyes, and with a sigh, she said, "Liam O'Cuinn promised the first daughter of the thirteenth generation born in Castle Gaelladgh to an entity named Zozo. It's not a demon I've seen in any of my father's books, and through my adventure in Faerie to find Mabd, I learned that the Fae courts did not know of this being before Liam summoned it on Old Tom's Hill. Also, the demon seems to be in league with a wannabe Jareth noble in the Court of Autumn named Bha'esi."

"The summoning contract and the working tonight," High Bard Murphy said. "They must be connected, but how?"

Sam shrugged her shoulders. "I don't know," she said, "but that demon is dangerous. He gets in your head and can just fuck you up from the inside out."

"That's why we need you, Miss Hain," he said. "We train our agents to detect and identify magical signatures and residues during their investigations. We are vulnerable to attacks such as this."

"I'm no magician," Sam said through tears, "I know a few spells and rituals, but I don't have the discipline to focus my intent to be as powerful as we might need. But a child died, and my father appears to be in league with its killer. Happy fucking birthday to me. Well, if it means an end to your investigation of the banshee sighting, I guess I'm in."

Chapter 10

"Samantha, you're alive! I painted the sun as it set while I waited for you to call," Carmilla shouted after answering my call on the first ring. I felt like I was in a cartoon, waiting for her to leap through the phone as she spoke.

Her voice sounded ravenous and frantic. She hadn't fed, likely waiting for me to call. I felt bad, mainly for her servants and for whoever she encountered as she sought a meal, because 'Milla always got hangry when unfed. I've seen her rip a fledgling's head off, because he chose to amble in front of her while she stalked toward the dining chamber. And my fucking heart skipped a beat when she said she painted the sunset waiting for me. She woke before sunset, knowing that sunlight – even evening light – could burn her if she watched through a window.

"You didn't have to do that, 'Milla, you could have hurt yourself, and you sound hungry." I said, smiling into the phone and twirling my hair around my finger.

"Samantha Blake Hain," she said. Her use of my full name caused me to immediately snap to attention. She softened her voice and continued, "I care about you. I truly do. And when I heard that several of the ghost hunters were shot, I feared you may have been among their number. What happened? Do you

213

need protection? I can send soldiers or thralls. No. I will go myself."

I blinked. She was serious. Countess Carmilla Karnstein offered to travel to Ireland to protect me. My heart raced, and I blushed. "I'm flattered, 'Milla," I said, "but you don't need to trouble yourself. I wasn't in Bannagh when the ghost hunters were killed. I was, by a strange coincidence in Faerie rescuing Mabd Donovan."

"The strangest things happen to you," she said, chuckling. "I hope that soon you will tell me the entire story."

"Well, I hear Christmastime in Austria is nice," I blurted without thinking.

"So, you are accepting my invitation, Sam?" She asked. After all this time, my body still twitched when called me "Sam." And I've spent enough time around Carmilla to know that she was gloating through the phone.

I nodded, not that she could see, and said, "I am. And I suppose I have you to thank for the aid you gave Destiny the other day."

"That little Grimm never enters The Four Winds without you," she purred. "So, I listened from my table, and when she fled into the powder room, I followed. It seemed you were in trouble, and I had information that I thought might be worth something to Samael. I am happy that I was correct."

"Well," I said, hoping she couldn't hear my shallow, rapid breathing, "that's another coincidence I'm thankful for. And I'm looking forward to Christmas."

"I will handle your arrangements, then," Carmilla said. "And I promise that we will spend the holiday together as friends unless you change your mind."

I chuckled at her persistence, biting my lip for a second

before saying, "You know my feelings, 'Milla. And we tried that once. It just didn't work out."

"I know, Samantha," she said, "but those months were, and your friendship is, a bright moment in my long, dark immortality. Stay safe, and I will see you on your birthday."

"I will." I ended the call and sighed, adding, "It's not that I don't want it to work out, 'Milla. I just can't handle the loneliness of the days when you're a corpse."

I fell backwards into the bed in my room at The Slouching Giant and stretched my muscles. With a sigh I folded my arms behind my head and closed my eyes. I felt like I hadn't slept in a week, but I didn't have the time for a full night's rest. From my adventure in Faerie rescuing Mabd to negotiating a deal with the Duilearga to end to innocent bloodshed in Bannagh to preparing to attack the Astrum Argentum and the Order of the Dragon during some midnight ritual, it's been one fucking long day. If I managed to survive this, I promised myself that I would take a vacation.

Destiny sent the pictures of that mind shielding ritual, and I still needed to call my father. Yet given what I've learned from the Duilearga, from Nick Scratch, from the Vernal Prince, and even from Donal fucking Hain himself, I doubted it would be in anyone's best interests to tell him. I wanted to give him a chance, but now I wasn't sure if that was anything more than wishful thinking. But he was still my father, so I scheduled an email to be sent at midnight to let him know I was safe and alive. I sighed and stared at the ceiling, wondering what I had gotten myself into this time. I set my alarm and drifted into a nap.

That was the first dreamless sleep I've had in a month, which I needed. I still haven't had that legendary riding a white horse dream that all my friends claimed to have had as teenagers. I tore through a small bag of potato chips and then freshened up for the night's events. I reloaded my Walther with the blessed cold iron rounds. While the blessing on them should help against Zozo, I had prepared to intimidate and fight against the Fae, but I neither mentally nor physically prepared for demons. And I had no idea I'd be facing one who could fuck with my mind like that. I sighed as I ran my fingers through my hair. This was going to be a long night.

So much death for what I thought this would be a standard fix. I actually didn't plan to kill anyone. I thought I could save everyone. Hell, I thought I could save my relationship with my father. I thought I was strong enough and smart enough. And to hear a young mother cry when her baby was taken – taken because her ancestor did a shitty thing out of lust and greed – that broken, warbling wail, which I've heard before when I wasn't quick enough to help a woman whose coke addict husband decided to use a drain cleaner and bleach cocktail to ease their toddler's toothache. I wasn't ready to confront a vision of my own death, accompanied by my own mother's mourning.

"And it's not over yet," I sighed, standing. "Time to rendezvous with the fucking Duilearga of all people."

I organized everything I planned to take with me and then sat at the foot of the bed. I visualized a ball of white light in my heart, a warm, comforting, safe light. Focusing my intent, I transformed the ball into a kite shield like those in the Bayeux Tapestry. The shield circled around me, spinning faster and growing larger with each revolution. When the shield's movements created a sphere of continuous energy around me, I directed it to pulse in rhythm with my breathing, charging it. My breathing quickened. My body swayed as my energy moved with the energies of the universe, and when our energies peaked, I pulsed the energy once more and then drew it into myself, covering my body in a layer of white light. With one final exhalation, I gathered my things and headed to meet the Duilearga.

* * *

Sam arrived at Mister Crowley's old farmhouse at half-past eleven. She tensed momentarily when Mister Crowley answered the door wearing the same sweater and deerstalker hat he wore the night he accidentally shot Frank Caldwell. She smiled gingerly and followed him into his sitting room where High Bard Murphy sat in one of the leather chairs sipping from a pint glass filled with a mocha colored beer. Dressed in a brown, green, and navy argyle sweater and a gray plaid driving cap, both he and Crowley looked more like grandfathers than high ranking special operatives legally charged to keep dangerous secrets from the public. His eyebrows raised as he noted Sam wore an orange cropped cardigan over a blue swing dress. An orange ribbon kept her hair tied in a ponytail.

"Interesting choice for tonight's operation, Miss Hain," he said.

"Well," she said, sitting in a chair opposite him and crossing her legs and smiling at him, "this type of operation is new for me. Had I known that my only pair of trousers would have gotten torn while searching through two Faerie courts for a kidnapped girl and that I would be fighting against assholes conspiring to summon a demon for whatever purposes they have, I would have packed different clothes."

As the High Bard opened his mouth to respond, Mister Crowley interjected, "Would you like a beer, Miss Hain? I don't have any of your American lagers, but I have a few bottles of wine and some whiskies."

"If you have a good bourbon, I'll take that," she replied. "If not, a nice, smoky whiskey that's strong enough to numb me to the fact that I might kill my father tonight."

"That won't happen," the High Bard interjected. His voice trembled as he continued. "I left Sinn Féin in seventy-six after shrapnel from a bomb I set killed my own father, who took a different walking path than usual. I joined the Duilearga nine years later after the nightmares became less frequent. I won't let you suffer that. Leave him to one of us if it comes to that."

Sam nodded. They spent the next few minutes finalizing plans for the night's operation. They planned to observe the ritual long enough to learn its purpose and then try to disrupt the working. Through the Duilearga's influence and legal standing, the Garda had received orders to stay away from Old Tom's Hill until the thirty-first. Both men consoled Sam on the reality that situations like this called for deadly force. Ignoring her protests due to lack of knowledge and experience, the High Bard convinced Sam to take charge of any magical attacks and defenses. With their plan devised, they headed to Old Tom's Hill.

Clouds filled the late October sky above Bannagh as Sam Hain, High Bard Murphy, and archivist George Crowley walked through the forest north of town toward Old Tom's Hill. They kept their flashlights low to the ground, giving them minimal visibility. Aside from the orange, yellow, and brown leaves rustling in the cold north wind, silence blanketed the air. The earthy smells of the forest danced in the wind. After

218

a few minutes of walking, an owl hooted from a nearby tree, and they heard the howl of a lone wolf coming from the west.

Sam observed the emotionless faces of the Duilearga men as they walked. Her heart pushed against her throat as she focused on her breathing to both calm herself and maintain her psychic shield. She winced as images of Mabd in her cell, Zozo snapping her rapier like a toothpick, Sarah Ellison crying as she sat alone in court, and Sam's own mother weeping over her corpse, assaulted her mind. She smiled wistfully as she recalled her fifth birthday; her father took her to the Shetland Islands so she could ride the ponies. Her shoulders slumped as she sighed, realizing that, regardless of the outcome, any chance of a relationship with her father died tonight. She searched her companions' faces again and found them unchanged.

When they saw what appeared to be torchlight ahead, the High Bard held out his hand. They stopped. He pointed to three trees ahead, and they crept toward them. Peering around the trees, they saw six figured in the midnight blue robes of the Astrum Argentum and six figures in the black doublets and crimson tabards of the Order of the Dragon carrying torches on long poles as they marched to form a circle. On the High Bard's signal, the three of them advanced to trees closer to the circle. From here, they saw a figure, Seamus Creevy, standing near an altar within the circle. He wore a ceremonial breastplate under his tabard and carried a sword on his belt. Donal Hain, the hood of his robe down, leaned over the altar and arranged the tools from his bag. Sam tensed.

As Donal Hain finished, he turned to Seamus Creevy. The two began talking, but neither Sam nor the Duilearga men could understand their words. The High Bard raised two fingers and then pointed at each of them. As he pointed, they moved two trees forward to reach a more advantageous position. A Murphy and Crowley raised their rifles, Sam unholstered her Walther. The High Bard pointed at his ear, then pointed at Sam, and then pointed forward. She nodded and crept forward until she could hear the conversation.

"Ten minutes until the hour arrives, correct?" Seamus asked.

Donal Hain nodded, opening his pocket watch and setting it on the altar. "In ten minutes, we begin walking the path to bring the world peace and order. If only Samantha were standing at my side."

"Still haven't heard from her, I guess?" Seamus asked.

The Arch Magus shook his head, saying, "No." He sighed and continued, "At least her name has not been listed among those killed yesterday and this morning. So, whatever her whereabouts, I hope she's safe."

Sam rolled her eyes as she listened to Creevy respond, "Well, as long as she does not interfere tonight, perhaps we can keep her safe."

"Perhaps," Donal nodded. "However, Bha'esi seemed to be of the opinion that I would need to kill her."

Sam's ears perked at these words. She knew that Bha'esi and Zozo were somehow connected, but she did not know her father, and by implication, the Astrum Argentum were connected to that eccentric fae noble. She dropped low to the ground and crept one tree closer. She smelled the burning wood from the torches. Her heartbeat rose. Her breathing quickened. She looked back at the Duilearga men and motioned for them to come closer. They nodded and crept forward until they were one tree behind Sam.

"At any rate," Donal continued, "this working would be much easier if I had been able to obtain Liam O'Cuinn's contract, as all evidence indicates that it contains the only known imprint of Zozo's sigil written by the fiend itself."

"Are you confident that you can still control the fiend without it?" Creevy asked.

Donal Hain nodded and said, "Summoning and commanding demons is a matter of confidence and focus. If you've dominated one, you can dominate any of them." He paused and checked his pocket watch before adding, "Well, it's time to begin."

Arch Magus Donal Hain raised his hood over his head. He lit the charcoal in his censor and sprinkled his incense blend atop it. After a few moments, the heated resins perfumed the air with their spicy, earthy, and sweet scents. Taking his dagger in his right hand so the pommel faced downward, he knocked on the altar three times. He performed a pair of basic rituals, one to banish and one to invoke, that he had taught Sam. Then he performed an intricate ritual involving his wand, his chalice, some earthen disk with markings on it, and then his dagger where he made several passes and chanted phrases in a language Sam did not understand.

Sam's mind wandered as her father performed this long, intricate ritual. She recalled the first time her father taught her a basic banishing ritual when she was twenty. They stood in his hidden ritual room in his Dublin home where he explained the history of the ritual, the symbolism of each gesture, the meaning of each phrase, and the importance of focused intent. He restarted his lecture several times, because Sam's mind drifted to the fight she had with her girlfriend at the time. After the fourth interruption, he lectured her on how dangerous her lack of focus could be; she raised her middle finger to him and stormed off. Eventually, she managed to focus enough to learn the ritual, but that only happened when Ronan Fingal stepped in and trained her.

Sam snapped back to attention when her father stated that he named Zozo. Sam recognized the opening of a Goetic evocation. She listened. Her mind raced as she listened while trying to remember the words. She shook her head, certain that those were not the correct words. Her eyes widened, and she whispered a string of expletives as she realized he had altered the incantation, replacing the kabbalistic references and names of power with Sumerian and Akkadian ones.

The beating of wings tore through the night sky. Sam searched the sky but saw no birds. The torches flared, releasing a lingering scent of cedar and brimstone. Sam spun to face the Duilearga men and jerked her head. They advanced to her position. All readied their weapons. The smoke tendrils from the torches twisted toward the center of the circle, coalescing into the form of a giant, smoky door. As the smoke dissipated from the center outward, Zozo's four-winged, bipedal goat form strode through the opening.

Sam narrowed her eyes. She exhaled upon seeing both High Bard Murphy and Mister Crowley taken aback by the sight of the fiend. She took a deep breath and focused on her psychic shield. Seamus Creevy slid his hand onto the hilt of his sword. Donal Hain extended his arms and said, "Welcome, Zozo, warrior of Pazuzu, breaker of armies, deceiver, and slayer. I, Donal Hain, Arch Magus of the Hermetic Order of the Astrum Argentum, have this night summoned you–"

"Do you have the contract?" Zozo's growl echoed in everyone's mind.

"No," Donal Hain admitted. "The contract was not in the location specified."

222

Zozo narrowed his eyes and growled. "Then," he said, "name your sacrifice."

The Arch Magus closed his eyes and exhaled, nodding. He said, "The offering I give to you, given willingly, rests in Sligo University Hospital. His name is Frank, ah!"

A gunshot rang through the night. The Arch Magus screamed and grabbed his right knee. He hobbled in a circle to see the shooter. His eyes widened, and his jaw dropped as his daughter strode into view. Sam's narrowed eyes blazed with greater intensity than the torches, and she pointed her Walther at his forehead. Blood spurted from his knee. He winced, applying pressure as fire and electricity shot through his leg.

"Samantha," he said, his voice trembling.

"Hello, father," she spat.

The torchbearers scrambled, jamming their torch poles into the ground. High Bard Murphy and Mister Crowley rushed forward, flanking Sam as they fired at the scrambling torchbearers. One member of the Order of the Dragon fell. Zozo cackled and bleated in delight. Seamus Creevy spun around. Sam's bullet pierced his ceremonial armor. He sputtered. His body crashed onto the ground.

Sam returned her attention to her father. He hobbled back toward the altar. She fired again. He rolled to the side. The bullet kicked up dirt at the base of Old Tom's Hill. Donal Hain fumbled around in his doctor's bag, grabbing the portal stone. Sam took two steps forward, her focus unwavering. One of the Astrum Argentum torchbearers slammed his shoulder into her, knocking her to the side. She kicked the torchbearer in the stomach and then shot him in the knee. She spun toward her father as the torchbearer rolled on the ground, crying in pain.

223

Her gaze returned to her father as he activated the portal stone and disappeared, saying, "Great Zozo, accept our torchbearers as your sacrifice."

"Focus on the demon," High Bard Murphy bellowed as he shot another of the torchbearers.

"You sure about that?" Sam shouted.

"You've got the most experience with magic," he said. "It has to be you."

"Alright," Sam muttered, adding, "That's like saying a kindergartner is more educated than a toddler.

Sam tensed her muscles and breathed deeply. Zozo kicked one of the Order of the Dragon torchbearers to the ground, grabbed the torch pole, and shoved the fire into the young woman's mouth. Sam winced as her muffled screams and the burning flesh tore through the air. As he stalked toward her, Zozo grabbed an Astrum Argentum torchbearer by the throat, drew the pleading young man close to him, and tore into the young man's throat with his rotten, yellow fangs. Sam's breathing became shallow and rapid. Zozo tossed the corpse to the side with the disdain a human reserves for litter.

"You could run," his voice growled into Sam's mind. "I'm speaking to you alone now. You can't win."

"Get out of my head and back into that Ouija board," she replied.

Zozo chuckled menacingly and said, "A simple shield. No ward is impenetrable."

"Fuck you," Sam said, firing her handgun.

The muzzle flashed. Zozo growled. He grabbed his right arm, wincing as the path of his blood vessels glowed. Sam wrinkled her nose as the smell of singed fur pushed its way into her nose. Zozo growled as his midnight blue blood glistened against his fur.

Sam smirked and said, "You bleed."

The fiend growled and narrowed his eyes as he glared at her. Sam heard crying – her mother's crying – in her mind. She pushed back against it and shot Zozo in his left shoulder. The fiend howled. The crying returned, and Sam covered her ears with her hands, wincing and shutting her eyes tightly.

"No," she said, focusing on her breathing and her shield. "This isn't real."

Zozo growled as the torchbearers, Mister Crowley, and High Bard Murphy screamed. Guns fired. Bones broke. Sam's focus remained steadfast, and her breaths marched purposefully from her lungs. The smells of gunpowder, burning flesh, rot, and sulfur bored their way into Sam's nose. She coughed, reflexively covering her mouth while keeping her eyes shut. Her body trembled as the crying inside her mind and the sounds and smells outside her mind assaulted her.

"Samantha," her mother's voice spoke into her mind.

"That's not you, Mom," Sam answered, shaking her head.

"Samantha," the voice continued, "it' okay, darling."

Sam trembled and exhaled slowly as tears formed in her eyes. "You're not real," she said. "Get out of my head."

"Samantha, dear," the voice pleaded, "just open your eyes. You'll see me."

Tears fell as Sam trembled. She exhaled and opened her eyes. Death surrounded her. As she surveyed the scene, she tripped over Professor Creevy's body and squealed. The torchbearers' mangled bodies had been set aflame. Long poles of sharpened bones, bound in sinew, supported the High Bard's and George Crowley's heads. Their decapitated bodies lay in a pool of blood at the sides of the altar. Zozo perched atop the altar, his rotting yellow fangs twisted into a mocking smile. She raised a trembling hand to her mouth and blinked wildly. She fired two shots. One grazed Zozo's left horn, but the other missed.

"We're all alone, Samantha dear," her mother's voice slowly darkened into Zozo's growl as he spoke into her mind.

"No," Sam whispered, "not again."

Smirking, Zozo leapt from his perch atop the altar. The fires in his eyes cackled as he growled hungrily. Blood dripped from his yellowed fangs and elongated claws. Sam's breathing became rapid and shallow. She backed away as he stalked toward her. She raised a trembling hand and fired twice. Both missed. She cursed. Her shoulders slumped as she panted, glaring at the fiend whose brittle laughter mocked her.

She cried, gnashing her teeth as his low, dark growl entered her mind, "Every wall has a weak point, and you have already shown me yours."

Sam gritted her teeth. She held her rapid breaths, trying to stabilize them, as her hands trembled. Zozo strode forward; a torchbearer's rib cage snapped as the fiend stepped through it. Sam shrieked, firing two wild shots that kicked up small clouds of dirt. Her heart thundered against her chest. Her breathing quickened. Trembling, she slammed her eyes shut and tensed her muscles.

"Go ahead, Samantha," her mother's voice rang alongside Zozo's growl. Zozo's voice faded into white noise as her mother's rang clearly, "It's okay. We can be together again. I want that. Don't you?"

Through her tears, Sam croaked her response, "Nothing more."

"Then you know what to do," the voice said.

Her mother's voice soothed her. Sam took one deep breath,

holding the air in her lungs before releasing it. Zozo was right. Her failure and death were inevitable. She clenched her jaw as she inhaled. She held her breath for a few seconds, letting her mind simply exist, and then exhaled. She turned her Walther over in her hand, sliding the other hand along its warm barrel. Only one round remained. She surveyed the surrounding carnage, focusing on the deaths she caused and the deaths of those who trusted her. If Zozo killed her, she died. If she ended her life, she could be with her mother forever.

She wiped the tears from her eyes and nodded. Her eyes closed, she breathed deeply, coughing as smells of smoke, burnt flesh, and fading incense filled her nose. Bile rose in her stomach, causing her eyes to water. Faint white light flashed in her mind.

"Miss Hain, open your eyes," a familiar but distant voice called out.

Sam blinked. That was not her mother's voice. The taste of bile hung in the back of her throat as she looked around. The torchbearers were all dead, but the Duilearga men were not. Mister Crowley writhed on the ground; his left leg bent at an unnatural angle. High Bard Murphy crawled on his elbows, his face bloodied and scratched. Zozo looked up from licking human blood from his fingers and smiled at Sam. He licked his lips. She shuddered.

"Please, Miss Hain," the High Bard said, "you've got to stop him."

Sam shook her head violently and holstered her handgun. "I can't," she said. "I'm not strong enough."

They both turned as Mister Crowley sputtered, twitched, and ceased writhing. His chest struggled to rise and fall. The High Bard turned back toward Sam, his eyes pleading, and

227

said, "You have to. George won't last much longer without aid, and I can't signal an emergency airlift without this being clear. Please."

Zozo's dark, brittle laughter shook the trees. Sam closed her eyes and focused on her breathing. As he stalked toward her, Zozo spoke into all their minds, "You should have run away, little lamb. I've broken into your mind twice. I know how to destroy your wards. Before the dawn breaks, I will feast on your flesh and devour your soul, a truly wonderful sacrifice."

High Bard Murphy grasped Zozo's right ankle. The fiend contorted his body and stepped on the old man's wrist, snapping it. Sam's breathing quickened again. Her eyes darted from the wounded and writhing High Bard to the unconscious and struggling George Crowley to Zozo. Sam tensed her muscles as she inhaled. As she released, she untied the ribbon around her ponytail. She focused her mind on the orange silk ribbon, Zozo straddled the High Bard, growled, and raked his six-fingered claw across the back of the man's neck. Murphy screamed and writhed beneath the fiend's body as it continued raking its claws down his back.

Breathing deeply, Sam held the ribbon in front of her with both hands. She narrowed her eyes on the fiend's wrists and, while tying a knot in the ribbon, said, "Zozo, Pazuzu's Warrior, Deceiver, Slayer of Armies, I, Samantha Hain, bind you."

Zozo's left hand froze in the middle of its strike. The fiend's eyes jerked to meet Sam's glare with their own. She smirked and raised a challenging eyebrow. Zozo stood and kicked the High Bard in his kidney before taking a step toward Sam.

"Zozo, by the name of the Tetragrammaton, I bind you." Sam said as she tied another knot in the ribbon.

The fiend's right hand froze a few inches above its bloodied

228

and shredded target. The High Bard rolled a few feet away and sat against a nearby tree. He panted and groaned. Zozo continued his path toward Sam, but he found himself unable to move as invisible chains shackled his hands. His eyes flared, and his howl rattled all the rib cages of those north of Old Tom's Hill.

"That conjuror's trick won't hold me forever," he bellowed.

Sam sauntered to the altar. She knelt and took the traveling grimoire her father left when he teleported to safety. She set it atop the altar, flipped through the pages, and unholstered her Walther. Pivoting to face Zozo, she winked, aimed at his chest, and said, "Oh thou Zozo, because you have diligently answered unto my demands of binding, and because so bound you may take no action to harm any mortal living or dead, I grant thee license to depart, returning to your proper place without causing either harm or danger to human or animal. Depart now. I charge thee to withdraw peaceably and quietly, and the peace of God be ever continued between thee and me. You are fucking dismissed."

A peal of thunder ripped through the sky as she fired. The bullet struck Zozo in his breastbone. His bleating shriek caused Sam and High Bard Murphy to wince. The flames from the handful of still-burning torches flared, creating smoke tendrils that curled and slithered toward Zozo. They swirled counterclockwise around the fiend. Zozo writhed and screamed as the smoke formed a swirling vortex that pulled him into its thick, gray darkness. The magical bindings snapped, and Zozo plummeted into the vortex. The smoke dissipated, and silence filled the air. Sam exhaled and collapsed against the altar.

* * *

Sam awoke in a hospital bed inside a windowless room with robin egg blue stucco walls. George Crowley snored in the bed to her left, and High Bard Murphy sat upright in the bed on her right, reading a newspaper. Both men were connected to intravenous fluid machines and ECG machines. The room was cool but smelled of bleach. She winced and groaned as she moved, stretching her muscles as she sat up.

"Fuck," she said, "where am I?"

"Ah, you're awake," the High Bard said. "I thought the snoring had lowered to an acceptable volume. Welcome to our headquarters in a manor donated and maintained by one of our ranking member families."

"Yeah, well fuck you too," she muttered through a yawn. Her eyes shot wide, and she added, "Wait! What day is it?"

The High Bard grunted and winced as he turned toward her. Peeking from under his green and gold pajamas, she saw the bandages covering most of his torso. "The thirty-first," he said, "and our breakfast will be here soon."

Sam sighed. "Guess this'll be a slow birthday," she said, rolling her eyes.

The High Bard chuckled and said, "Well, may the anniversary of your birth be a day of joy and love, Miss Hain. Also, a young Miss Grimm should be here by noon to collect you for your celebration."

She smiled and exhaled. "I wouldn't call spending the evening at The Four Winds talking with my mother a 'celebration,' Mister Murphy," she said, "but there's no other way I'd want to spend the evening."

He sipped his tea and asked, "I was under the impression that your mother had passed on. Was my information incorrect?"

Sam smiled and shook her head, saying, "No. She took her own life almost a decade ago. It's about time I repaid Nick for granting me this request."

"An unspecified price for a boon," he said, "you play a dangerous game."

"I wasn't in a good headspace," Sam replied. She shrugged and said, "But it does give me a little more time with her, and it's less sad than if I just walked to her grave and talked to her that way."

Sam teared up as she thought about her mother. A young man in green and gold scrubs pushed a cart with food trays into the room. He placed a tray of sausages, poached eggs, grilled tomatoes, orange marmalade, and toasted soda bread. He also provided each of them with coffee, tea, and apple juice. The young man and the High Bard stared in awe as Sam chugged the hot black coffee as if it were a light beer. He refilled her cup and then left the room.

"I know it's not much, Miss Hain," the High Bard said, "but should you wish to serve as an occult consultant, we would welcome you as one of our own."

She snorted and said, "I think I'll pass, Mister Murphy. I know I told to you that I'm not an expert. I know four basic rituals, and I bullshitted everything I did the other night. If things were different, I could've suggested a few people. But now, I don't know if I can trust any of them."

He nodded solemnly as she sighed, running her fingers through her hair. "It must be hard for you," he said. "Even with your – and if I'm out of line, please tell me – problematic relationship with your father, this must be hard for you."

"Yeah," she said as she counted the textured marks on the

stucco ceiling, "I didn't grow up around these people. Donal was rarely involved in my life until after mom passed. He tried to teach me a few things, but I wasn't the best student. Didn't care for my teacher."

"There are other esoteric orders," the High Bard said, "and my offer still stands."

She shook her head. "I don't know," she said. "Did we – what happened that night? I remember the firefight starting and Zozo being summoned. But I have this massive blank between that and when I kicked him to the curb like an abusive ex."

Before he could respond, a young, svelte brunette wearing a green polo shirt, black trousers, and a bronze beret burst through the door. She saluted Eric Murphy and said, "High Bard, Sir, we have a situation at the gate, Sir."

The High Bard stroked his beard and asked, "What kind of situation, agent?"

She removed her beret and said, "There's a German woman demanding admittance, Sir. I know it sounds crazy, but I think she's a vampire."

Sam perked up at the young agent's words. The High Bard tilted his head and squinted. "Impossible, agent," he said, "a vampire would be foolish to come here, and the sun is out. Only clan elders are powerful enough to withstand sunlight for short periods of time. Besides that, we don't publicize our locations. There must be some other explanation. What does she want?"

The agent shifted her gaze and said, "She claims to be here for Miss Hain, Sir."

He waived a dismissive hand and said, "Then it's young Miss Grimm. Let her in."

The agent saluted and left. A few moments later, she returned, escorting a gorgeous woman who looked no older than twenty. This woman wore a black sheath dress under a black leather blazer with lace accents, large black sunglasses, and a wide-brimmed black hat from which a lace veil descended over her face. Sam inhaled sharply, smiling and biting her lip as she entered. The High Bard eyed her curiously as she dismissed the young agent with a hand gesture.

"Welcome, Miss Grimm," he said, "We did not expect you so early."

The woman removed her hat and sunglasses, revealing her bloodshot emerald eyes. Sam smiled and inhaled sharply. "Miss Grimm has been detained in Dublin awaiting a missing suitcase," she said. "I am Countess Carmilla Karnstein, and I am here to ensure Samantha's safety."

The High Bard scoffed and asked, "And how did you find us, Countess? It's not like we are public about who we are."

Carmilla sauntered beside him and leaned forward. As she spoke, she bared her fangs as clearly as possible while still enunciating, "The Le Fanu family, who owns this estate, has repaid a centuries' old debt."

"Vampire," the High Bard whispered. He steeled himself, glared at her, and said, "State your business quickly, or I will have a dozen stakes driven through your shriveled, blackened heart."

"If my business were adversarial," she shot back, "you would already have become my thrall. My business, as I have stated, is ensuring that Samantha is safe. The last time she found her path and yours entwined, your agent shot her."

They locked glares. It appeared that the High Bard wanted to say something. As he produced his first syllable, Sam interrupted, "'Milla, I'm glad to see you, but I told you I would be fine."

Countess Karnstein glided next to Sam and hugged her, planting a blush-inducing kiss on her cheek. "I know, Sam," she said, "but then I heard that there was a fight with the Order of the Dragon and your father's people and that you were lifted by helicopter to this manor. I have mortal and thrall agents surrounding this manor, but I could get no one inside. So, I came myself. I had hoped to avoid suspicion by coming during daylight. Even on your birthday, the sun is so wretched."

"You remembered?" Sam asked, beaming.

"Of course, I remembered," the Countess replied. "Knowing you has brought joy to my immortality. Your…friendship means more to me than you will know. Your present is in my car. Now, I will wait for you in the reception area as you finish your business here. I have a car, and I will inform Miss Grimm where to meet us for lunch."

The High Bard raised his hand and began to speak, but before he could sputter a sentence, Carmilla had glided from the room. He scratched his head, chuckled, and said, "You owe the devil a favor, and the matriarch of a vampire clan values your friendship. You are an unusual person, Miss Hain."

"You don't know the half of it," she mumbled through her coffee cup. She set the cup down and sighed. "Look, as much as I hate to admit it, Michael Cormack was right. I'm a loose cannon. We had our plan, but when my father offered Frank – one of the ghost hunters and a probationer in the Astrum Argentum – to Zozo as a sacrifice, I let my emotions get the better of me. I wanted to protect him. And," she paused and sighed, swirling her index finger around the rim of the cup. "After all I've been through on this fix, I had resolved to give him another chance. I was hurt. I felt betrayed. All that anger from all those years rushed forward. I endangered us. And, in the end, there was so much death. I still killed people."

"You did," he said without emotion. "Were you one of my agents, I would have lectured and reprimanded you for that. You acted on impulse. You were reckless. And you endangered both our lives and the mission. You behaved like a civilian untrained in our tactics," he paused before adding, "which you are. If we are to collaborate again in the field, you will need training."

Sam shook her head and replied, "Not happening. Too much overzealous killing. I told Werther the same thing when he asked me to work for him. I'm going to need a strong drink after this."

"And you think our agents don't?" When she looked puzzled, he said, "The act of killing is easy. You saw that two days ago. What's a challenge is living with it. And drink is a dangerous but temporary balm."

"So, what do you do then?" she asked in a soft, contemplative voice.

He sighed and scratched his chin. "Learn to find meaning in it," he said. "Why do you think heroic tales exist but to help young warriors make sense of why they have to kill someone they've never met and who has likely done nothing to them personally?"

She shook her head and said, "But all that killing does is preserve the status quo. The secret of the Veil is maintained, sure. Have you ever wondered that, if we learned to live alongside these non-human beings, there would be no need to kill so many people after the adjustment period?"

He smiled bemusedly and said, "Harmony is a poet's dream, Miss Hain. Look around you. We humans can't stop hating, hurting, and killing ourselves over trivialities like skin color, choice of lover, and house of worship. What we do, protecting humans from both these supernatural threats and from themselves, is heroic. We defend humanity from all forms of darkness, even if idealists like you won't see that. Perhaps now that you've taken life, the scales on your eyes will loosen."

"No," she said, "I hope they never loosen." She looked around and said, "Since I'm not connected to any machines, how long before I'm allowed to leave?"

"At any time," he said. "I can send for a doctor to examine you, escort you to a private room to change, and let you depart with your little vampire friend. Are you sure that you won't reconsider joining us? You'd make a fine agent."

She shook her head and smiled, saying, "No. But, if you ever decide you want to walk away from the blood, I'll leave my card."

High Bard Murphy kept his promise, and orderlies came and escorted Sam to an examination chamber. A female doctor examined her and pronounced her healthy, albeit with bruises and minor lacerations on her body. She handed Sam some strong non-prescription painkillers to take as needed and allowed Sam to dress. Not only had they brought all of her belongings from The Slouching Giant, but they had repaired the sweater and trousers that had been damaged during her trip to Faerie. She dressed, did her makeup, and brushed her hair. She and Carmilla shared a long hug before entering Carmilla's black BMW 750i-G12 to travel to Dublin. While traveling, Sam opened her present from Carmilla, a receipt for first class round trip airfare from Charleston to Innsbruck for this December and a blue and gold hounds tooth wool trench coat with removable hood and matching mittens .

They entered the underground parking garage of a windowless gray building. Carmilla informed Sam that this was FAI, short for *Fuil agus Ispíní*, or Blood and Sausages, a vampire-run establishment for vampires, their thralls, and select trustworthy friends. A nervous Destiny Grimm waited for them by the hostess stand. Sam and Destiny hugged upon seeing each other. While they dined, Sam recounted her experiences in Faerie and the fight against the Order of the Dragon and the Astrum Argentum. Carmilla drank her meal from a crystal wine glass. After lunch, Destiny and Sam headed to Dublin, and Carmilla returned to her castle in Austria.

* * *

Sam's birthday evening began as a small celebration with Destiny, Kina, Laura, and Laura's girlfriend Adrianne at Adam's Apple Wine Bar & Bistro. Sam enjoyed the company, but her mind drifted to the events of the past week. After a few rounds of wine and cocktails and large slices of almond cream cake, Destiny drove Sam back to her apartment. After a few minutes of petting Sandy and promising that they would return in a few hours, Sam performed the ritual to open the portal to The Four Winds.

A larger crowd than Sam expected gathered in The Four Winds to celebrate her thirtieth birthday. Lilith displayed her full vocal range as Mephistopheles led his infernal chamber quartet through his virtuosic performance on the violin. The entire Vernal Court made an appearance, thanking her for her assistance and delivering the final payment for her services. Carmilla, dressed in a sheer black sheath dress with her hair in a braided bun, joined Sam and Destiny at their table along with Aoki Kin, a three-tailed, auburn-furred kitsune whose food stealing deceptions ran her afoul of the Yanagitas.

They passed most of the night with drinking and friendly conversation, allowing laughter to harmonize with the performance from the stage. When the clock struck eleven, the party guests slowly dispersed. Being the last to leave, Destiny promised to watch Sandy until Sam returned. The music fell silent. Nick Scratch nodded and walked through a door. Sam inhaled deeply, smiling as her stomach turned over several times. A few moments later, he returned, escorting a middle-aged woman with graying brown hair and bloated, slightly blued skin. She walked over to the table. As she and Sam hugged, Mister Scratch returned to the bar and busied himself cleaning glasses.

"Happy birthday, Samantha," Amelia Burnside said while still holding her daughter tightly.

"Thanks, mom," Sam said, tears filling her eyes. "It's so good to see you again."

They sat the table, and Mister Scratch brought each of them a drink that he said was on the house. Amelia smiled and asked, "So what's new?"

Sam downed half of her cocktail before saying, "Well, the year hasn't been as fucked up as 2020 was, but I almost didn't make it here. And that's the summary, I guess."

"What do you mean? This is our one day each year," her mother said, concern adding traces of living coloration to her face.

Sam hid her face in her hands and cried. She bit her lip to the point she tasted iron. She took a deep breath and said, "It's been hard, Mom. I've missed you so much, and things haven't gone my way for the most part. The car's barely holding on.

We've been behind on bills at the office, and we need new computers and lighting there too. And as I watched my friends get married, it's been hard realizing that you won't be there if I ever get married. And things with Donal have gone to fucking hell. Even before this last fix, I wrote my note, which Destiny found and confronted me on, and I was going to join you in the forest yesterday."

Amelia's face fell. She reached across the table and took her daughter's hands in her own. "Sam," she said, "I understand your feelings, but what I did is not a path I would want you to follow. The Woods is not a pleasant place. It's dark. It's lonely. The harpies come and break our branches, which feels like having your arms or legs snapped in half. The only sounds are our screams. We would be there together, but we could not speak unless we bleed; and even then, we can only speak so long as blood flows." She sighed and looked toward the bar where Mister Scratch had his back turned to them. "And you know how Hell works. We would be allowed to see each other but not communicate with each other. And that would be another hell for both of us."

Sam's eyes glassed over. She nodded and said, "Yeah, he enjoys the irony of his punishments. This last fix has given me a little perspective on things."

Sam spent half an hour detailing the investigation in Bannagh, her adventure in Faerie, and then the fight at Old Tom's Hill. Amelia listened attentively as Sam described the events in the Forlorn Cavern. She squeezed Sam's hand during the depiction of Sam's lifeless body. Her jaw hit the table, and her eyes widened when Sam described her father's involvement with both the Order of the Dragon, the fiend Zozo, and, likely, Count Bha'esi. Sam finished telling the story, and they sat in silence.

After a few moments, Amelia said, "Well, you said that you and Donal were having trouble, but I never thought he would be involved in something like this. And you're sure it was him?"

Sam nodded and said, "I saw his face, mom, and I collected the ritual tools that he left behind when he teleported."

"Was his grimoire there too?" Amelia asked.

"The one he takes when he does a working outside his private office," Sam said. "I don't know what I'm going to do with this stuff."

"You know," her mom said with a smile, "you could always learn the spells and rituals in there. I mean, Samantha, it seems that you may need them."

Sam shook her head and shrugged. She took a sip from her cocktail and said, "I don't know. I don't think I have the discipline to be a magician like dad or even like Mister Fingal. Even before whatever Donal's involved in, I didn't want to join any order, since I'm his daughter. I don't need the pressure."

Amelia nodded and glanced over at Nicholas Scratch. He winked and turned his back to them again. She turned to her daughter and asked, "Maybe you should think about settling down then. Is there a woman you'll be introducing me to next year?"

Sam ran her fingers through her hair and sighed. "Rachel dumped me two weeks ago. So, given the past four years, it's looking like I won't be bringing a woman to meet you next year"

"What about Carmilla? You're still friends with her, aren't you? You were so happy when you were with her." Amelia asked, taking a few sips of her drink.

"Mom," Sam whined, "not this again."

"Don't you 'Mom' me, Samantha Blake," Amelia replied, causing Sam to bolt to attention. "I want you to be happy with whatever path you take."

Sam's right leg bounced against the table. She twirled her hair around her finger and sighed. She said, "It won't work. I wish it would, but I just can't handle waking up next to her while she's asleep. She's a corpse, cold, silent, and lifeless. And our natural schedules just don't align."

Amelia smiled bemusedly at her daughter. Chuckling, she shook her head and said, "And yet, you talk about her every year, she's always at your celebration here, and it seems she's willing to risk her health to protect you." Sam started to protest, but her mother held up her index finger and said, "Samantha Blake Hain, you ended that relationship, because you weren't ready for what it would require. Every woman you've dated since then has dumped you, and I think we both know why. Be honest with yourself. Be honest with her. Be willing to compromise and work."

The clock struck twelve dissonant bells. Nicholas Scratch sauntered to the table and said, "I hope you've enjoyed your talk, ladies, but it is midnight." He presented his open hand to Sam's mother and said, "Amelia, it's time to return."

She nodded. She and Sam hugged and said their goodbyes. Amelia took Mister Scratch's hand, and he led her through the door against the southern wall. Sam walked to the bar, sat, and finished her drink. After a few minutes, Mister Scratch returned, slid behind the bar, and poured two glasses of a dark, sanguine wine He passed one to Samantha and sipped the other.

"I don't have any information for you, Nick," she said

"On the house, Miss Hain," he said. "You've had a rather trying week."

She sipped the wine, holding it in her mouth as she pondered its taste. She swallowed and said, "Interesting choice, why does it have a subtle bloody aftertaste?"

He smiled. Leaning forward, he asked, "With all the time you've spent with Countess Karnstein, have you never had blood wine?"

"The blood taste was never this subtle," she said.

He chuckled. "Are you surprised," he asked, "that you can't find drinks on earth as perfect as you can find them here?"

Sam tilted her head in thought. After a moment, her eyes shot open, and she said, "Do you mean that this wine is, you know?"

He tilted the crystal wineglass to his lips and said, "That information isn't free." He set the glass on the bar and added, "I hope you enjoyed your hour with your mother."

Sam smiled and said, "I did. Thank you." She finished her wine and added, "About that. I think it's time we discussed that favor you want as payment."

Nick Scratch shook his head, saying, "Not tonight, dear. Though it is technically the first of November, it's still the night of your birthday. No business on a celebratory day."

She eyed him suspiciously and then chuckled, "I'll say it again, Nick. You're not so bad."

He smiled and said, "Tell anyone, Miss Hain, and I will send an infernal legion to destroy that giant bag of cereal marshmallows in your kitchen."

9 781636 842974